HISTORICAL NOVELS BY ALETHEA WILLIAMS

Willow Vale

From opposite sides of an ocean, two people wounded by the Great War are fated to meet and try to rebuild their lives.

Náápiikoan Winter

The woman. The man. The land. Changes unimagined are about to unfold.

<u>The Irish Blessings series:</u>

Walls for the Wind

A group of orphans leaves New York City to land in Hell on Wheels, Cheyenne, Wyoming, as a family.

Joy that Long Endures

As the transcontinental railroad is finished and its hell towns move on, the people who call Wyoming Territory home must find new ways to survive. Some earn a living by their sweat. Some drift from scheme to scheme. And some make a fortune.

Embers of the Hearth

Coming soon!

Joy That Long Endures

Alethea

Alethea Williams

Joy That Long Endures

Copyright © 2018 by Christine Alethea Williams

Edited by Andre'lle Hummel
Cover by Brigida Blasi

Joy That Long Endures

An Irish blessing:

May love and laughter light your days,
and warm your heart and home.
May good and faithful friends be yours
wherever you may roam.
May peace and plenty bless your world
with joy that long endures.

Chapter *1*
A Morning's Amusement

*H*AAWWWW. HAAAWWWWW!

Well might the mule sound amused, Devin Cavanaugh thought, as he pondered the present state of his life while hoisting another bag atop the pile in the wagon. It took only a glance for the man to resolve anew that this Wyoming Territory was a rough, raw place. The harsh landscape proved hospitable to equally raw weather: the wind had finally let up after an earlier blow so ferocious that loose dirt spiraled in a brown cloud two miles high. Now, with a sudden streak of lightning and vicious crack of thunder, rain cascaded in blinding sheets, turning the normally mindless job of loading the wagons into a wet, miserable business indeed. And to top off the whole soggy mess, there was Caleb Wilson and his fit of temper, accompanied by a veritable geyser of raw language. Wilson's tantrum was coarse enough that Devin almost expected clouds of steam to emanate from the man's mouth along with the steady flow of heated cussing aimed at one of the lead mules.

"Ya bacon-faced baggage, I'll strip the hide from yer jingle-brained gawdamned bones! Hold still, ya stinkin' Tom turd jilt! By gawd, I'll whip the skin clean off from yer scrawny fundament once I get ya fully hitched, ya useless scraggy whorepipe!"

Haawwww. HAAAWWW! Tiberius didn't whinny like a horse or bray like a donkey, but instead emitted a loud, distinctive trumpet of sound something in between the two. Devin stood idly by now, trying to stifle the grin he felt spreading across his face as Tiberius, the smartest of all the mules, once again slipped the collar and stepped backwards away from Wilson as they danced around each other in the slop of the corral. The big gray mule, displaying a large, impressive set of yellow dentition, even dared to taunt Wilson again with his signature bellow while the man once more responded by filling the wet, stinking air surrounding them with a new roar of helpless, angry curses. Recently employed at the freighting company, Devin had asked about the mule's unusual name. Cal had replied, "Old Beery? Why are you so all-fired eager to know about what some addled army officer called his cussed, sulky mule? Maybe ya ought to read your Bible."

"So you think Tiberius might be a name from the Bible?"

"I said so, didn't I? Ti-beery-us was an Old Testament king, if you're so almighty eager know. Now stop wasting time with chin music and get back to work."

It hardly seemed likely that Cal passed time reading his Bible any more than Devin did. He probably just asked someone with some education where the name originated. Although Tiberius didn't seem to mind the whole majestic moniker, he didn't appear to appreciate the nickname Cal bestowed on him. Just to show who was in charge, sometimes Tiberius refused to cooperate after a bout of Cal's sneering. Today was a good example. When the august-named mule continued to tease an increasingly frustrated Wilson, who was not yet fully recovered after a night of hard drinking, the man finally gave up and threw down the collar with a rather sodden jangle of hame bells. Eyeing the mule as he deliberately uncoiled a long, braided black whip he carried tied to his belt, he growled in a low voice, "I'm warnin' ya now, Beery. I've had enough, ya two-handed slack-baked put. I'm about to lay open yer no account hide, if yer full and total cooperation ain't *im-mejit-ly* forthcoming. Understand me, ya addle-pated scummy effusion: we are *done* playin'! We will get down to business *now*, and that's my last word on it."

The pole corral containing the man issuing the ultimatum to the mule, located in the little settlement of Bryan City in Wyoming Territory, was one of the West's ubiquitous, hurriedly built "magic" towns—slapdash settlements of raw buildings and raw roads that rose seemingly overnight. Its unpainted shacks of splintery up-and-down planks faced the tracks of the recently completed Great National Highway in a long lane of equal parts rutted, gooey mud and smelly, disintegrating horse droppings. This type of settlement typically petered out at the far edge with a hastily dug cemetery, and Bryan was no exception. After the completion of the Pacific road and the sudden collapse of employment as well as population in the territory, the little town had settled into a regular, if small, grid of shops and canvas dwellings. Bryan clung to life as a supply and service settlement that sold goods of every kind to the railroad workers who remained in the area, as well as haulage to the gold mines to the north. Others of its kind, not so lucky as to be sited near such irresistible lures—the hellhole named Benton came to mind—faded into railroad history just as quickly as they had blossomed.

Devin was equal parts grateful to have found steady work in Bryan upon completion of the road, and ashamed at having to accept such demeaning labor. He had most recently been an iron man to the Casement Brothers, contractors building the Union Pacific, and still had the brawny arms to prove it. In his own opinion he had taken a mighty tumble since the road building crews disbanded after the race to finish ended at Promontory a few years before. The last thing he ever dreamed he might eventually end up doing for a living, while he had been busy helping to build the road, was stoop to tending mules. Although if he did say so himself, he thought he was a sight better at the job than Wilson. He had gotten pretty good at convincing the animals to cooperate without resorting to violence, but fortunately or unfortunately—it remained to be seen which for Tiberius—it was actually Wilson who attempted the harnessing as Devin stood by and watched. The winner of a little bet the two men had made could name his prize, and since Devin was aware Wilson typically had little money in his pocket, he had asked instead that the boss take the job of harnessing the team on the next trip out. Devin hadn't expected that such a minor wager would pay off so well in terms of entertainment alone. But now, eyes rolling in their sockets toward the sight of the whip, bedraggled with the continuing heavy downpour and apparently judging the wiry muleskinner truly wearied of his latest performance, Tiberius suddenly turned meekly obedient, finally allowing Wilson to get down to the business of collaring.

Devin glanced sidelong through the rain at the narrow porch of the freight office adjoining the corrals. The little boy waiting there hadn't changed expression, no matter if his ears were being singed red by Wilson's swearing or his tender feelings assaulted by the threat of mule blood mixed with mud. He stood patiently, as if the long minutes he had been staring through the deluge, watching the business of getting the mule team into their proper places to pull the wagons, was what every boy of about six years of age should be doing on this miserable morning of what Devin was fairly sure was a school day.

Although he couldn't of a certainty have sworn what day of the week it truly might be. Odds were equal for it being a weekday or even a Sabbath. School could be in session or out. After all, it made no difference to him. At twenty years old—at least as near as he could determine he was about that age—Devin Cavanaugh had less than a month's formal schooling under his belt. And for sure he had never in his life been kitted out like the little boy waiting behind the porch rail. The lad, apparently without a twinge of embarrassment, sported matching coat and cap and knickers of a fine summer weight blue wool, a pair of navy-striped stockings, and high button boots. At an age approximate to what he judged the boy was now, Devin had already been living on filthy New York City streets, ragged and dirty and surviving the best he could on his ability to quickly determine whether the better part of valor involved standing up for his bit of territory carved out of the Five Points area or else turning tail to run, and so live to fight another day. This little lad here now, clothes growing more darkly damp by the minute no matter that he stood under the shelter of the porch overhang, didn't look as if he had ever had to fight for, or run from, anything in his short life.

But, in fact, the small boy did call up a tiny bit of sympathetic reminiscence in the former iron man, reminding Devin just a touch of that familiar boy from long ago boy. Perhaps it was merely the child's wretched, dogged persistence, standing there with his clothes soaking up moisture in the wet early morning, uncomplaining as he watched the capture and collaring of the team. Perhaps it was no more than the suitcase at his feet, a nice, unscuffed, oxblood-dyed leather valise secured with shiny brass clasps. To be sure it did not resemble at all the grim pasteboard specimen of the several trips Devin had carried while chasing his destiny as the rails were laid west. The fancy valise belonging to the boy surely must be a fond farewell gift to a beloved child, not an anonymous handout courtesy of one or another of the big city charitable organizations trying to help rid the streets of the teeming Eastern cities of orphans, half orphans, and other assorted unwanted children who lived in the underworld like so many rats.

"That useless little doodle still standing about?" Wilson raised his chin questioningly in the boy's direction, breaking into Devin's musings, as on the street outside the corral he backed a now meek and docile Tiberius into the traces.

"Sure looks like it," Devin agreed. After all, Wilson was the boss. If the man wanted to ask stupid questions about what was plain to anyone with eyes to see, and to call their passenger names to boot, it was his own business.

"What does the young coxcomb want?"

"He says he's meant to go to South Pass, Cal. With us."

Wilson bristled, straightening from his task. "My foxy naked ass he'll go with us! On whose authority? We ain't a stage line. Folks can't just come up and hitch a ride."

Devin shrugged. "I already told him much the same."

"Come here, shaver." Wilson marched back into the muddy corral, raising his voice and waving his hand. The boy stepped obediently if somewhat reluctantly off the porch. Devin looked away and observed that at least the rain seemed to be starting to let up. Maybe the ground would soon dry out and even become dusty again, all the moisture wicked away as if it had never been, and they could be on their way. "Who told you to loaf around here this morning?" Wilson demanded of the boy.

The lad cringed. Still, he stood his ground and lifted his chin. "My grandmama says so."

"Your gran'ma? Pshaw. What's some old frump got to say that anybody would listen to about anything?"

The boy removed his hand from his jacket pocket, extending toward Wilson a tightly clutched, soggy bit of folded paper.

Wilson looked at Devin. "What's this?"

"Dunno." Again, Devin shrugged.

"I *tried* to show him," the boy said, nodding toward Devin. "He wouldn't look."

"So what's it say, then?" Wilson asked, eyeing Devin with a touch of malicious advantage reflected in his eyes.

Devin said, "I couldn't make it out. My eyes are bothering me. Must be all the rain."

"I told you what it says." The boy craned his neck to look up at the men's faces. "It says my grandmama wants you to take me to South Pass City."

"The hell you say. What monkey shines is this?" Wilson turned his head to disgorge a gob of phlegm, snatched the paper from the boy's hand, unfolded it, and squinted at the penciled words. Reluctantly, he glanced up from the paper. "Well, I'll be an unwashed gap stopper. This paper says exactly what the little feller says it does."

"And so, then? We're expected to tend a child all the way to South Pass City like a couple of English governesses?" At least hauling grain and sugar and flour and liquor to the gold miners at South Pass was a man's job. Wilson and Devin didn't haul people, and they especially didn't provide passage for little children.

"Looks like we ain't got a lot to say about it." It was Wilson's turn to shrug.

It was a worrisome situation indeed when Wilson suddenly stopped cursing. Devin demanded, "Why? We aren't nannies. It sometimes takes us more than a week to make the Sweetwater. Why are we stuck with a small boy? It doesn't make sense, Cal."

Wilson lowered his voice to a gravelly whisper and waggled his bushy eyebrows. "Here's why, ya blockhead: 'Cause his grandma's Lou Schering, that's why. Lou does what she wants, when she wants, and without consulting the likes of us. She owns most of this town, in case you ain't aware of that fact by now, sonny boy. She owns a distillery back in St. Louie, has fingers in one or two other pies like this here shipping outfit. Not to mention the local brothel, by the bye."

Devin gritted his teeth. He didn't need reminding where Wilson spent his spare time and most of his pay. "So then I take it you owe the woman."

"A bit, yeah." Wilson grinned weakly, showing the nubs of his brown and rotting teeth. He glanced once more at the boy. "At the moment it looks like I owe her grandson a ride to South Pass City. If you'da read the damned note, you could have had the kid wait inside the office where it's dry at least, instead of making him stand out here in the rain. Lou's grandson, for chrissake. Yer head stuck fast between yer legs or what, Cavanaugh?"

"I? It's hardly my place to decide what to do with him. You're supposed to be the boss. And besides, I told you my eyes are bothering me so I couldn't read what the paper said."

"Yeah, yeah. Yer eyes. My ass. That's not all that's going to be bothering you if the kid's gran'ma decides to fire the both of us for letting him catch his death of cold from standing out here in all weathers." Wilson turned fiery red-veined eyes back toward the boy. "What's your name, kid?"

"Luther Brandingham, sir. The Third. My daddy, Luther Brandingham, Junior, was killed in the Rebellion."

Devin didn't bother adding up on mental fingers the number of years since the start of the War Between the States and the apparent age of this little boy. It was within the realm of possibility that the child could be a war orphan. But again, maybe he wasn't. Devin had knowledge that he hadn't shared with Wilson: he happened to remember old Lou Schering from Julesburg, from the days of the construction of the Pacific railroad and its traveling den of thieves and whores, Hell on Wheels. Old Lou had thrown in her lot wholeheartedly where she had made her fortune, with the Union Pacific. She, as well as Devin and many others, had followed along as the tracks progressed. Lou had settled in Bryan when the railroad bypassed Green River, the railroad being primarily a land company and its officials in a proper fit of high dander over S. I. Field beating them to the punch and establishing a prior claim on the land near the river. So Bryan on the Black's Fork subsequently became the permanent site of the railroad's operations in this part of the territory, even to constructing a roundhouse and machine shops of brick, while Green River City's optimistic half-built adobe walls started slowly sinking back into the sand from which they'd arisen.

Hell on Wheels had eventually moved on—albeit without Lou Schering—to its place in history at the final end o' track where the rails east and west met up in Utah. So Devin knew Bryan wasn't the first location where Lou had dipped her fingers in the fleshpot pie, and he had his doubts about any daughter of Lou's landing any scion of a distinguished Southern family, deceased soldier or no. He suspected someone, probably Grandma herself, had been spinning this kid a yarn about his true origins. But people making their way out West to seek their fortune often invented just such highly embroidered pasts. It didn't really make a difference to Devin if Luther was first or second or third of the Brandingham name or any other, and it certainly wasn't his place to enlighten him if his past was a tall tale his grandma made up. Not if the smart conclusion to draw was that the boy's grandma's hand worked the spinning wheel that presently wove the pattern of Devin's own fate, as well as that same hand signing his paychecks.

"Daylight's a-wasting. Get the young'un heaved on up there, and let's go," Wilson said, nodding toward the high-sided wagon.

"Me? Are we leaving already? It's still muddy! And how come I've got to take care of him?" Devin found himself sputtering at the nonsensical nature of the entire situation.

"Because I am the boss tycoon, and because I said so. Stop yer whining. Do as I say." Wilson turned his back on them and mounted one of the wheelers, a pair of huge horses rearmost of the teams of mules, and nearest the lead wagon. Devin, swamper, and in all ways except perhaps native intelligence inferior in status to Wilson, hurried to take his place on the brake of the trail wagon—after shoving the boy up under the canvas cover and pitching his shiny little oxblood valise in after him.

~

Wilson cracked the blacksnake over the mules' backs with a sound like the pop of a firecracker. Despite the threat, the team moved out at a sluggish pace because of the morass of the road, eventually dragging the big iron-shod wheels out of the ruts with an audible sucking sound. But soon enough the little town of Bryan began to disappear in the distance. It took a few hours, but after the sun came out and the road started to dry, the mules finally stepped with a bit livelier stride. They knew very well how far the river was, they could probably smell it and acted eager now to make for it. Unfortunately for them, unless they got a really late start Wilson usually crossed the water and went on, their first night out typically being a dry camp.

As the wagons rolled on after the soaking rain the smell of sage scented the air. The countryside boasted few trees beyond the cottonwoods lining the distant river, and the land on both sides of the trail was covered in sagebrush. It was a good smell, a clean smell that rose when the moisture so unpredictable in this country saturated the leaves and roots of the tough desert plants.

Most freighters out on the frontier used ox teams, pairs of longhorns broken to the yoke and willing and able to pull tremendous loads. And most other teamsters in this particular corner of the territory used the Point of Rocks to South Pass City route, which was shorter, if also shorter of water. As well, there was the Green River to Sweetwater route, which followed the river all the way but which often flooded, making the route all but impassable in the spring.

Anyway, it was Wilson's decision about the animals, and Wilson preferred mules. Mules were a faster, although more expensive means of transport, since they had to haul their own feed. Oxen were a slower and cheaper means of moving goods, which saved money since they fed on prairie grass. Wilson and "St. Louie Lou" Schering had gone back and forth about all the pros and cons for a while, but once he got his mules Wilson began lobbying for the longer route from Bryan to the gold mines to the north. The two of them finally reasoned that despite, and in fact because of, all the water crossings on this route, Wilson could haul more goods worth more money, and yes, some boxes of corn and oats for feed, but also fewer heavy barrels of water. And so far, with flour at thirty dollars a hundredweight, and sugar and coffee selling for seventy-five cents a pound, the two of them had been proved right. They had made lots of money and everybody was happy. There were two breweries in South Pass City, so the saloons had no lack of beer. But hard liquor was another matter—and another money maker for Lou. The formula of the whiskey she bottled was a secret known only to her and perhaps her distiller, but her hush-hush ingredients made a drink vastly superior to Valley Tan, a vile, murky, potato-and-wheat decoction hauled by oxen up the route from Green River. Lou's sipping whiskey was so much more appreciated by the miners of South Pass City they waited to get it, readily plunking down a premium in coin and paper and nuggets.

This morning, with nothing much to do since the flat stretch of road didn't require any braking action from him, Devin tipped back his broad brimmed sombrero to pull out his guns for some long delayed inspection and admiration. They weren't new exactly, but new to him, a pistol and a Springfield rifled musket of War vintage. The weapons were more booty Devin had won off Wilson, who seemed to have slight-to-no luck at gambling but nevertheless diligently kept at it, as if he could devise better fortune through practice not to mention sheer determination, washed down with lots of evil smelling spirits.

The boy, Luther, watched from his high perch as Devin sighted along the rifle barrel out into a stand of greasewood and mountain mahogany, and then put it back in its case hung on the side of the wagon. Devin then took up spinning the cylinder of the Colt's Army Model.

"Hey, mister, what's your name?" Luther called down.

"Devin Cavanaugh." He spun the cylinder once more, all his attention on the weapon.

"Are you a desperado?"

"No." Devin hoped the kid wouldn't persist in trying to make conversation for the entire journey. He tossed the boy a glance from a gimlet eye, hoping the idea of having small holes bored into him by Devin's gaze would terrify Luther into silence. Devin wasn't about to give this stripling a historical account of the adventures of Devin Cavanaugh—a tale heretofore lacking any firearms at all—in the slums of New York City. For good measure he added, "Your grandma don't hire outlaws."

"Well, why do you have a gun at your hip and another to hand there on the side of the wagon, if you aren't a desperado?"

Devin pulled his hat brim down on his forehead and stuck out his chin. "There are road agents and Indians always on the lookout for their chance to steal this valuable merchandise, which it just happens to be my duty to guard against."

"Merchandise that belongs to my grandmama," Luther observed.

"I just said so, didn't I?"

"Is there any chance we might encounter any real desperados?" Luther shivered at the thought.

"There's always a chance," Devin said with an air of wisdom he didn't really feel. Just the idea of encountering gunfire from white brigands or whizzing arrows from Indians in the performance of his duties gave him chills down his spine and an accompanying hollow feeling in his gut. He certainly was no accomplished gunslinger. He practiced sliding his pistol in and out of his belt several times, just to be sure it would appear quickly in his hand should he need it.

"I should like to be an outlaw when I grow up," the boy said, peering over the side of the high wagon while cocking his finger and pointing it at Devin.

Devin almost laughed, until he thought of some of the well-educated and apparently wealthy individuals he had seen in Cheyenne, having a high old time carelessly shooting off guns in every direction in drunken celebration of any minor event. He thought of the twelve- and fourteen-year-old farm boys who ran away from homes in Iowa or Illinois, aspiring to become the next hero of a dime novel, who often enough ended up dead for their trouble or else stuck in boring manual labor jobs that didn't make their lives any better than what they'd left behind. When he would admit the truth, Devin had been lucky, very lucky, in all his own western endeavors so far. It was mere fate he had met up with the people—the good and perhaps those not so angelic—who smoothed his way for him so he had not had to try to make his living with the grip end of a gun.

"Your grandma wouldn't like you to be an outlaw," he said to the boy. "You better just be a good lad. Do what she says, and give up any thought of becoming a villain."

Luther Brandingham III deliberated for a time, flipping over to lie on his back on the grain sacks under the folded-back canvas tarp, staring at the sky as the wagons rolled along through the sage-perfumed air toward their destination.

"I suppose you're right, Mr. Devin," he said eventually, heaving a big, disappointed sigh before closing his eyes for a nap.

Chapter 2
The Soda

*A*S THE WAGONS MOVED away from the river, the company left behind the tall, jagged cliffs of compressed layers of rock in colors of yellow and white and orange. Twice the lumbering wagons were overtaken by lighter, swifter conveyances, a sight often to be seen now that the winter snow had melted in the high country. Stagecoaches full to overflowing with men lured by tales of instant riches were all bent on dashing to the goldfields. Previously, while the work and the pay had been steady during the building, the railroad had lured young men away from the mines. Now, drawn by newspaper accounts of the Sweetwater district and advertisements by those same railroads, the tide of adventurous youth flowed in the opposite direction.

One day the two freighters, the boy, and the freight wagons were met by a dirty, wild-eyed apparition hurtling back the way they had come, toward Bryan. "Indians!" the terrified man shrieked as he passed, pointing over his shoulder as he galloped past. "Ride for your lives!" He lifted his felt hat long enough to show them a glimpse of daylight peeping through a hole in its crown, and then he was gone, swaybacked old mare beneath him clopping madly away, leaving behind a small cloud of dust. As man and beast disappeared into the distance Luther looked at Devin with wide eyes, his mouth a round *O* of astonishment and fear as he clutched for a secure perch on the fabric of the bag of grain beneath him. Devin drew his rifle from its scabbard, watching as Wilson looked cautiously all around them before dismounting to walk ahead of the mules to scout the country. The intelligent animals plodded on without supervision, Devin remaining alert for any movement on the sides of the road, expecting ambush from every shrub or rock or mounded hill.

The ground turned to powdery grit as they climbed to a stretch of empty terrain, alkali that rose in puffs and then clouds, tasting like saleratus on the tongue. Wilson pulled his neckerchief up over his nose and mouth in meager defense against the choking dust kicked up by the team as he came to walk alongside them. Devin pulled off his own bandana and climbed up to wrap it around Luther's face until only the boy's eyes showed beneath his newsboy-style cap. Devin stayed up top with the boy for a time, glad to be riding for the most part above the cloud of fine white dirt instead of striding along in the midst of it. Sometimes Devin aspired to be boss, but although he hated to admit it at other times his inferior status had its own reward.

"Now we look like bandits for sure!" Luther was wriggling with excitement, one hand splayed across the kerchief covering the lower part of his face. "We could be real desperados."

"Well, we aren't," Devin said. "The scarf is to keep you from choking, and to protect your lungs. I've told you before we're on the side of law and order. Even if in truth there isn't much that can be called real law around these parts." He turned his head once more to survey the country for any sight of Indians before climbing down to take up his post by the wagon brake.

"So if we're held up, the bandits will just go away free while our bones are thrown by the wayside to be picked clean by coyotes?" the boy asked.

Devin turned back to eye the boy. "You're certainly one for big fancies, Third. Where do you get such notions?"

"My proper name is Luther Brandingham III," he reminded Devin with an air of highbrow dignity.

"Yeah, that's what I said—Third." Devin grinned to himself. He had no expectation of ever having children of his own, but secretly he liked them okay. He especially liked their ingenuousness, it was such easy work to twit them.

"And I have quite an extensive library," the boy continued. "I've read about many things."

"This extensive library of yours, is it back there in the big municipality of Bryan City?" Devin scoffed, making a rude noise in his throat.

"It just so happens I had to leave most of my things behind. In St. Louis, Missouri. Where my home is . . . was. Used to be." The boy shook his head, and to Devin's utter astonishment, pulled the borrowed neckerchief up past his eyes to hide his entire face. From underneath it there came a telltale sob.

~

Dulcinetta Jackson sat at a green baize-covered table in the Goldust Saloon and Dance Hall. It was one of several such places situated on the half-mile-long main thoroughfare in South Pass City. Thirteen spades from one deck of cards were fanned out in front of her as, on a desultory midweek morning, she dealt faro from a second deck for the three men who sat across the table from her. Business was slow yet, but she had no doubt it would pick up as soon as daylight began to fade and the miners who worked individual claims straggled into town, picks and shovels balanced over their shoulders. Luckily for those who serviced their needs, other men with steady jobs who worked for the big quartz outfits reported in regular shifts, and came into town at predictable intervals for their daily libations, as well as the other pleasures the establishment offered. As yet most of the people associated with the Goldust's nighttime commerce slumbered on, even amidst the constant reverberations of the ten-stamp mill of the Carissa which, except for periods of shutdown to clean up the pans and batteries, ran almost continuously, day and night, the pounding accompanied by the rattling of glasses and bottles on the back bar of the Goldust.

Some of the doxies who worked at the saloon complained the constant racket ruined their sleep, but Dulcie quite liked the steady pounding. The noise and vibration meant a continuous stream of gold dust, coin of the realm, and paper money wending its inexorable way into her expanding bank account. The Carissa, which had morphed into the affectionate name feminized from the original Cariso, as well as the Morning Star, Melrose, Copperopolis, Last Chance, Miner's Delight, and the other gold and silver mines of the district, were Dulcie's personal tickets to a shining carousel of wealth, and she meant to ride the boom as long as it lasted. There were once over fifteen hundred lodes nearby, but almost from the beginning the Sweetwater had been declared a "flash in the pan," a "bilk," a "deadbeat." All of which Dulcinetta had heard numerous times and felt she could safely ignore. Still, she was having trouble completely disregarding the niggling mental observation that the seasonal population of the area was this spring already showing a slight but noticeable—and yes, admit it, worrisome—decline.

Formerly no more than a stage and telegraph station on the old Oregon Trail, South Pass City had moved north and in the last two years grown to a population of a few thousand souls. The little settlement tried hard to be a real town, but the Goldust and Billy Wilson's Hotel and Saloon were as yet the only two-story buildings in town. Hampered by a lack of lumber, save for the output of a small sawmill that couldn't handle the demand, plus the distance from the railhead necessitating almost all supplies being hauled in by wagon, the town was still largely made up of half-canvas structures, tents, and dugouts. A group of speculators had erected a few cozy one-room cabins with a view to selling them to the miners at a profit, but for the most part they still sat unoccupied. Very few local residents made their fortunes at the actual business of mining, a story familiar to Dulcie and her compatriots. The people who made a living serving the miners generally did better financially than the miners themselves. It was a lesson she had learned early, at the knee—so to speak—of her aunt and foster mother, St. Louie Lou. Lou Schering was a decent enough parent, all things considered, but she had been an excellent teacher of finance. And Dulcinetta Jackson had been an outstanding student.

"Gentlemen, place your bets." Stacks of chips appeared on the spades, and Dulcinetta shuffled the deck of cards with an expert riffle. She offered the cut to a florid-faced man sitting opposite her, who was steadily puffing clouds of bluish smoke from a huge, smelly cigar. As she bent toward him with the cards she deliberately pressed her upper arms against her breasts, offering a quick glimpse of the dark shadow of her cleavage.

With one eye on the action directly in front of her, still she kept track of the other activities of the barroom. Without having completely sobered up from the previous night, one of the town's intrepid gold seekers, known as a rip-roaring drunk, was arguing that the bartender should serve him another shot. The barkeep, swarthy of skin and dark of eye, curly hair cut short and oiled to his skull down both sides of his head from a middle part, caught Dulcie's eye on him over the shoulder of the inebriated customer. Wordlessly, Dulcinetta cut her gaze in the direction of the door.

"You've had all you're going to get for now, Hank," the bartender, Josiah Jackson, said in a reasonable tone, heeding Dulcie's silent direction. "Go on now, get sobered up and come back later."

"The hell you shay!" Hank the Sot shouted, pounding his fist on the bar. "I ain't nearly drunk enough yet. Gimme another!"

Dressed in an immaculate, high-collared and gartered striped shirt, with clean, pressed pants, white apron, and gleaming black boots, Josiah casually reached below the bar for his Enforcer, a length of stout hickory which had followed him from place to place in his long career serving up liquor to patrons sober, well-oiled, and all stages in between. He laid it, without ceremony and without a word, on the bar top between Hank and himself.

Hank, though, was a little too far gone to heed the silent warning. Swaying, he managed to steady himself enough to grab the empty glass in front of him, turn, and hurl it against the wall near where Dulcinetta sat. The glass shattered, a few drops spattering the skirt of her low-cut green satin gown. She looked at the wet spots staining her dress, then raised her eyes once more to the barkeep's. The expression on her face didn't alter, but Josiah responded instantly by hurrying around the bar to seize the hapless Hank Smith by collar and belt. Rushing him toward the door—in the end dragging the man once he lost his balance—Josiah kicked open the double doors and flung Hank face first out into the muck of the street. Then he brushed his palms together, straightened his apron, and sauntered back to his post behind the cherry wood bar that had cost Dulcie a small fortune to ship from Chicago by rail and then by freight wagon.

It was still a few minutes shy of eleven o'clock in the morning. Dulcinetta sighed, feeling from all indications this might prove to be a long day. She turned the soda, the top card of the deck in the dealing box, and placed it to her left. The second card of the deck she placed face up to her right. The third card went on soda. Each player was betting against the house. The first card was ignored, the second was a loser, and the third a winner. Patrons could bet for or against any of the numbers. A copper placed on the chips was an indicator that particular number would lose. With no limit on the number of players, Dulcie was skilled enough that she could take on many more at a time than just these three at her table. She kept track of all cards played on a wooden-spindled casekeeper, so everyone playing knew which cards formed the winning and losing piles, and which remained to be dealt. By now the game was nearing its end, with only three cards remaining. The men sitting in front of her could bet on the order that the cards would be turned up, instead of on the layout. Two of the men watched her hands as they eagerly awaited the turn of the cards. The other man, apparently already despairing of any good luck coming his way this morning, instead turned his hot gaze on the slope of the dealer's breasts, the twin mounds of which rose and fell gently with each inhale and exhale. Dulcinetta knew very well where the player's regard had strayed. Deliberately, she dragged out the moment to give the loser a good look before turning the last three cards face up.

Her livelihood depended on knowing how to get men to play, and how to interest them in continuing to play. And the odds were always in Dulcinetta's favor: odds of any of the men successfully calling the last turn were at best five to one. The odds of the man presently eyeing her assets having any luck in luring her where his thoughts wandered were much, much higher—and likewise always in Dulcinetta's favor. She not only had Josiah guarding her. Her secret, favorite little derringer resided, loaded and ready, in a handy pocket of her otherwise enticing, black lace-trimmed emerald frock. The little gun looked harmless, and the few times she had been forced to display it some men had dared to laugh outright at the sight of it. But Dulcie knew it was anything but a toy, and she was as skilled with firearms as she was with games of chance.

She had paid off the gamblers and was raking in the house winnings with the edge of a card when the front door opened and a splash of yellow light lit up her gown. She expected that Hank had sobered enough to have crawled out of the road by now and was coming back for another try at getting more whiskey from Josiah. Nothing new in that, it happened on average twice a day, so she couldn't have said what caused her to actually look up. Her pert breasts rose high on an indrawn breath, threatening to spill from her bodice as she held her breath, the urge to exhale suddenly failing her in her shock. She held that one breath for a long moment, long enough to take in every detail of the sight of the rumpled, dirty man clutching the hand of a little boy with a head of hair the exact same black color and crinkled texture as hers and Josiah's. The pair just stood there backlit in a wash of morning sunlight, in the open doorway of the Goldust Saloon. As they let their eyes adjust in the smoky dimness, Dulcinetta Jackson stared at the pair with a wide-eyed, unbelieving gaze.

~

Just because Devin and Cal Wilson had seen no Indians out on the trail, didn't mean Indians hadn't actually been there. South Pass City had its share of Sioux raiders who ran off stock and appropriated material goods whenever the chance presented itself. But generally the trip from Bryan to the gold district was uneventful, and the freighters had grown to expect it to be so. Soon enough when nothing further occurred to alarm them, the two had dropped their guard and the trip proceeded as usual. Wilson climbed back on the wheeler and Devin resumed his admiring examination of his guns. Third had eventually gained control of himself and quit crying for the things he had been forced to leave behind in the big city. Except for a few complaints from the boy about the monotonous diet of beans and salt pork giving him gas and a belly ache, the final few days of the trip had passed uneventfully.

There was a minor struggle, a difference of opinion, between the men when they descended into the little valley containing South Pass City. "Take care of the animals," Wilson ordered Devin, dismounting and moving hurriedly toward the boy.

"You still owe me another turn," Devin objected. "It was part of the payoff."

"Are ya looking for a good socdolager?" He grinned as Devin held up a hand forestalling a fight. "Ya know that word, huh? I thought you'd funk out when push come to shove. Be off with ya now. We'll worry about paying ya later."

Funk out, indeed. Cal had a nerve calling him a coward given the disparity in their sizes, Devin thought. At any other time a physical threat from Wilson might have struck Devin as comical, but he wasn't given the leisure to think about it. All of a sudden Wilson, who had wanted nothing to do with the boy for the entire eleven days previous, took proprietary hold of the kid's arm with one hand and the handle of his little leather valise in the other, and started towing him down the street. Man and boy marched past the hotel, the bakery, and the Masonic Lodge, several saloons including that belonging to John Morris, the judge's husband, as well as the W. L. Scholes Overland Saloon.

"Hey, just where are you supposed to deliver him?" Devin hollered.

"You shoulda read the letter, ya dumb, ignorant coot," Wilson tossed back over his shoulder.

It wasn't as if the new little city had grown so big he wouldn't be able to find them later, Devin consoled himself as they disappeared from sight. Droop-shouldered with weariness even though it wasn't much past noon, he led the team to the warehouse to see to getting the wagons unloaded and the horses and mules turned over to George

Dean's Black Horse Livery Stable to be curried and fed. When the work was finished, he was degrees more dirty, sweaty, and tired than when they'd rolled into town. He thought about taking a dip in Willow Creek just to get the worst of the grime off, but he knew from experience how teeth-chatteringly cold its swift waters were, and put off bathing in favor of finding Wilson, and perhaps some liquid refreshment to help unglue his tongue from the dry roof of his mouth.

As soon as he entered the double front doors of the Goldust Saloon and Dance Hall, he was sorry he'd changed his mind about a dip in the creek. Sitting across the room with Luther Brandingham III perched on her knee was the prettiest woman Devin had ever espied. He knew it was small of him, but he was pleased to see that even after all the time that had passed since Wilson left him to take care of the wagons, the imperious lady had yet to offer to let Cal sit in her presence. She kept him standing in front of her dealer's table like a petitioner to a royal court. Several sheets of creased paper lay on the table in front of her. Devin was guessing one of them was probably Third's initial letter to Wilson from Lou. From the evidence, the boy had been tasked with delivering the remainder of the missives only to the lady, probably tucked away this whole time in his little leather valise.

Devin continued studying the woman, hoping to catch his breath. He had never had his breath stolen by the sight of a female before, but this one was a truly extraordinary example of the species. The sight of her simply knocked the wind out of him. With shiny, curly hair cascading in ringlets down to her sun-kissed bare shoulders, she wore an expensive-looking, low cut green gown, and was undeniably beautiful—but she was also obviously upset. It seemed to Devin that perhaps Third had been deposited into her keeping without prior warning, which would explain the need for the missives strewn on the table. At any rate, her ruby lips wore a slight pout and her dark eyes kept shooting accusatory glances at Wilson as if he'd delivered a most unwelcome package, even as she continued to hold the boy on her knee. She might not want Luther perched there, but it didn't look like anyone dared to suggest an alternative to her.

The barkeep stood behind the bar polishing glasses with a cloth and trying to pretend he wasn't eavesdropping. Devin had no such compunction. He went to stand beside Wilson so he could listen. He wanted a closer look at the woman. He especially admired the smooth flesh above the ruffle of black lace adorning her décolletage. He had a brief urge to scoff at himself for even knowing that highbrow word, but he'd picked it up from a fellow refugee from New York City, Ailis Tierney, who had high ambitions and whose fondest wish was to have her own dress shop. Thinking of Ailis, Devin spared a passing hope that his friend, at least, had begun to realize her dream by now.

"That's him, Mama," Third shouted, pointing at Devin. "The desperado!"

Devin, as had become his habit to tease the boy, turned to glance over his shoulder as if he didn't realize Third was pointing at him. The woman, who looked to Devin to be perhaps in her mid-twenties in age, a few years older than himself if he had to make a guess—but he didn't know much about women and his estimate could be way off—raised a manicured hand to grasp the boy's rude pointing finger and lower it to his lap. Her dark eyes studied Devin even more closely. He tried not to reveal any hint of reciprocal admiration, running a finger underneath his grimy collar. He had started to sweat under her scrutiny, and he wished even more sincerely that he had taken time to bathe before showing up here.

"I hope you realize the boy is just having a little fun, ma'am." Devin's skin itched under her steady gaze but he resisted the urge to scratch.

"I want to thank you, sir," she answered in a sultry voice as her grip on Third, who was now squirming, tightened. "I'm afraid my son hasn't had much opportunity for amusement in his short life. He has been relating how you kindly took him under your wing for his journey here, even to indulging him by enacting some of the most exciting parts of his library of adventure novels by the light of your campfires at night."

Wilson rolled his eyes, rocking back on his boot heels. Devin would bet almost anything that Wilson wanted pretty urgently by this time to just get over to the bar and sink his mustache into a mug of foamy beer instead of standing here like a truant in front of a lecturing schoolmarm. Although with his admittedly limited experience of school, Devin had never glimpsed, or even imagined in his most outlandish fevered adolescent dreams, a school teacher who might in the least resemble this woman.

She extended her hand for Devin to shake. He hesitated to touch it with one of his own dirty paws but when he did he found it warm and dry and clean and soft. "Dulcinetta Jackson," she purred while Third seized the opportunity to slip from his mother's satin clutch and run to pitch his arms around one of Devin's thighs.

"Pleased, I'm sure, ma'am," Devin muttered, as he allowed his begrimed hand to barely brush the tips of her delicate fingers. Still feeling a bit stunned by the sight of her, he sucked in a deep breath through his nostrils. Her scent wafted toward him, a subtle flowery perfume he could detect even above the heavy saloon odors of male sweat, alcohol, sawdust, and cigar smoke.

"And you are Devin Cavanaugh." She smiled, lips shiny and red as garnets parting to show two rows of perfect, small white teeth. She indicated the papers on the table. "As well as our Mr. Wilson here, you are aware of the import of these letters?"

Devin shook his head. Until entering the premises he had had no idea there was more than one letter. That sneak Wilson had apparently been rifling through the boy's little valise while he slept to have discovered that there were more. Wilson was quick to snatch any advantage, Devin well knew by now. He suspected that the facts that Wilson had hustled off with the boy as soon as they hit town, and that he was still standing here minus a dripping mug in his hand, meant that he awaited something, probably a reward as yet unattained for delivering the boy and the letters.

"I see." Dulcinetta's gaze settled on a point behind the waiting men's heads as she paused in thought. Perhaps she studied the opulent painted curves of the redhead reclining invitingly atop a rumpled coverlet in the large gold-framed portrait over the bar. But in Devin's opinion, if the comparison entered her head she needn't harbor a single worry that she didn't measure up. She was much more beautiful than the nude in the painting, if perhaps not quite so voluptuous.

But Dulcinetta's gaze suddenly lowered from the picture.

Devin and Wilson both turned to see what she was looking at. A vision in scarlet crepe de chine descended the stairs, a tiny Chinese woman of unimaginable delicacy and grace, jet black mane of hair confined with two ivory pins and eyes kept demurely lowered.

The whole place grew absolutely silent as this dream made her way toward them. No one, with the possible exception of Dulcinetta, spared a glance for the man who followed her down the stairs, melting into the gathering of other men in the saloon. The boy Third wasn't overawed by the entrance of the woman either. "Xiang Ju!" Luther yelled, releasing his grip on Devin to rush and throw his arms around the small woman's waist.

From where he stood next to Wilson, Devin very clearly heard him swallow, the only other sound in the saloon being the faint rustle of embroidered fabric as the newcomer lifted a languid hand to stroke the boy's hair.

"Fragrant Chrysanthemum," Third hollered.

The woman smiled down into the boy's excited face. "That is correct, small master," she said in a musical voice. "You remember. Xiang Ju—Fragrant Chrysanthemum."

Dulcinetta sighed. "Ju, I have told you numerous times that you have no master. Please don't put such an idea into my son's head, even by a term of address."

"As you wish." The tiny woman bowed in Dulcinetta's direction. "But I still have a debt, nevertheless."

Dulcinetta chose to ignore the comment. She indicated the two men. "These gentlemen have delivered Luther to me. Xiang Ju, please meet Caleb Wilson and Devin Cavanaugh."

The woman bowed to Wilson and then in turn to Devin. From the continued dry gulping sounds issuing from Wilson's direction, Devin suspected his boss was as affected by this beauty as much as he himself had been by Dulcinetta Jackson. It was truly a day of wonders.

"I have some consulting to do," Dulcinetta said. "Ju, could you see that these fellows get a nice bath and something to eat? Not you, young man. You stay with me," she added, rising to halt Third by grasping his shoulder as he forgot himself and relaxed his grip on Fragrant Chrysanthemum, allowing the Chinese woman to escape his hold and leave the barroom.

Luther Brandingham III stood still and appeared to consider his options as he watched his friend Devin, and Wilson, walk out of sight, following Xiang Ju.

"All right, Mama," the boy agreed eventually, with a heavily weighted sigh.

Chapter *3*
Double Eagle

FRAGRANT CHRYSANTHEMUM LED WILSON and Devin to a door set in a wall at one side of the bar. Josiah Jackson watched their passing reflections in the mirror as he straightened bottles and lined up glassware. Then his eyes once again sought the reflections of the card dealer and her son. Dulcinetta caught the man's glance of repressed longing, and after the others disappeared, gave Luther a nudge. "Be a good boy and go greet your grandfather," she said in a low tone.

Dulcie watched Luther's transformation from exuberance to shyness and formality at the departure of his new best friend and apparent role model, Devin Cavanaugh.

"Go on," she urged, although she could hardly blame the child for his ambivalence toward the stern-looking old man standing behind the bar. She knew Josiah remembered his grandson, at least a much smaller version of this same boy, but it was doubtful if Luther had any memory of Josiah.

Josiah's expression began to thaw a bit as the boy came forward and obediently extended his hand.

"How do you do, sir?" Luther said.

"Very well. Very well, indeed." Josiah clasped the smaller hand in his own. From across the room the man's upright posture and limber movements had hinted of a younger man. Up close, one could begin to tell his true age from the fine wrinkling of his brown skin and the threads of silver in his hair. He shook the hand of the youngster who looked very much like a smaller, lighter-skinned version of himself. "And how are you this fine day, young sir?"

There were few patrons in the saloon, but they already had enough to talk about this day and Dulcinetta didn't want the meeting between Josiah and Luther to become more grist for the gossip mill. She approached the bar, lifting her skirt slightly to avoid the aromatic layer of sawdust on the floor. Because the wood shavings were fresh, they had a tendency to stick to her hem and slippers, and consequently aggravated her when they made a mess of the carpets of her private rooms.

"You heard?" She cocked her head in the direction of her faro table where the letters still lay. Josiah nodded in reply. "What would you advise me to do now?" she asked.

"Let it ride for a day or two," her father said. "Watch the two of them and see how it pans out. Just because they delivered this fine young man to us doesn't mean you have to choose either of the messengers. There are lots of other eligible candidates."

"Yes, I'd say we have quite a selection of quality contenders walk in the door every day of the week," Dulcie commented wryly, letting her gaze slide over the patrons of the saloon, most of them already in various stages of inebriation. "Papa, there's not a single one of them I would trust with my business for even a single hour. By sending my child to us through these teamsters, she was sending a message. You know that. You know Lou. Why the mystery? She could have simply put Luther on a stage."

"I do indeed know Lou." The hard creases bracketing Josiah's mouth softened. "It's been many a year now. Since St. Louis, and before that, even. I knew that yellow-haired gal in Mississippi."

"I know. Where I was born," Dulcinetta said in a voice pitched for his ears only.

"Yes, you were born the child of a beautiful mama," Josiah reminisced softly, the focus of his eyes softening as he remembered. "It was a very dangerous time for us."

"I know, Papa. And the blood of that child of mine is diluted even more than mine." Dulcinetta tipped her head in Luther's direction, not wanting to draw the boy's attention to matters he was better off not knowing. The comparison of Josiah's sienna-colored skin, her own *café au lait* color, and Luther's pinkish-beige complexion was a subject too obvious to be often discussed when he was near. It was one reason among many that the boy usually resided far from his natural family. The situation with Lou must be of an extremely dire nature for her to send Luther to his mother and grandfather.

"We owe Aunt Lou a lot," Dulcinetta continued. "For the future of us all, it is incumbent upon me to make the right decision."

"I realize that. We owe her our lives, child," Josiah said. "If she trusts your judgment, I can do no less."

~

Ju led the men down a short hallway, opening a door to a small room behind what Devin thought must be a kitchen, judging from the mouth-watering smells emanating from the gaps around the door. The tight space they entered held a bench, a copper tub, and a chair. There were a few pegs on a board nailed to the wall. Ju gestured them inside. "I will bring water for bath, sirs," she said. "If you remove shirt, I will also shave and cut hair."

Devin propped his rifle against the wall, happy to oblige and hoping he could be first to get shaved. He hated the feel of what little facial hair he did grow. Now, after days on the trail, it was lying in stiff patches against his sticky skin. The only reason for allowing the hair on his jaw to grow while on the trail was that it tended to help keep the bugs off his face. As for the state of the hair on his head, he had no excuse. He just hadn't taken the time to have it cut in a while. It hung in a wild carrot-colored bush past his shoulders, as if he'd been away from civilization for months instead of little more than a week. It was no wonder young Third thought he looked like an outlaw. But up to this point he hadn't seen fit to spend much of his pay on sprucing up. He'd had no reason to worry about his appearance. Who had any inkling he would meet up with someone he would care to impress as much as Dulcinetta Jackson? If it wasn't already too late for anything like a revised first impression, he thought miserably.

Ju left while Wilson began unbuttoning his shirt. "I'd sure like to get me a piece of that cunning little petticoat, yessir." Wilson smirked.

"She looks pretty high-class to me," Devin answered, dismissing Cal's chances. "And even if you had any money in your pocket, how do you know she's for sale?"

"Don't you worry none about that. She is in the trade, that's a certainty. I just wish I had the correct wherewithal. Can you front me a bit?"

"No, I won't lend you any money. How can you tell she's for sale?" Devin persisted.

"I just know women, that's all. For instance, the one out front, the snooty baggage in the green dress, the card dealer. That one don't never go upstairs. Take my word, that one definitely ain't in the market. The Chinee gal, now, she come sashayin' down the stairs with a happified shopper following along behind her like a well-fed dog. They came directly out the sheets. I could almost smell it—didn't you take note?" Wilson removed his shirt and hung it on a peg.

The odor wafting toward him as Wilson raised his arms gave Devin the urge to lift his own to find out how bad his armpit stench was. It occurred to him that he should return to the freight office for his carpetbag. It would be a crying shame to get all spiffed up and then put the same dusty, smelly clothes back on. Dirty duds hardly seemed destined to impress the likes of Dulcinetta Jackson any more than a dirty muleskinner inside them might.

"Tell you what, Cal," Devin said, "why don't you go first with the bath and the shave? I'm going back to get a change of clothes."

"Ya still lookin' to impress that high class piece of muslin out in the saloon—no matter what I tell ya about her? Well, I can't blame you there, but good luck to ya is all I can say. I got a better chance with no money and the Chinee than you got flashing a month's wage for that fancy piece." Wilson turned away and began unbuttoning his trousers as the door opened and Ju returned, a protective cloth wrapped around the bail of the large kettle of hot water she toted so she wouldn't burn her hands.

Devin turned and left them to the business at hand. As he made his way back to the freight office, he found himself hoping Wilson was right about what kind of woman Dulcinetta Jackson was. He wanted to believe she held herself above such dissolute goings on as he had witnessed in the temporary towns during the building of the new railway. Why he wanted to believe she was better than the blowsy type of woman common out West, he couldn't say. As if it could make a single difference in the world to his chances concerning Dulcinetta what his standards might be, Devin thought, shaking his head at his own foolishness.

He took his time returning to the Goldust. He had no desire to walk in on a naked Caleb Wilson. He also didn't want to hear Cal's attempts to persuade Fragrant Chrysanthemum to tender him a bit of rocking buttock action on credit, or more predictably in the case of the Wilson that Devin knew, on the house. In Devin's estimation, based on what small success he himself had ever had with women, paid or otherwise, he suspected the favors of an exotic like Xiang Ju would be darned expensive.

When he returned to the Goldust, Dulcinetta and Third had disappeared and only the bartender remained in the saloon. Devin passed him with a nod, and headed back to the room where the bath was set up. Upon entering the room, glad to see Wilson fully dressed, Devin had to admit the man looked and smelled a lot better. But Wilson's attitude was considerably soured, and so Devin assumed he had had no luck in talking Ju into a free or reduced-price upstairs romp.

"I'm gonna go get me a beer and something to eat," Wilson said, brushing past Devin. Those two things could be got without cash money, the freighting company taking care of board within reason for the men for the duration of their stay in South Pass City, and their bed consisting of sleeping on the wagon tarps on the freight office floor. Devin had to stifle a smile at the very idea of shrewd old St. Louie Lou providing the services of one of her girls free of charge to a smelly old mule-whacker like Wilson. Or even a spanking clean mule-whacker, come to that.

Devin removed his shirt and took a seat on the chair Wilson had recently vacated. Fragrant Chrysanthemum put her fingers on his forehead and gave a gentle push, urging him to tip his head back. When he obliged, she slapped a hot towel around the lower half of his face and let him steam while she stropped the razor and then whipped a cake of soap in a mug into a lather. She removed the towel, brushed a layer of thick shaving foam on his face, and then began scraping at his cheeks with the straight razor. When she was done, she wiped his face with the wet towel and motioned for him to turn the chair around. She picked up a thick comb, and dipping it in a glass of water, began working the snarls from his tangled mat of red hair.

"I apologize for the rat's nest," Devin said. "You have very gentle hands but you can pull my hair hard if you need to. I don't mind."

She said, "Missy not allow rat nest here." Her small hands steadily continued their task.

Devin smiled at her literal misinterpretation. "How did you come to live in South Pass City, Ju?"

"Missy Jackson bring me. From San Francisco."

"And now you work for her?" Devin tried to square what Wilson said about Ju with what little she seemed willing to admit.

"I stay here. I work." Ju wrapped another towel around his shoulders, took up a pair of scissors, and began snipping at his hair. "Missy Jackson buy my debt. I belong Missy Jackson."

"Nobody owns you. Slavery is outlawed in this country, Ju, in case nobody told you. A big, bloody war was recently fought so all people could be free." Devin resisted the urge to shake his head while she was cutting his hair in case he ended up with a bald patch or two through his own carelessness.

"Missy Jackson buy my debt. My family honor. I go now for water for bath."

Devin found it hard to believe that Dulcinetta Jackson would force Xiang Ju to come from San Francisco to South Pass City just to embark on a life of prostitution. Something didn't quite add up. But all that could wait. As Ju disappeared with the basin and towels and scissors, he thought that all he really cared about right now was the hot bath he'd been promised.

He emerged, dressed, a short while later. Clean and shorn, he was ready for a good meal and maybe a beer and some socializing in the saloon. As he was passing the door from where the enticing smells originated, it suddenly opened and he found himself face to face with the object of his curiosity. Dulcinetta had also freshened up and changed her clothes; she now wore a stunning peach taffeta ensemble that brought out a similar blush in her cheeks. Her shoulders were bare, the gown apparently held up by some whalebone contraption over her ribs that also lifted the top of her golden bosom to his appreciative view. A drape of fine mesh of a matching color adorned the tops of her shapely arms. Devin sucked in a breath at the sight of all that creamy flesh on display, unable to tear his eyes away even if he'd wanted to.

"Mr. Cavanaugh," Dulcinetta exclaimed. "I would hardly have recognized you. You do clean up well—you look simply dashing."

"Well, ma'am," Devin said, feeling heat rising up his neck to his cheeks as he finally looked into her eyes instead of elsewhere at her person, "I'd say you're looking mighty fine yourself."

"Oh, do you like it?" She twirled once, her skirt flaring to display a pair of trim ankles. "I stumbled upon the most divine dressmaker. She was traveling with the hurdy gurdy girls on the dance circuit, of all things. She's Irish, rather like yourself, I think, Mr. Cavanaugh."

Devin murmured, "Let me guess. Not Ailis?" When Dulcinetta started to nod, he asked, "For certain? Ailis Tierney?"

"Why, yes, I think that was her name. Do you know her?" Dulcinetta examined him from the corner of her eye as she took his arm and steered him into the small space set up as a dining room, easing the door closed behind her.

"I knew her a bit in Cheyenne," Devin said. Upon catching the quirk of one of Dulcinetta's raven-wing eyebrows, he added, "I wintered in Cheyenne in late '67 and early '68, waiting for track laying to resume in the spring."

Third jumped up and left his place at the table to race across the room and clamp Devin's leg with both arms as had become his habit. "Hello, Devin!" he yelled.

Devin smiled down at the boy. "Hello, squirt."

"You know that's not my name!"

"Oh, that's right, I forgot. You're Third. I remember now."

"Luther Brandingham III," the boy shouted.

His mother frowned. "Luther, would it be possible for you to lower your voice from a screech so we might dine in a civilized manner? And why don't you be a good boy and let Mr. Cavanaugh free of your frantic clutch?"

Devin admitted to himself it was rather a difficult task to negotiate the floor of the dining room, even as small as it was, with Dulcinetta clinging to one arm and her son riding like a stick horse the leg on his opposite side, grasping him tightly around the waist so he wouldn't tumble off. Still, he said, "That's all right, ma'am. It's just a lad's high spirits. He'll settle down eventually." He managed to pull out a chair and get her properly seated. Then he rounded the table, pried each of Luther's hands off, got him plunked on the seat of a chair, and finally sat down next to him.

Dulcinetta took it all in with her dark eyes. Devin felt the weight of her judgment. He could only hope he wasn't found wanting.

"You're very good with him," she said, nodding toward her son.

"Oh, I've been around kids most of my life." Devin squirmed at the thought of enlightening this sophisticated woman about his dodgy exploits as a New York City street Arab or the questionable doings of the other members of his gang. Luckily, Ju entered at that moment, bearing a big, steaming bowl of elk stew and dumplings, and saving him from further evasion on the subject of his past.

"Seems like for her size that woman can pack around her weight in kettles of water and bowls of victuals," Devin observed.

"Yes, our Chrysanthemum. Small but mighty." Dulcinetta smiled indulgently, shaking out her napkin to place it on her lap. "Dinner smells wonderful, as usual, Ju. Will you join us?"

Fragrant Chrysanthemum shook her head, tucking her chin against her chest. Dulcinetta sighed as if this was the usual course of events between them, and raised her glass to her lips for a dainty sip of water.

Devin was grateful once again for his exposure to dinner table manners in the orphanage. Now he copied Dulcinetta's motions instead of tucking the cloth into the neck of his shirt, even though that course of action still seemed more logical to him than having his napkin lying uselessly across his knees. Ju served them and then backed out of the room.

Dulcinetta picked up her spoon and Devin did the same. Luther was still squirming around in his seat, every once in a while clinking his spoon against his glass, as if testing to see if anyone would pay attention to small instances of misbehavior or if he must escalate in order to become the center of attention.

"Why are you so wriggly? Do you need to go out back?" Dulcinetta asked him with a sharp glance.

The boy shook his head negatively.

"Then stop fidgeting and eat, or I will excuse you from the table and you can go to bed," Dulcinetta said to the boy. Third looked hopefully in Devin's direction as if he thought maybe his grown-up friend had the authority to countermand his mother's threats. "I mean it, Luther," Dulcinetta said. "I am due in the saloon in a few minutes, and some of us who must work have not yet had their suppers. If you don't take the opportunity to eat now while the food is hot on the table, you may go hungry."

They set to eating, and the adults were soon finished. Patting her lips with her napkin, Dulcinetta rose. Luther was still in the process of dragging out going off to bed as long as possible by dawdling over his meal. When Ju came in to clear the table, Dulcinetta gestured to the boy and said to Ju, "I leave him entirely to you."

Ju nodded, smiling in Luther's direction.

As Dulcinetta and Devin left the small living quarters, she whispered with a glance from beneath her lashes, "I must confess Ju is actually better with my son than I have ever been."

Devin was beginning to get the idea that almost anyone was better with Third than his pretty mother. They entered the main part of the saloon from the little hall, Dulcinetta clinging to his arm. Things were starting to liven up as the sun set and darkness fell outside. Inside, lamps had been lit, there were several card games in progress, and beer and whiskey were flowing. Devin caught sight of Wilson leaning against the bar, one foot propped on the brass rail.

Dulcie, folding her skirts against her legs, went behind the bar and nodded back toward the way she had come. The bartender apparently took her wordless meaning, and left to follow the rich stew smell toward his own waiting dinner.

Devin stood next to Wilson, who raised his glass in salute. "Ain't you going to get anything to eat?" Wilson asked. "The restaurant has a pretty good venison steak. Or they got bear, if you've a mind to try it."

"I already ate." Once again Devin had the impression Dulcinetta was weighing his behavior as she stood behind the bar watching them in the mirror, so he did not enlighten Wilson as to the location of the meal he had eaten. For some reason, he thought she approved of that omission.

"I'm glad I caught you both together," Dulcinetta said over her shoulder, drawing Devin a beer. "I wanted to give you a little something for seeing my boy safe on the road."

"Why, that's not neces—" Devin began, when Wilson's pointy elbow suddenly spiked him in the ribs.

"That's mighty kind of you, ma'am," Wilson said. Dulcinetta set the mug in front of Devin, who gave her a weak grin and slight shrug as explanation for not continuing his protest. When she dug into her pocket and came up with two shiny twenty-dollar gold pieces and set one in front of each man, Devin caught the greedy gleam in Wilson's eye. The double eagle in front of Wilson disappeared so swiftly, he might have been a circus practitioner of legerdemain.

"Take it," Dulcinetta urged Devin when he failed to pick up his own reward. "Please. I want you to have it."

"I'll be glad for it if you don't want it," Wilson offered, starting to reach for Devin's coin. Dulcinetta's eyes flashed in warning. Devin quickly pocketed the money, deflecting Wilson's grab for it, and once again an analytical spark appeared momentarily in Dulcinetta's eyes before she shuttered the expression.

With his pocket newly lined, Wilson wasted no time in switching to whiskey from the beer he had been drinking. Dulcinetta served him as quickly as he could swallow and re-order, and it wasn't long before

Wilson was slurring his words and grabbing the edge of the bar for support. There might have been just the tiniest bit of contempt for the muleskinner displayed in the point of Dulcinetta's tongue poking the inside of her cheek as she slid another shot across the bar. But she was much too practiced at controlling her feelings for Devin to be sure she wasn't just thinking of something else as she continued to serve Cal liquor. And he never did decide definitely as Wilson's loosened tongue prattled on about one inconsequential thing and another while he drank and Dulcinetta appeared to be listening.

When the bartender returned from his dinner to resume his duties, Dulcinetta yielded her place behind the bar and retired to her gaming table for the evening's play. Devin followed along, still nursing his solitary beer of the evening which already warm. He stood watching the card game for a while, until he caught a flash of red from the corner of his eye. His eyes widened as he watched Ju sidle up to Wilson and place her hand on his arm. Then she pulled his arm around her neck and after settlement on price was apparently reached, assisted him as he climbed the stairs on none-too-steady legs. The place grew quiet as activity ceased and every eye followed the pair. Ju and Wilson attained the landing and stumbled toward a room, she shutting the door behind them.

For once, Devin was positive he wasn't misreading Dulcinetta's expression. She seethed—steam fairly rose from her and her hands shook. The line of her jaw tightened and he knew she was clenching her teeth. For a while, he had suspected that she was merely intent on getting her gold back from Cal, and then he thought that perhaps Ju was part of a plot to recover what was left. But Dulcinetta was truly angry. He took a seat in front of her at the card table. "I thought Cal was wrong about her," he said in a low voice. "But he guessed right. Ju really is—"

"A whore. Yes, she most certainly is." Dulcinetta picked up her deck and let the cards cascade from one hand to the other before cutting and shuffling them. She regained her composure quickly, as if she had trained herself to show nothing but measured aplomb to the world. "Will you play, Mr. Cavanaugh?" she asked.

"Sure," he said uncertainly.

"How much do you want?" She brought out her tray of chips.

"Ten dollars?"

"You don't sound very confident. Do you want ten dollars or not?" Dulcinetta laughed, tipping back her head so her black ringlets bounced against her honeyed shoulders. The tinkle of her laugh sounded forced to Devin, but it had the effect of turning every male eye in the place in her direction. He wondered if, underneath it all, that was her true purpose, to focus attention on herself—and on her faro table.

"It's been a while since I did any formal gambling," Devin said. The urchins of his former street acquaintance often possessed only partial decks, which made difficult any game for which they didn't make up the rules themselves. "Dice is usually my game."

"Ah. Some other time, perhaps, we will cast the bones. If you haven't played faro before you'll pick it up fairly quickly, I'm sure." Dulcinetta handed him a stack of chips and his change. Another man seated himself to Devin's left and she handed him the deck to cut. The play began.

Devin watched, placing small wagers and absorbing the rules of the game as he won a few bets and lost a few more. He ignored the crowd of sluggards standing around the table, like a half circle of vultures on carrion, waiting for their chance to accost a winner and beg a few dollars for a meal. Several of these, young men like himself, indeed looked as skinny as if they hadn't eaten for weeks, bearing a gray sheen of desperation on their faces. They seemed to be trapped here in South Pass City, without hope, without any means of survival. Perhaps gold mining for a living wasn't all it was purported to be. Perhaps they had dug their fortunes and already gambled everything away. But Devin wasn't really interested in them. He was most interested in what was going on in front of him, the copper circles topping the chips on some of the spades. Very soon he understood their significance and was making the majority of his bets against any card's chance of winning. The pile of chips in front of him slowly grew. Dulcinetta smiled as he placed another copper on top of a card, murmuring, "A pessimist, are you, Mr. Cavanaugh?"

"I haven't had much occasion in my life to bet on anything positive, ma'am."

"But you must keep in mind, life is long." She flashed him a glimpse of her perfect white teeth. "You have much time yet to experience its virtues."

He glanced at her sharply, sure there were layers of meaning underlying the innocence of her words. She met his gaze without flinching, a slight smile still curving her lips. But whose virtue might she be commenting on if there was indeed another meaning to her words? His? Ju's? Perhaps Wilson's? Or maybe her own?

At last Wilson materialized from the upstairs room, exaggeratedly adjusting the fly of his trousers and scanning the barroom to ensure it was noticed from whose room he emerged. He smirked an "I told you so" message over the railing and down toward Devin, who averted his eyes and tried not to accept the communication. Wilson made it down the stairs on his own and back to the bar without stumbling too badly. He elbowed his way in among the men standing there and casually resumed his drinking.

Devin watched Fragrant Chrysanthemum as she came down the stairs a few moments later and again began working the room, allowing men to buy drinks for her that he noticed were poured from a different bottle, and that she set aside and did not consume as she smiled and bowed and sometimes let them paw her. Devin wasn't sure what to think. He made a point of watching Dulcinetta as she watched Ju, her lovely face determinedly neutral, until Ju once more disappeared upstairs with a man.

Ju had said she belonged to Dulcinetta Jackson, that Dulcinetta had bought her debt. If that were the case and Dulcinetta disapproved of Ju's activities, why didn't she just order her to stop? It was plain to Devin he had stumbled into some deep undercurrents here that he didn't understand. He was a simple man. Until the task of shepherding the child Luther to the care of his glamorous mother had been dumped in his lap, Devin had usually avoided becoming ensnared in the emotional affairs of others.

It was beginning to seem that most everyone in South Pass City had some mighty big secrets. So he wondered if the possibility of becoming more involved with a complex woman like Dulcinetta Jackson meant being willing to sink neck deep in complications whose depth he couldn't begin to guess yet.

Chapter *4*
The Position

*I*N THE EARLY HOURS of the morning the saloon finally emptied out completely, the last customer persuaded to wrap up his off-key ballad singing and go home to bed. Josiah locked the front doors for the few hours a day they closed the Goldust. Other South Pass City establishments stayed open around the clock, but Dulcie made enough money that she and those she employed could indulge in some well-deserved rest. The two headed wearily down the short hall to their living quarters—not to seek their own beds just yet, but to sink into chairs in the small dining room for a business meeting.

"Want coffee?" Josiah asked.

"Sounds good." Dulcinetta rested her forehead on her fingertips, elbows on the tabletop.

"I bring," Ju said from the shadows, where she had been dozing in a chair set against the wall since the hour had grown late and the saloon's patrons had passed the point where they could physically no longer make use of her services.

Dulcinetta raised her head. "Ju, just go to bed, would you? Hasn't your day been long enough already?"

"Long as yours, I bet, missy. I get coffee."

"She's hopeless." Dulcinetta sighed as Ju disappeared in the direction of the kitchen.

"You bought her contract and brought her here, to surroundings completely unfamiliar to her. Ergo, she is your creature, and her faults are yours," Josiah reminded.

"Of all the hurtful things you could imagine saying to me, Papa! I bought Ju to set her free, not to transfer ownership of her slave status from the tong to myself."

Josiah shrugged. "There is involuntary slavery, and then there is the kind that people choose for themselves. You know very well Ju's beliefs in this regard. You saved her life, you bought her debt. She belongs to you until her obligation is paid. Besides, it's not as if she has to put herself out to fetch us some coffee. All she has to do is pour, the pot has been on the stove all day."

Dulcinetta grimaced at that thought. "Wonderful. I am most

happy for Ju. But please let us tend to the matter at hand, Papa. I'm very tired and don't wish to waste any more time in hopeless reiteration of the inscrutable reasons for one small Chinese woman's immense obstinacy."

"Very well." Josiah seated himself, a slight groan of gratitude escaping his lips as he took the weight off his feet for the first time in many hours. "Have you made up your mind?"

"You saw for yourself. You served that sodden sot all night long. As soon as he had money in his pocket he spent it on drink and on satisfying his lust. Is there really any sort of decision I need to make?"

"The red-haired one is awful young for so much responsibility, Dulcie."

"It is hard to tell just by looking at him how old he is, Papa. That is true." She chewed a fingernail thoughtfully for a moment. "But beyond his sheer size, I get the feeling he has a lot of experience behind him no matter his real age."

"Perhaps you should ask him about it," Josiah said.

"Interview him for the position, you mean?" She laughed.

"Why not?" he countered as Ju entered with enameled coffee pot, cups and saucers, and a pitcher of cream on a tray. "Perhaps if you looked before leaping you would better understand the implications of that into which you're contemplating jumping." He smiled up at Ju where she stood next to Dulcinetta. "Isn't that right, Fragrant Chrysanthemum?"

It was obvious Ju had no idea what Josiah was asking her to confirm. She smiled, nodded agreement, and started to back away while bowing. Dulcinetta gripped one of the red silk-covered arms before Ju could make good her escape.

"Sit."

Ju tried to tug her arm away. Dulcinetta held on. "I insist."

After Ju reluctantly complied, Dulcinetta placed a cup and saucer in front of her and poured her a cup of coffee.

Ju reached into a hidden pocket and came up with some coins in a very small velvet sack which she placed in front of Dulcinetta. Dulcinetta shoved them back toward Ju, who pushed them back to Dulcinetta once more.

"I think you're aware by now that I have no need of your money or your gold dust," Dulcinetta said, casting Ju a fierce frown.

"Is room rent. White girl pay room rent. Ju pay room rent." Ju folded her silk clad arms across her bosom and averted her eyes.

Dulcinetta rolled her own eyes, letting the coins remain untouched where they sat. "I think you should go to Bryan City," she said to her father, turning her attention to the person she had a better chance of influencing. "Aunt Lou has probably already left for St. Louis. Someone needs to watch over her commerce there."

"I imagine she has returned home to seek expert advice. From what I gather in the little she reveals in her letters, I can only hope she survives the trip and is successful in finding a good surgeon. What about you, Dulcie? Is it safe to leave you here alone?"

"I can't predict the future, Papa. But what choice do we have? We can take care of Lou's concerns in her absence and profit thereby, or sit back and watch them go bust. And there's always the chance we could go bust along with them."

"Of course, you are right. I just hate the thought of leaving you here among so many vagabonds and ruffians." He added a large dollop of cream to his coffee and took a sip, looking at her over the rim of the Queensware cup before squinting his eyes in pleasure. "May God bless the ranchers of Brown's Park, the Mormons of Utah, and the Oregon settlers, who all send their fine cattle along the trail to South Pass City. Especially milk cows."

"Amen." Dulcinetta drank from her own cup, wrinkling her nose at the bitterness of the brew that had sat slowly turning to sludge on the back of the stove for many long hours now and whose acidic bite was discernable even diluted with cream. "So when do you leave?"

Josiah sighed. "The sooner, the better, I imagine. On the next stage."

Dulcinetta turned toward Ju. "And you, my fine miss, have a new job."

"I not 'miss'," Ju contended. "You 'miss'."

"Stop wasting time arguing with me this instant, Ju. If you insist I'm your missy, then you shall begin doing as I say." Dulcinetta gave the other woman a severe look. Ju responded with downcast eyes and a studied demeanor of subdued obedience. "Beginning right now, Xiang Ju, your job is to watch over my son. All day and all night. You will not leave him unattended. You will not loiter about the saloon soliciting men. You will not leave Luther alone while you accompany strangers upstairs for professional purposes. Is this all clear to you or must I repeat myself?"

"How I earn money then?" Ju asked.

"I have told you many times that I will pay you whatever sum you think you require for doing my cooking and cleaning. Now that offer extends to watching my son and keeping him safe. If you insist on returning my own money to me in some kind of self-imposed bargain for your soul, I suppose that is your affair. I can't stop you from throwing away your wages. But if Papa leaves, it will be just us two alone, Ju. You must agree to do as I say and not as your misguided heart leads you to do." She paused before adding, "I need your promise on that."

Ju sighed. "Okay."

"Okay, what?" Dulcinetta sometimes felt, when dealing with Ju, as if she negotiated with a person nearer Luther's age than her own. Fragrant Chrysanthemum might be small in stature, but she had survived her ordeal passed from hand to hand in San Francisco with a will forged of iron, which had over time tempered to steel.

"Okay, I watch boy and not go upstair with men."

"Very well," Dulcinetta said. "Papa, do you need us to get up early and help you pack?"

"I can manage, I'm sure," he said, finishing his coffee and trying not to smile at the pair who sat across from him. No two women could be more different in looks or background, yet scrap so much like sisters.

"Then I will rise in time to see you off. Ju, you may go to bed now."

"I wait here. Help missy," Ju said.

Dulcinetta pursed her lips and narrowed her eyes in Ju's direction, but let the other woman's determination ride this time. She really could use some help with the row of fancy buttons down the back of her dress and with the whalebone stays that were the sole support of the bodice of her stunning peach dress.

~

Wilson woke with a raging thirst and a mean look in his eye that Devin recognized all too well. "Get them mules harnessed," Wilson ordered. Holding his head, he stumbled outside.

"Are we headed back to Bryan?" Devin asked as Wilson retreated.

"Stop yammering at me. Just do as I say." Wilson rounded the corner of the freight office, a small building dug into the hillside and fronted with canvas and half walls of wood that had begun life as someone's one-room South Pass dwelling. The previous tenant wouldn't be the first who embarked on a gold-seeking adventure with more money than he possessed when he gave up and went home.

At this elevation mornings were chilly. Devin wrapped the flaps of his coat around his middle and slapped his hands against the fabric as he headed for the livery. He'd begin the process of gathering the animals and getting them hooked to the spreaders and harnesses he laid out in the road in front, spaced along both sides of the chain.

"I'll tell you but the once, Tiberius," he warned in a reasonable voice as he entered the corral and the big gray mule gave him an appraising look from one brown eye. "We ain't playing no games this morning. Cal is in a mood, and he'll take the hide from you in strips if you try to hold us up. Maybe you'd even receive an additional lash or two from me, who can tell? You wouldn't want that, would you?"

The mule snorted, shaking its head.

"Good," Devin said. "Let's get started then." Cooperation from the ringleader meant better cooperation from all, and Devin had the mules and horses hooked to the wagon and waiting when Wilson returned.

"Take the wheeler," Wilson ordered. "I'm gonna climb up and take a nap." He brushed back still-wet hair and Devin fought a grin. The older man had evidently soaked his aching head in the water trough on his visit to the privy.

And we'll both hope you sober up a bit, Devin thought. As Wilson headed toward the rearmost wheel to climb up into the wagon bed, Devin asked, "Cal, is it some kind of secret where we're going this morning or should I just decide on my own which direction to take?"

"There's a load of lumber up in the hills at that puny excuse for a sawmill, an opportunity waiting for us to haul it to town. Last night I collared us the job. Sing out if you need any help, won't you?" Devin took this to mean Wilson would be unavailable to pelt the team with rocks from the can on the seat to help get them moving. Devin mounted the left wheeler, one of a pair of huge draft horses whose job was to start pulling and get the wagon rolling. He hung his rifle so it would be ready if he needed it. Then he grasped the jerk line in one hand and snapped the blacksnake over the mules' backs with the other, careful not to actually hit them or, alternatively, to accidentally put out one of his own eyes. Today he would be the boss, the jerk line skinner, and Wilson the swamper—although it was doubtful Wilson would live up to the title by actually being any help.

Leave it to Wilson to drum up the means of making a bit of extra money on the side, even while sloshed to the gills. The man was truly a genius at finding ways to squeeze a clandestine dollar out of their official trips to and from Bryan. He just hadn't the talent to hold on to his furtive earnings. Where Devin had ended the previous evening richer than he had begun, thanks to the reward for delivering Luther and then his takings from the faro game, he was willing to bet Wilson hadn't two bits left in his pocket this morning.

But, on the climb up the road to the mill, he didn't need Wilson's help on the brake and so the man could sleep it off and leave Devin in peace to ponder his own thoughts. It was on the return journey, wagons loaded with heavy green lumber, that Devin was grateful Wilson had cleared his head enough that they could change places. He felt safer working the brake himself instead of relying on a half-sober Wilson. Back in South Pass City they left the wagons to be unloaded at the Joseph Marion Warehouse. Wilson collected his fee for delivering the lumber, the horses and mules were deposited at the livery, and the men returned to the same saloon that they each had been thinking about all through the day.

Devin had paused to wash up in the trough, slicking his newly shorn hair back with one hand and running the other over his cheeks to see if he could get away without shaving. He entered the saloon to see Wilson, elbow bent, already tipping one back at the bar. Devin nodded toward Dulcinetta at her table, and then joined Wilson, whose mood had scarcely improved throughout the day.

"Where's the regular barkeep?" Wilson asked.

"Gone to Bryan, or so I understand," answered the new bartender, a stranger Devin hadn't seen before.

"Where's that little Chinee gal?" Wilson demanded. "Ain't she working tonight?"

"That one, as I understand it, has a new position. One that requires her to remain upright." The bartender smirked. "She won't be coming in here anymore. But I hear some new girls arrived with the stage this morning. They're down the street at Billy Wilson's. You can try your luck there if the ones upstairs here don't please you. The new ones call themselves 'terpsichoreans,' if you please, but most of them earn their real money in the hills out back of Billy's and not the dance floor—if you take my meaning."

Wilson's eyes narrowed. "Well, don't that beat all. A new position, you say? Seems like people around here sure don't stick for long." The impermanence of South Pass City's population was legendary. As a term of his employment Wilson had made Devin promise that he would stay with the transfer company and not give into the temptation to abandon the wagons and run away to the goldfields. "What kind of occupation did Ju get, if you don't mind my askin'?"

The bartender paused in the action of polishing a glass. He eyed Wilson up and down. He seemed to be considering whether Fragrant Chrysanthemum's whereabouts and new duties were any of Wilson's concern. Devin tended to agree the man should be cautious. But the barkeep apparently decided the bellicose man facing him across the bar was in a position where it could invite trouble raining down on himself if he chose not to answer. "It seems she has taken up child care and domestic duties."

Wilson bared his rotten teeth in amazement. His forehead furrowed in a frown, as though he suspected he was being made the butt of a joke. "You telling me she up and got hitched just since last night? I can't hardly believe that."

"Who said anything about marriage? Xiang Ju has made a true change of occupation. She has initiated a new beginning," Dulcinetta said from behind them. Neither man had heard her approach. They'd failed to pick up on the whispered rustle of yellow silk brocade worn over a cage hoop. The hem of the gown was shorter than normal. It didn't quite touch the floor and instead danced over the mounds of sawdust, the particles hovering around Dulcinetta's feet as she glided toward them. Devin turned slowly, but Wilson whirled to face her, as if she represented some kind of threat.

Dulcinetta smiled a welcome, but Devin noticed the expression didn't reach her eyes as she looked at Wilson. "Have you gentlemen eaten? Might I interest you in a bite of supper?"

"That's mighty kind of you, ma'am." Wilson hurried to accept, eager to save the four bits he could charge the company for a meal, cutting off whatever Devin had begun opening his mouth to say.

But Dulcinetta had caught Devin's look. She eyed him quizzically. "What is it, Mr. Cavanaugh? Do you have an objection to dining with me?"

"Are you offering us supper at the restaurant?" he asked, trying to signal his worry with just his eyes.

"Why, no. Supper is already prepared. I thought we'd eat here." She studied his expression, as did Wilson.

Devin tore his gaze from her scrutiny. He had a pretty good idea whose home and child Ju would be giving up whoring to tend from now on. How could he say to Dulcinetta, in Wilson's hearing, that he didn't think it was a good idea to show the other man her family's living arrangements? He couldn't say exactly what it was that bothered him, only that Wilson's continued interest in Fragrant Chrysanthemum set Devin's internal alarm clanging. The best he could do now was to accompany Dulcinetta and Wilson, and try to head off any trouble that might arise.

Dulcinetta turned, floating down the hall toward her private quarters. Wilson followed, tossing a lofty grin over his shoulder at Devin who brought up the rear. She opened the door to the dining room, preceding the men into the room. Devin closed the door behind them and hurried to where she stood at the table, pulling out a chair for her before she could do it herself.

"Please, gentlemen, sit." She gestured with a slim honey-skinned hand and smiled.

Ju entered, head lowered and hands tucked into sleeves of sapphire blue silk. Wilson straightened in his chair, staring at her. Ju stood behind Dulcinetta, refusing to meet Cal's eyes.

"May I offer you gentlemen anything to drink? Wine, perhaps?" Dulcinetta's steely gaze headed off any untoward suggestion from Cal about what he might really be interested in as his attention turned away from watching Ju. His eyes gleamed ferally in the lamp light.

"I'll take whiskey if you've got it." Wilson's heavy-lidded gaze returned to Ju. She nodded without raising her head.

"Wine is fine by me, if you'll join me," Devin said to Dulcinetta. At her nod of acquiescence, Ju left to get the drinks. Devin had a glimpse of Third peering curiously through the doorway before he was apparently yanked backwards into the kitchen.

"You've had a pleasant day, I trust? When do you return to Bryan City?" Dulcinetta smiled in the men's direction.

"We hauled a nice load . . ." Devin began, when he felt the sharp toe of Wilson's boot giving his ankle a hard prod under the table. He frowned at Wilson, then made a point of raising the tablecloth to look pointedly at the man's scuffed boot. Wilson pulled his foot back under his own chair and rolled his eyes at Devin's refusal to take a hint. Devin returned his attention to Dulcinetta with a wide smile. "A nice load of wood from the sawmill," he concluded with stubborn determination.

Where before he had only suspected the load of wood hauled in Lou Schering's wagons had been a deal made under the table to enrich Cal Wilson and not his employer, who owned the wagons and the animals they'd used, now he was sure of it. Cal's actions left no doubt he didn't want Dulcinetta to know they'd used Lou's wagons without permission. Dulcinetta watched the interplay between the two men, her dark brown eyes missing nothing.

"We'll be heading out tomorrow," Wilson said as Ju entered carrying a tray with two stemmed glasses and a tumbler for Wilson. She rounded the table, setting the proper drink in front of each of them. As she leaned over Wilson, he leaned back, allowing his arm to brush her hip. Her eyes flew toward his face and he grinned at her, showing his decaying teeth in invitation. She quickly backed away, leaving the room without a word. "The extra run today will make a nice contribution to our month's screw, Devin's and mine. No sense wasting wagons and labor while we're here. I'll settle up with Lou as soon as we get back, don't you worry about that," he said, leaning forward toward Dulcinetta once more.

"Well, that's the thing, you see," Dulcinetta began. Ju entered with steaming platters of rice and vegetables, a whole roasted trout laid atop each serving. Dulcinetta unfolded her napkin and waited until Ju finished serving and withdrew again. Wilson's eyes tracked Ju's every move, while Dulcinetta silently observed.

"I'm afraid I have some bad news," she said, picking up her fork and stabbing delicately at the fish, whose flesh flaked away from its bones, wafting a tantalizing aroma over the table. "Lou is suffering a malady that requires specialized care. I assume she has already left for the East, to seek a doctor." She placed a bite of fish in her mouth.

"I'm right sorry to hear that," Wilson said, shaking his head in apparent sorrow and beginning to shovel food into his mouth with a silver spoon. "Lou's your ma, am I right? Good woman." A few grains of rice escaped his lips and fell to his lap as he talked and chewed at the same time.

"She is as close to a mother as I will ever get."

Wilson looked up from his plate, his eyes narrowed. "I thought she was the boy's grandma," he insisted.

"Lou is, in point of fact, my aunt. Not my mother." Dulcinetta's eyelids tightened slightly in response to Wilson's continued ill-mannered enquiry, but that was the only outward sign of her displeasure. "My mother was Lou's sister, although Lou does look on Luther as her grandchild."

Devin observed the reactions of Wilson and Dulcinetta as he ate and drank in silence. He could see Dulcinetta was perfectly capable of handling Wilson, and the safer course seemed to be to just stay out of her way and let her do it. He figured if Wilson was given enough rope, he'd be sure to hang himself with it, especially as a decanter of whiskey sat at his elbow from which he had already topped off his glass once. Not that Devin wouldn't like to get a few clarifications himself about the comely woman with the secrets, but he was fairly sure this wasn't the right time to start pestering her. He would leave that ill-advised activity to Wilson.

Dulcinetta set down her fork. "My purpose in asking you here tonight, in Lou's absence, is to see if we can begin to get a handle on her affairs. The freight transfer business must have a competent supervisor in order for operations to continue. Do you both agree?"

Wilson straightened up from his slouch. "Hell, yeah," he said, hiding a big grin of anticipation behind one of the hands sporting a sickle-shaped crust of black beneath each nail, which seemed a permanent fixture as the previous day's bath had failed to dissolve it. All his attention focused now on Dulcinetta. Even Ju returning to refill wine glasses and see if anything more was needed by the diners couldn't distract him.

Devin liked this turn of events even less than Wilson's inattention to anything but Ju. Devin caught Dulcinetta's eye as Wilson once more refilled his glass, but when she shook her head negatively he merely nodded assent and held his tongue while he waited to hear her whole plan. No one paid Ju any mind as she retreated to the shadows in a corner of the room near the door to the kitchen.

"I'm afraid I don't have a good grasp of the freighting portion of Lou's several business interests. You gentlemen are much more competent to assume this responsibility. But I'm thinking only one man should step up, one who will oversee different aspects of transporting goods from Bryan City to South Pass City. One who will manage the other employees and all operations." She looked at each of the two men in turn. "Does this idea meet with your approval?"

Wilson bobbed his head, grinning. Again Devin gave Dulcinetta a slight nod.

"Good. You lighten my burden immensely. I am happy that we all agree."

Wilson took a big swig of his whiskey, seeming to anticipate cause for celebration. Devin watched Dulcinetta's lips curve just the tiniest bit before she announced, "I am therefore pleased to offer the position of superintendent of Schering Forwarding to Mr. Devin Cavanaugh."

She smiled across the table at Devin. Taken completely by surprise, Devin felt the fork slip from his hand and land with a clatter on his plate, scattering fish bones and rice grains.

Whiskey spewed from Wilson's lips over his shirt front, the tablecloth, and the plate in front of him. He wiped his slack lips and glared at Dulcinetta, then shoved his plate aside to stab the table with a blunt forefinger to emphasize his words. "Let's just back up a step here. Ain't you making a mistake, ma'am? My name happens to be Cal Wilson. I'm Lou's foreman. That there's Devin Cavanaugh. He's a swamper, which means helper." He pointed to Devin. "He ain't worked for your ma—your aunt, I mean—for but a few months. I been with Lou for a couple years now. I was a teamster before that, even, in Omaha. I know all about the freighting business."

Dulcinetta bestowed a dazzling smile on Wilson. "I'm sure you do. Your experience is a valuable asset to Lou's company, and your store of knowledge will be consulted often, I'm sure, by Mr. Cavanaugh."

"An 'asset,' am I?" Wilson fairly growled. "You say I'll be *consulted*?" He pushed his chair back from the table. It toppled unheeded to the floor. "*In*-sulted is more like it. You can't do this to Caleb Wilson!"

Dulcinetta folded her hands under her chin. "Mr. Wilson. Understand me. I can, and I have. From this moment on, all decisions pertaining to Schering Forwarding are to be made by Mr. Cavanaugh, and only by Mr. Cavanaugh."

"Ya tallow-faced, wiry-haired bitch," Wilson said under his breath. He whirled toward Devin, grasping a handful of shirt front in a none-too-clean paw, trying to lift the much more substantial young man from his chair. A button popped off Devin's shirt and rolled away across the plank floor toward the sideboard, but Devin remained seated no matter how Cal strained. "And you, ya bastard pup, going behind my back to sweet talk the boss's daughter. I shoulda known."

"Niece," Devin corrected. Smiling and rising to his feet, he aimed an unmistakable challenge into Wilson's bloodshot eyes. "You will apologize to the lady, Cal."

"Aargh! I'll kill you both first!" Wilson tried to fling Devin away from himself, emitting a good whiff of rancid breath in his ineffectual effort. Devin waited for another attack, which never materialized, before subsiding once more to the seat of his chair.

"You'll both be sorry, I'll tell ya that much," Wilson yelled over his shoulder, stomping across the small room to yank open the door.

Devin calmly righted his position on the chair too dainty for his bulk, watching as Wilson disappeared, the door slapping shut behind him.

Chapter 5
The Snare

WELL, THAT DIDN'T GO as I had hoped. Do you think Mr. Wilson meant what he said? Or will he be able to lower his lofty opinion of himself enough to take orders from you—and not ultimately kill us both?" Dulcinetta raised a forkful of rice toward her lips, tilting her head and slanting a mischievous look at Devin.

"I guess it depends on how bad he needs money." Although amazed at the woman's composure, Devin supposed she had in her line of work been exposed on occasion to the bad behavior of men, and didn't intend to allow Cal to ruin her dinner. So he tried emulate her by remaining unruffled, resuming his consumption of his own meal.

The kitchen door popped open and Third escaped Ju's grasping hand as he raced across to Devin and seized him by the wrist. Devin moved his chair back and swung the boy up onto his lap. "How you doing, squirt?"

"Luther!" the boy screeched. "Devin, you know my name is Luther Brandingham III."

"Oh, yeah. I don't know how I can keep forgetting that. Sorry, Third." Devin grinned. The boy grinned back at the familiar joke between them.

"*Luther Brandingham the Third.*" Dulcinetta's voice dripped ice. "Would it be possible just once for you to contain yourself around Mr. Cavanaugh and not be showing him what an uncivilized young bear cub you are?"

"Uh-oh. Sounds like your mam doesn't have any trouble remembering your whole name," Devin whispered. His lip quirked on one side as he tried to hold back a laugh. He hadn't been around families much, but he knew it was a bad idea to even unintentionally cross a scolding mother.

Suddenly sobered by his mother's tone, the boy slid off Devin's lap. "Yes, Mama. Sorry, Devin."

"You will call him Mr. Cavanaugh," his mother insisted.

Luther looked to Devin, who merely shrugged. "Sorry, Mr. Devin," the boy temporized. "Ju said I could come and say good night. So, good night." He turned toward twin doors set in the wall behind

Devin, and started to march off.

"Kiss," Dulcinetta called after him before he could make good his escape. The boy ran to fling himself, with great passion, at his mother. Dulcinetta covered his face with kisses and then set him back on his feet.

"Good night," she said. "I love you, Luther. Off to bed now."

"'Night, Mama. 'Night, Mr. Devin. I love you, too."

Devin fidgeted uneasily with his wine glass as the boy closed the door between the rooms. He hazarded a glance at the attractive woman, hoping his heart wasn't displayed on his sleeve much as a schoolboy's might be.

"Don't look so tentative. I think Luther meant that just the way it sounded. He does love you. Welcome to Lou Schering's cobbled-together family of relatives and employees, Mr. Cavanaugh."

He looked up, meeting eyes that were openly studying him once more. "I want to thank you for your confidence in me, ma'am," he began. "I will do my best to earn your continued belief in my abilities."

He hoped he sounded more assured than he felt. As much as he had coveted Wilson's job in the past, now that it had been dropped in his lap he wondered if he could really do it. He remembered his fellow New York City escapee—pretty, supremely self-confident Ailis Tierney. She had tossed her auburn curls and narrowed her eyes evilly at him, saying in a sneering voice when he innocently asked if she really thought she could make a living by sewing women's clothes in Cheyenne, Wyoming, "Certainly it doesn't take a giant intellect to *drive a wagon* or *herd cattle* or some sweaty occupation such as that." Now, he would finally see if he was a better man than Ailis's low estimation of his abilities.

Dulcinetta's laugh yanked him back to the present. She tipped her head back slightly, which emphasized the long, graceful line of her neck. "Rest assured you will have no trouble ever discerning if I am displeased with the quality of your work. If you don't get any raises in your pay for long stretches at a time you will be correct in suspecting that I am not happy. At worst, if I send you a letter rescinding the offer of employment you can be certain that I am most supremely dissatisfied with you."

Devin swallowed a dry lump in his throat. He had no doubt this young relative of St. Louie Lou's was as tough inside as that old woman, and would have no reluctance about throwing him out on his ear if he didn't perform up to her great expectations. Just the thought of receiving a letter of dismissal from Dulcinetta Jackson brought nervous moisture to his palms and armpits. "I prefer that you tell me in person how to improve if I'm not doing a good enough job for you," he said.

"Oh, I hope you're not just worrying about second chances." Dulcinetta tipped her glass toward him in salute. "People generally have a second, and perhaps even a third opportunity to disappoint me. But *positively* no more than that."

"No ma'am," Devin said, agreeing to her terms while raising his own glass and swallowing down the last ruby drops. He thought she might be flirting with him, but he wasn't sure—and so didn't know how to respond. He had no experience with sophisticated ladies of Dulcinetta's style and education. He would have to think about his next step, decide for certain if she might be issuing some kind of invitation.

He took his leave of her soon after that, wanting to get a good night's sleep before taking off in the morning with the wagons. He had money, but instead of heading for the hotel and paying for a room, he unlocked the freight office, lit a lamp and unrolled his blankets there on the dirt floor. The accommodations fell within his preferred price range. He had become used to sleeping without too many other people around to disturb him with their noises and smells, and sleeping on hard surfaces didn't much bother him, although he preferred a bed with not too many rocks. He gave a passing thought to wondering where Wilson was spending the night since he'd walked out on Dulcinetta's offer of employment. But Wilson's choices were really of no consequence to Devin. Almost immediately upon stretching out on a wagon tarp, he fell asleep.

~

Having awakened several times to the sounds of late night revelers and at least one instance of gunfire, Devin nevertheless rose early in order to get on the road. He gathered the papers on the trestle desk and stuffed them into a saddlebag so there would be nothing of importance left in the office during his absence. People generally left their doors unlocked and their possessions unguarded in South Pass City, an informal brotherhood of faith in each others' better nature. But that didn't mean he trusted Cal Wilson. He took a hard whiff of the bacon wrapped in a length of muslin left over from the trip north. Giving it a sniff, he decided the meat smelled all right and would do him well enough for the return trip. He jammed it in the opposite saddlebag. He hoisted the saddlebags, his bedroll and his carpetbag to his shoulders and headed for the livery.

He had the lines laid out and most of the animals necessary to pull empty wagons harnessed when he noticed Tiberius leaning up against the fence on the far side of the corral. If he had been in a questioning mood, he would have noticed things were a mite too quiet and the animals too cooperative this morning. The large gray leader was standing on three legs, taking the weight off his right front foot. The sky was beginning to lighten, and as Devin approached he spotted the rust red of dried blood on Tiberius's pastern. The mule heaved himself away from the fence, rolling his eyes and baring huge yellow teeth in warning.

Still Devin came on. "If you threaten to bite me with that set of tombstones, Tiberius, I can't be helping you," he said in a conversational tone. "You understand me? If you fight me, we won't be able to tell what is the trouble here." He placed a hand on the mule's shoulder. Tiberius turned his big head and eyed Devin with what looked like suspicion, but consented to close his lips over his teeth for now and Devin felt safe in bending over to examine the animal's sore foot.

He sucked in a breath as he detected the wire snare encircling the mule's leg below the fetlock, cinched cruelly tight. Leaving Tiberius for the moment, Devin crossed the corral to bang on the livery man's door. The proprietor, George Dean himself, answered with a scowl, cinching up his trousers and yanking his suspenders over his shoulders. "If you'd given me time I would be dressed and outside in a few more minutes. What's the rush?"

"You've got to come now and hold my mule's head while I get a length of wire off his leg."

"Wire? He didn't get no wire at George Dean's, I'll tell ya that much. No wire is left carelessly laying around my corrals." Quick to come to his own defense, at least the man didn't hesitate in following Devin to aid Tiberius.

"Doesn't matter at the moment exactly how it came about," Devin tossed over his shoulder. "But we've got to get it off. Grab a pair of pliers, will you?"

"Oh, it's that one, is it?" Dean looked sidelong at Tiberius, but he exited the livery a few moments later with a pair of pliers and a length of rope, and commenced slowly sidling up to the mule. "He bites, if you aren't aware of that fact."

"He does bite. Sometimes. His name's Tiberius."

White rimmed the mule's eyes and his nostrils flared. He eyed with evident fear and distrust the implement in the livery man's hand. Dean stood with the rope dangling, hesitating to approach and place it over the mule's head. Impatiently, Devin reached for the rope, fashioned a quick halter, and did the job himself.

"Tiberius, indeed," Dean muttered under his breath. "His name should rightly be Trouble."

"You just get that wire off his foot. I'll hold his head and chance a nip," Devin said.

George Dean took a step toward the mule and Tiberius lifted his head, pulling Devin's hand up in the air. But Devin clung to the lead and mildly but forcefully pulled the mule's head back down. "Easy," he said. "You know we got to get it off in order to help you, Tiberius."

In fits and starts, between attempts where Devin finally succeeded in calming the mule, they got the snare off and some salve pasted on the wound. It was clear Tiberius wouldn't be making the trip back to Bryan, not even a quick trip with empty wagons. Devin debated whether to leave behind Tiberius's partner, Milly, as well. But Milly was the near leader, the line mule, the one that got the rest of the team to turn when the skinner pulled on the jerk line. Other mules had their places, as pointers, sixes, eights, tens, as well as the two massive horses directly in front of the wagon, the wheelers. None was as smart as Tiberius or Milly.

As well, there was the fact that he would have to pay to leave Tiberius, and pay double if he left Milly. He would have to hire a swamper to work the brake if Wilson failed to show up, although he could put off paying the new helper until they reached Bryan. He could put in a request for reimbursement for Tiberius's expenses with Dulcinetta when he got back here to South Pass City in a few weeks' time. If worse came to worst and George Dean asked for money up front to keep Tiberius for a month or so, Devin still had his reward money and his gambling earnings in his pocket.

In the end he gave Milly a new partner from the team, and tied the extra mule to the back of the wagon. He hired a helper, a former farm boy who knew how to handle mules. The boy had given up on striking it rich and was ready to go home, thankful for a free ride to the railway.

As the road climbed the fold of land that cradled South Pass City in its embrace, Devin turned briefly to look back. He thought it was silly to be hoping for a glimpse of Dulcinetta before he left, as if he could just crane his neck around and she would appear at the door of the Goldust to wave good-bye. She kept late hours, and even if he had been almost half the morning seeing to Tiberius's needs and hiring help for the journey back to Bryan City, Dulcinetta was probably still soundly asleep. But he did catch a brief flash of red in the distance, and wondered if Ju would be out at this hour, maybe taking the morning air with Third. He hoped, for her sake, she wasn't out working the notorious cribs behind the bar while Third was sleeping. He was sure there would be hell to pay if Dulcinetta found out that's what her friend was up to.

~

That first night on the road after Devin led the mules to water and then got them hobbled, he looked for the cleft in the rocks that hid the cache he and Wilson had hidden on the way up to South Pass City. He had the swamper start the fire, and then went to retrieve the hidden store of grain for the animals. The caches also held extra clothing, sacks of dried beans and corn, and whatever sundries Wilson and Devin had thought they might need in a pinch.

It was empty.

Devin cursed aloud. He wasn't sure what to think of the cache's disappearance. Wild animals such as a bear might conceivably have got to the food stores, just as uncharacteristic carelessness concerning his corrals on the livery man's part in South Pass City might have led to Tiberius's lameness. But to Devin's way of thinking the site of the empty hoard was too clean for animals to have robbed it. There were no claw marks, and no evidence of unrestrained digging.

These daily occurrences of bad luck were getting to feel a bit too coincidental to him. The loss of the stores wasn't severe this first night out. The animals had grass, like it or not, and he and the former farm worker and gold miner had a pot of beans and the hunk of bacon. He kept a wary eye ahead on the road the next day, casting glances over his shoulder, a nervous hand on the butt of the pistol thrust in his belt. The way remained clear and the animals kept up a good pace, their hooves clopping away the miles to the jingle of hame bells that seemed to help them maintain the pace.

The company had no trouble reaching its destination for the second night's camp. Devin hesitated only slightly before leaving the wagons to check the cache, not knowing what he would find but praying the store was untouched. He levered aside the big rock with a handy cottonwood branch. Just as he had half expected there was nothing left of the supplies he had previously hidden there. Not only was the cache robbed, there was a shiny black obsidian arrowhead lying at the bottom of the otherwise empty dirt hole, as out of place as a diamond in an outhouse.

He returned to the campfire and stood gazing at the flames. At last he sat down, wondering if his suspicions about what was going on were correct and what he might do about the situation if they were.

"Somethin' wrong?" the farm boy asked.

Devin passed a hand over his eyes, blaming the burning behind the lids on sitting too near the heat of the fire. "Nothin' to worry about. Hope you're not too hungry because the store's been cleaned out," he said gruffly. He could only hope there truly was nothing much to worry about.

Chapter 6
The Terpsichoreans

AILIS TIERNEY LEANED HER head against the coach wall, watching through the window as the Western landscape passed by. A huge herd of pronghorns was bisected by the road, the tan-and-white animals lifting their heads to watch the wheeled vehicle pass before springing up and coming down to earth at a dead run on spindly legs. They were gone so swiftly she was left with only a glimpse of their heart-shaped, white-tufted behinds. The air smelled of sage. The sun-warmed, sandy earth yielded grass in sparse clumps, as if seeds had been flung far and wide by the hands of the wind. Wildflowers grew along the ground, most with desert-colored grayish green leaves, but bearing tiny flowers of yellows and whites and blues, unexpected bursts of startling color in this brown, high desert landscape. Some of the most beautiful yellow and pink blooms were guarded by long sharp spines of cactus. Looking out over the land in the distance from the height of the coach seat, Ailis thought the landscape appeared sere and rocky and inhospitable. So she kept her eyes lowered to what she could see near the ruts of the road, discovering the small treasures hidden in plain sight.

The girls traveling with her broke into screeches of shrill laughter again, causing her head to pound as they passed the whiskey bottle around. She pushed it away when one of the hurdy gurdy girls continued to wave it in front of her face. "Ah, come on, Ailis Stick-in-the-Mud. Have a drink with us. It helps make the time passsh."

"Leave me alone. I said I don't want it." Ailis resisted pulling her head away from the open window even to look at the woman offering the bottle. The coach rocked and reeked, of the road and dust, of stale perfume and the body odors of a gaggle of tightly packed women. There was also the astringent tang of spilled whiskey, and, a tad less pungent now since it had been wiped up, the underlying sharp whiff of vomit. The way stations for the stage line were dim, dirty affairs most often built of stacked stone with few or no windows. Here the coaches halted long enough for a change of horses or driver, and perhaps a bowl of indescribably bad slop for the passengers. Otherwise they were on the road twenty-four hours a day, and by this time all of the women, including Ailis, were in desperate need of a long soak in a hot tub.

"Let her be," one of the women said, slurring her words a bit. Ailis thought it had to be Bethenia coming to her aid, the only one of all the girls she could truly call friend. Bethie was much like the others and nothing at all like Ailis, and yet the two had remained close since their first meeting in Cheyenne more than a year ago. The remainder of the troupe merely tolerated Ailis and her purportedly snooty ways, and she tried her best to be tolerant in return, of both them and their sometimes deplorable habits.

Once more the women started the rousing chorus:

> *She'll be coming round the mountain when she comes*
> *She'll be coming round the* moun-*tain when she comes*
> *She'll be coming round the mountain . . .*

Ailis thought she might lose her mind before they arrived at their destination. She clapped her hands over her ears, hoping she wouldn't start screaming, but that was hardly an effective deterrent against the loud, off-key voices of eight drunken women. Well, seven if the truth be known. Agatha had passed out cold some time ago and was now in danger of sliding insensibly from the seat to the filthy floor with every rocking side-to-side sway of the coach. Riding in a Concorde with this bunch of women from Fort Bridger to South Pass City on this last leg of their latest circuit was like being cooped up with a mob of expensively silk-clad, inebriated toddlers sporting heavily-painted faces, scandalously low-cut dresses, and tightly curled if dull, frightfully dusty hair. She would have found it amusing, once upon a time, to see the rats that were supposed to hide the sad natural thinness of Dolly's mousy brown hair lying askew and flopping by their pins over her ears like small shaggy snakes or large fuzzy caterpillars. Now she merely found the state of her companion's coiffure a sorry, if accurate, illustration of the unhappy vagrant life these girls led. If up to the present time they hadn't already had their blinders stripped off by domineering, abusive spouses, they doggedly still expected that the one-and-only, handsome true love, who would sweep them off their feet and marry them, was surely to be found in the very next town down the line. Soon they wouldn't have to be dancing and pushing drinks in one saloon after another until they all blurred together into one town and one dance floor and one big drunken spree. One day—

any day now—they would stand up and take the straight road, no longer allowing alcohol and exhaustion and despair to lead them astray. When that time came, and it would—yes, it surely would—never again would they lift their skirts and lower their drawers for yet one more handsome incarnation of Mr. Wrong.

Ailis was part of the troupe, and yet set far apart from them. She rarely danced, never pushed drinks on the customers, and had not even once lifted her skirts for a man since the day she began traveling with the dance company. She stayed with the group only because they visited the best places to make money—mining towns. It had once been railroad settlements that nurtured the acquisitive aspirations of young women like these, but with the completion of the transcontinental railroad most of the workers had dispersed to parts unknown, as nomadic as the dancers themselves. These days it was mostly gold that drew the girls, although silver being brought to the surface at Nevada's Comstock and Colorado's Central City had its own shiny allure. The group tolerated Ailis because she made more money than any of them, and also she was generous—with loans of small sums of money when needed, and with her sewing skills and any extra length of lace or ribbon she might have on hand. Ailis could spiff up a faded old frock to look like new with a few well-placed stitches and some tatting, or if a girl had the money Ailis could whip her up a fresh dress of fantastic color and attractive cut and style. She was their magician seamstress, and wearing her flattering creations allowed the lot of them to make even more money. So their unspoken bargain to abide with each other's peculiarities was observed by all, even as she acknowledged it was truly no small feat in a company of such disparate personalities.

Ailis happened to be looking when they passed a multiple-animal mule team and two high-sided wagons going the other way, its long chain jangling and bells ringing. The man perched on the saddle of a giant horse trailing the mules and just in front of the lead wagon raised a curious face toward the sound of the raucous, inebriated female voices emanating from the stagecoach. For a moment, Ailis's gaze met the man's and a spark of recognition passed between them. Out from under the wide-brimmed hat peeked trimmed burnsides of carrot-colored curls. The cheeks were hidden beneath a few days' scruff of reddish beard, but she thought surely she recognized the eyes, the lines of the face—but no, it couldn't be. For just a flash she thought she knew those familiar features, the face of her fellow Irish expatriate, Devin Cavanaugh, another of New York City's castoffs like herself, who had journeyed west to seek their fortunes. It was just possible, she thought, she had actually seen the very man himself. After all, the entire population of the territory would fit into one neighborhood in the big city. But if the stranger was not who he seemed, it was most unusual that she would think she saw Devin passing the other way on the road between Bryan and South Pass City. Why would she conjure him of all people out of the thin air of southwestern Wyoming Territory? They had been friends once upon a time, but now she barely remembered the man.

She tried to take a breath, but abruptly halted a deep inhalation. If she was having visions, they were probably the result of the overpowering smell of alcohol residing in her nostrils, strong enough to make her drunk on fumes alone. Shaking her head, she dismissed the likely mirage, and concentrated on how much work she would probably have to do in the days the company stayed in the little mining town of South Pass City. The town was now the biggest settlement in all of big Carter County, which stretched from Montana to Colorado and Utah territories, second in population in Wyoming only to Cheyenne. By now Ailis knew not to expect too much of these mostly canvas settlements sprouting like fields of white mushrooms on the Western landscape, and just as quickly fading. Still, despite her jaded outlook, life had a way of surprising her sometimes, and one never knew what might happen in a different place. Ailis and Bethie had been here before, but some of the girls were new since their last rotation through here. Perhaps Bethie's girls were correct this time, and something wonderful would happen to them in South Pass City. Ailis's lips curved slightly at her own cynical fancy.

At last the stage descended a gentle grade into the little city. All up and down the single long main street men stopped what they were doing to observe the boisterous progress of Bethenia's girls making their way into town. The welcoming whoop and holler started even before the coach came to a complete stop. As Ailis climbed over her companions to be the first out before her willpower gave out and she too heaved up her last meal, there were several willing hands offering to help her step down.

She waited while the rest of the women stumbled and tumbled to the street behind her, crinolines and the newer American crinolettes, their so-called cages ballooning to display shapely lower limbs up to gartered, dimpled knees. Eager hands splayed out to catch the women, men shoving each other aside to be the first to offer assistance should any of the ladies actually threaten to tip over on her face. Two kindhearted gentlemen climbed into the coach to haul out poor incapacitated Agatha, her arms and legs flopping nervelessly since she had yet to rouse from her stupor.

Ailis lingered only long enough for her bag and her machine to be unloaded from the boot before straining to lift both and starting to head down the rutted street for the saloon. "Here, let me help you with that," one of the eager men offered, following her and taking hold of the handle of her machine. Wearing a broad smile, he wrested it from her grip. "Where to?"

"The Goldust," Ailis said. The hand-cranked machine was one of a few of its kind ever made, and she'd gone to great trouble to locate it and have a special case made for it. Not strictly what could be called portable—she would never become used to the little cast iron machine's weight—still she could, with some effort, carry it herself. However, she was tired and not in the mood to continue to contest the man's insistent grasp on it. She offered a weary smile of thanks and allowed him to assume the burden of carrying her belongings down the street. Little powdery puffs of yellow dust coated their shoes with each step. She lagged a little behind him, mindful of piles of various droppings, large and small, left in the street by the animal residents of South Pass City.

The rest of the dance troupe followed along behind, screeching laughter and tripping over their own feet, accompanied by a line of male admirers toting luggage. Agatha still hadn't awakened, and was being carried slung over the shoulder of one of the men, her posterior tilted toward the sky and her white hands flapping in the region of his kidneys.

Inside the Goldust, as the rest of the girls headed straight for the bar to continue their revels and Agatha was deposited in a precarious slump in a chair with her head lolling to one side, Ailis stopped only long enough to get a room key. She forcefully wrested her bag and her machine in its custom wood case from the gentleman who held them, thanked him politely, and headed for the stairs. Alone.

"Say, will I see you later?" he hollered after her. "What's your name anyway?" He watched, rubbing his chin and frowning as she continued climbing the staircase and his hopes faded. She didn't speak until she heard another voice, one that was more familiar. At the sound of Dulcinetta Jackson calling to her, she turned. She put down her burdens and leaned on the rail to smile down at the sweet creature attired in one of Ailis's very own best creations.

"Leave your things in the room and come down," Dulcie cupped her hand around her mouth and yelled over the growing din. Ailis nodded agreement, turned and unlocked her door, and put her things inside. The iron bedstead looked so inviting, but the glazed flower pitcher and bowl on the washstand looked hardly capable of providing the thorough wash she so desperately wanted.

The first thing Dulcie said as Ailis descended and they locked arms to head toward Dulcinetta's private quarters in the back was, "I'll ask Ju to draw you a bath before we eat."

"Bless you, my dear child," Ailis breathed.

Dulcinetta laughed. "I've missed you, Ailis. Ju will be glad to see you as well. Oh, and I have a little surprise for you, one whom I was not expecting. My son, Luther, has arrived."

Ailis cast a sideways look at her friend. Neither of them had been endowed with many observable maternal traits, and Ailis couldn't imagine Dulcie raising a child, let alone trying to raise one in the often wanton atmosphere of a saloon in a gold district in Wyoming Territory. "I thought you said he was safe in Missouri?"

"And so he was, until just recently, when circumstances changed. Go on, wash off the dust of your journey. We'll talk more over dinner tonight." Dulcie waved her friend into the familiar little room off the kitchen which contained the copper tub.

Ailis was already undressing when Ju came in with the first of several pails of hot water.

"Ju!" Ailis stood, tossing her shoes under the room's lone chair, and tried to hug the smaller woman after she emptied the pail into the tub. But Ju avoided her arms. "Ju," Ailis said uncertainly, "what's wrong?"

"I missy servant now. White girl don't make fuss over cook." Ju tilted her little chin and departed.

Ailis, bemused at the unwelcoming greeting, didn't let it stop her in the quest to get clean. She sat to roll her garters down and pulled off her stockings, draping them over the back of the chair along with a limp, travel-worn jacket. As she took off her skirt and untied the crinolette, she watched Ju enter once more and exit wordlessly, gaze averted and head bowed.

When the tub was almost full and Ailis judged it would be the last trip for Ju and the bucket, she seized the woman's arm. "Ju, what's going on? I ordered the material you wanted, the indigo silk. When will you have time for the final measurements so I can get started?"

She noticed Ju was wearing some old pajama-type Chinese outfit with fraying cuffs and torn seams. Of course, it wouldn't make sense for her to wear any of the beautiful, colorful silk tunics and trousers, and unusual form-fitting, split-skirt dresses just to work in the kitchen. But Ailis had seen Ju doing housework before, and Ju had never looked quite so ragged.

"Ju, talk to me," Ailis begged when Chrysanthemum refused to speak. It was only when Ailis tugged on Ju's arm and turned the other woman in her direction did she see the tears streaming down her friend's face.

~

Ailis emerged sometime later, refreshed and in clean clothes that Ju had fetched for her from her luggage. Her damp auburn hair hung in dark red ringlets down her back. She could detect dinner cooking, and the aroma coming from the kitchen made her stomach growl. The hour was early yet, but dinner was almost always served in late afternoon at Dulcinetta's. In this place, everyone's livelihood meant being primped and fed and ready for business by early evening, seven days a week.

Ailis sat at the table, and soon Dulcie and a boy of about five or six years of age joined her. The boy bore the family trademark crinkly black hair, and his face was a miniature of Dulcie's, with high forehead, button nose, and eyes brimming with intelligent curiosity.

Dulcie was dressed for the evening in another of Ailis's creations, a maroon velvet off-the-shoulder gown that hugged the curves of her upper body to her waist, where it flared out behind in a soft bustle. The style was becoming all the rage in fashion now, and the gown emphasized Dulcie's womanly charms. "That color selection was inspired, it complements your skin to perfection," Ailis said.

"The style is all yours," Dulcie replied. "And as you say, perfection. As always." She kissed her fingertips in Ailis's direction.

Ailis nodded. She hadn't a shred of false modesty when it came to her dressmaking talent.

"This is my son Luther. Luther, say hello nicely to Miss Ailis."

"Luther Brandingham III," he said, holding out his hand. "Pleased to meet you. How do you do, Miss Ailis?"

"Very well. Thank you, Luther." She nodded approval of the boy's manners to his mother.

"I'm afraid I can't take credit," Dulcinetta confessed. "Until a short while ago, he was in St. Louis in the care of a tutor and a governess. We actually don't know each other all that well, do we, Luther?" Turning to Ailis, she said in a low voice, "I have never thought this type of place was the proper milieu to raise a child."

Luther climbed up on a chair next to Ailis, who didn't pay him much attention. She wasn't very good with small children and would be the first to admit it. She had no desire to become a mother, and wondered how Dulcinetta, who displayed as little of a nurturing bent as Ailis, had become entrapped in the role of maternal goddess.

"And yet here he is, at the Goldust," Ailis observed.

"Grandmama took sick," Luther informed her. "I couldn't stay at her house in St. Louis anymore."

"I'm sorry to hear that," Ailis said, although in truth she had no fond memories of Lou Schering from the time when they had both been following the progress of the tracks toward Cheyenne. To young Ailis Tierney, St. Louie Lou had appeared a slatternly old madam, a purveyor to the railroad workers of barrels of rotgut liquor and provider of quick forays with none-too-clean women behind the blanket walls of a half-board Hell on Wheels tent.

But Ailis kept her opinion of Lou to herself, especially once she learned of Dulcinetta's family connection to the woman. She still couldn't quite figure out all the details of how Dulcie came to regard Lou as her mother, and Dulcie's child to regard her as his grandmother, when Dulcie herself said Lou wasn't her real mother. It just seemed out of character for the old woman to have adopted a mulatto girl, which Ailis knew very well Dulcie was since she had previously met Josiah, Dulcie's father, and there was no question the man was a negro. None of which made any difference to Ailis. Dulcie was her friend, and

Dulcie also spent a lot of money on Ailis's fashions, so Dulcie was a valued customer as well. It was just curious, that's all, that a crusty old bird like St. Louie Lou would be claimed as family by someone as obviously cultured and educated as Dulcie. And yet, here were Dulcinetta the faro dealer and Josiah Jackson the barkeep and now Dulcie's child, Luther Brandingham III, all living, and the adults working, in Lou's saloon at the outermost fringe of civilization. Life's twists and turns were indeed strange.

"Ju is watching him until I can make some kind of arrangement for a new tutor," Dulcie said as Ju herself entered the room with a platter of food and a pitcher of cold water. With exaggerated motions of care that spoke more eloquently than if she had dropped the platter an inch from the table, Ju gingerly placed the meal on its surface between the adults and very carefully set the pitcher down directly in front of Dulcinetta.

"And none too happy about the situation, I take it?" Ailis helped herself to a slice of medium rare beef and some roasted potatoes, and then served the boy, saying nothing of previously witnessing Ju in tears.

"Ju, please sit and eat with us," Dulcie said.

"Servants not eat with family," Ju said, turning a stiff back on Dulcinetta.

Dulcie sighed. "As you see, Ailis, I have been a failure at explaining American customs to our Fragrant Chrysanthemum. She seems to think cook, housekeeper, and nanny are much inferior situations to that of hooker."

"What's hooker mean, Mama?" Luther asked.

"Never you mind. Eat your dinner," Dulcie said, reaching to plop another few pieces of potato on his plate.

Ju turned back to face the table and make her stand. "Inferior cook don't make enough money to buy pretty dress. Ailis promise to sew Ju pretty dress. Now Ju not make enough money to pay Ailis for pretty new dress."

"I presume that explains those rags you're wearing? A form of protest against your supposed enslavement in my household?" Dulcie's lips thinned.

"Whatever you say, missy. I don't understand all that. I not slave."

"That's right, Ju. Not anymore, you're not. I saved you from that life in San Francisco. Or would you prefer to return to the rather desolate conditions where I found you, about to be passed on to your next Chinese master? I bought your contract, Ju, to set you free from that fate."

"I promise to be bride to China man. Not hooker." Tears were once again tracking down Ju's cheeks. "Now I never be bride. So I want be hooker. I want be pretty, wear pretty clothes like white girl. But Ju not good enough to go upstair with white man anymore."

Ailis felt bad for Ju, but although the offer was on the tip of her tongue she couldn't propose to make clothes for Ju without charging her regular fee. If word got out to the other girls that the dressmaker was so softhearted she gave away her fabulous creations for the price of no more than a sad tale of woe, they would all plead for the same bargain rate with their own anguished stories. Eventually a first small urge toward tenderheartedness would lead to Ailis's complete financial ruin.

"I apologize for this scene. Please, continue eating," Dulcie said to Ailis, rising from her place at the table. She took Ju's arm and led her forcefully toward the kitchen, hissing in a low voice, "Just what are you hoping to accomplish with this performance?"

Luther looked at Ailis. "Did you understand that?" he asked. "Do you think Ju really wants to be a hooker—or not?"

Ailis almost choked on a bite of potato. Clearing her throat, she said, "I think not. I think Ju only wants the new clothes she ordered. I also think you should forget you ever heard the conversation that has just taken place here."

Luther thought about that for a minute. At last, his gaze turning toward the closed door to the kitchen where his mother and Ju could be heard still arguing in muted voices, he raised his fork in a salute to her, observing in a disconcertingly adult manner, "I think you could be right about that, Miss Ailis."

Chapter 7
The Bryan Boardinghouse for Young Ladies

FEW OF BETHENIA'S GIRLS made it to the dance floor that night, most of them too tipsy to endure being whirled around for hours without risking some truly vile results. Instead they encouraged the Goldust's patrons to drink up, and continued their own imbibing at the gentlemen's expense. As the afternoon wore into evening, and then to the late hours of the night, several of the girls disappeared upstairs for a short time, or outside for an even more brief interval with men who had been heard boasting of bulging pockets, pockets full of gold or otherwise. The fiddler worked the bow for an unusually lackluster audience, and the banjo player strummed to middling response. The master of ceremonies did his best to cajole the crowd, which consisted of single men packed almost to the door, but the dance floor of the Goldust wasn't its biggest draw that night.

Ailis spent some time at ten cents a dance, only because the long hours of the evening stretched in front of her and she had nothing else to do. She had many enthusiastic prospective partners. A dime was poor pay indeed compared to what she could make with her sewing, but as she was prevented from sewing since she had no supplies yet she might as well earn a dollar or two dancing. Her smile encouraged tips and she made a few more dollars that way, but it purposely wasn't so bright it invited the wrong kind of attention. She had grown cautiously adept at discouraging overly amorous advances from lonely men whose sweethearts were far distant. When she finally retired for the night, she locked the door and also tipped a chair back under the handle as reinforcement. In the morning, she was the first to rise. She wanted to get to the dry goods store and make sure the material she had on order had arrived. As well, she had been furnished a shopping list for the rest of Bethie's girls.

Ailis had grown used to the looks she got from store proprietors when she went shopping. She had vowed that one day she would show them all who they had dealt with in such cavalier manner. Although liberated women were attracted to the little Wyoming settlement by the promise of equality with woman suffrage, in Ailis's experience it was easier for most proper women to just lump her in with the dancing girls and their questionable morals. At least at this hour of the morning in the Lightburn and Company store she didn't have to put up with the supercilious, icy manner of the owner's spouse.

"Two bottles of Samaritan Nervine, three of Paragoric Elixir, two Dr. Raphael's Cordial Invigorant, two of the good doctor's Galvanic Love Powders, and two Dr. Brown's Renovating Pills." One of Bethie's girls was an opium addict, one was prone to nervous fits, and the other items were for those who insisted various cordials and powders and pills helped move matters along more expeditiously during the most intimate portion of their business enterprise.

One of the male clerk's eyebrows rose and kept rising until it almost touched his hairline. As Ailis wound down from her recital, his mouth pursed. "Would you care to repeat that? More slowly, if you please."

Ailis reiterated the list, giving him time between each item to fetch it from the shelves or from beneath the counter. Once he had the nostrums arrayed in front of her, he said in an unctuous voice, "I trust that will be all, madam?"

"No, I'm afraid that will not be all." Ailis raised her chin and stared directly at him, causing him to lower his gaze first. "I've come to inquire if my fabrics have arrived. Two bolts sage green faille, one brown moire, one olive wool and six yards olive chenille, as well as the one hundred twenty yards of black lace and seventy of olive green ribbon. And the matching thread. As well as a packet of sewing machine needles." She plunked several gold eagles down on the counter, and said, "Have it all delivered to the Goldust, if you please. The sooner, the better."

As usual, and unlike female sales people who never warmed to a supposed fallen woman, the sight of her gold improved the man's condescending manner toward her. "I'll see what I can do. You know how hard help is to find around here. Everyone's out working their claims. No one wants a tedious job as a delivery boy."

"Watch what you wish for. I've heard some say that men are starting to pull out of the Sweetwater. If the rumors go around that few are finding color, you'll have many men looking for work enough to pay a passage back home."

"As you say, madam." He nodded his head as he leaned conspiratorially toward her. "Er, is that what you hear in the Goldust? Is South Pass being called a humbug for certain?"

"Not for certain. I've only heard whispers here and there. It's no stampede out of here and on to the next big strike. Yet. So far, I understand Dulcinetta is holding her own and doesn't seem to have seen her business falling off any."

"That's good. Good news indeed. I wish Miss Jackson all good fortune." He looked around his store, a sad, reflective look on his face as if he imagined the shelves bare and the windows boarded up. It was a look that sent a shiver as of icy fingers up Ailis's spine. Not for herself, the special case she had paid to have made meant her little hand-cranked machine could be carried anywhere. But a saloon and dance hall, or a dry goods store for that matter, weren't so easy to pick up and move. She feared for Dulcinetta and Ju if South Pass City's supply of eager would-be miners should dry up. Drawn to this place by glowing newspaper articles and railroad advertisements, they could just as easily be directed elsewhere, on to the next big gold discovery.

Ailis didn't mean to be hardhearted, but she thought she should make every effort to get the dresses finished that her two friends had ordered. She thought it might be best to be paid and ready to move on, just in case South Pass City's figurative ceiling of gold quartz fell sooner than anyone expected on those who remained.

~

Everything went all right until Devin was handed a stack of bills of lading at the railroad station. The papers detailed the number of boxes and barrels, their weight and how to identify them by the marks on them, and a contract for their transport to their destination. He had been so pleased to have made it back to Bryan without further incident, he hadn't considered how he would actually carry out the important duties of a freight office superintendent.

He had paid off the farm boy when they got back to town, the lad happy he could take off back to Iowa or Ohio or wherever he called home. Devin had meanwhile managed to hire a replacement swamper. The new boy was about Devin's own age and untested, but as he had never held a job before outside of agricultural work he wasn't a candidate for employment on the railroad or as much more than a stock boy in the mercantile.

The boy, Moroni Smythe by name, was one of the young Mormons forced out of the sect's Salt Lake City headquarters by older men who didn't want younger competition for the limited supply of wives. Upon being hired by Devin, the young man expressed pathetic gratitude and relief. He readily confessed an inordinate fear of being entombed underground and so had avoided seeking work in the coal mines at Carbon and Rock Springs. The wage Devin promised wasn't as high as what the mines or the railroad paid, but it was more than Moroni could have earned clerking.

And the boy was literate. He could easily have read the papers for Devin, but Devin didn't know him well yet and was afraid that letting him do any paperwork would give Moroni an unfair advantage over the boss. As they took possession of the teetering stacks of boxes and barrels at the train depot, Devin tried to keep track in his head what should end up where. He had the freight company's warehouse organized by destination, and pointed this out to Moroni as the young man began unloading the day's freight they had picked up at the dock. And so the loading and unloading went smoothly, but as the pile of documentation grew it constantly threatened to topple over . . . and to topple Devin as manager as well.

He had to figure out some way to decipher the papers. But how, without revealing his profound secret? He felt sick at the thought that he didn't begin to deserve the trust Dulcinetta Jackson had placed in him. Dulcie had promoted him to manager. She hadn't specified how to run the business, only that he should. Was it possible to hire someone to take care of the office side of the business? Someone to organize all the freight by who had ordered what, and explain it all slowly enough that Devin would retain the information in memory?

Who might that person be, the one who wouldn't betray his shortcoming? And where might one go about finding a person like that? Where might he turn, and who in Bryan would have Dulcinetta's interests at heart as much as he did himself? A person, say, who had Lou Schering's interests at heart as well. That person was Josiah Jackson. Devin left Moroni to the unloading and turned his own steps toward the local bordello. He was a large, rather conspicuous figure to anyone who might observe him on the street of Bryan City, marching determinedly toward the whorehouse in the early afternoon. But that couldn't be helped. He'd rather have people think he needed to take care of a certain kind of private business than to discover him completely incapable of taking care of the real business entrusted to him.

Set in the first cross street near the tracks, well away from the respectable businesses crossing Evans at Tenth and Eleventh, the blue-painted bordello with its vivid purple door was still nicknamed the White House. Its original white canvas had been transformed into a sturdy Victorian dwelling with curlicue-decorated gables. Devin climbed the steps of the porch and, without knocking, opened the door of the two-story building. Stepping inside the establishment's front parlor, he discovered things were mighty quiet at the Bryan Boardinghouse for Young Ladies at this hour of the day.

"Help you, honey?" a husky voice asked from the shadows. Devin made out a voluptuous figure dressed in not much more than a belted satin wrapper, her assets threatening to spill from carelessly crossed lapels. A mass of tumbled red hair was piled loosely on her head and her makeup smeared. She looked as if she had just crawled out of bed.

"I need to talk to Mr. Jackson," Devin said, clearing his throat and taking another tentative step into the room so that he might see her features better as they spoke.

The woman rose, drawing near enough to Devin that he could smell her, a mixture of bottled scent and what she exuded from her own pores. At this small distance, he could see she was older than he had thought her at first, her skin coarse and beginning to wrinkle, the red of her hair obviously enhanced and of a pinkish tint near the roots. "Josiah's probably sleeping at this time of day. You can find him bedded down over at Lou's. Or you can wait until tonight when he'll be here. In fact, you could wait right here with me if you like, until he shows up." She ran an appreciative gaze over the entire length of Devin's considerable form, head to toe.

"Uh, I think I'll go and search him up. Thank you very much."

"Any time, honey. You know whereat Lou's place is?"

"I think I do. I can find it, anyhow. This town isn't big enough to get lost in."

Painted red lips stretched over yellow teeth. "Now that you know where we are, you come on back and see us, hear?"

Devin hastily backed out the door. Fitting his sombrero back on his head, he traced his steps back toward the wooden warehouse, and the row of impermanent tent dwellings erected next to it. Anyone who worked nights and slept days in this town had to be a fairly heavy sleeper. All the dwellings, canvas and wood alike, strung out along

Bryan's main street stretching from the rails to the Black's Fork sat mere feet from the rumble and screech of iron wheels on iron tracks, the clamor of the engine's bells, and the noise and bustle of people and animals and conveyances. He could only hope it was possible to awaken Josiah Jackson at this hour since he certainly didn't want to have to go back again to Lou's White House to conduct his business.

At Lou's domicile, he pulled a string to sound a cowbell attached to the inside of the door. He waited a bit, got no response, then rang it again. As he was lifting his hand to ring it a third time, the door was whipped open. Josiah Jackson stood there, frowning and squinting against the light, wearing only a pair of trousers and pulling one strap of his leather galluses over his shoulder.

"Devin Cavanaugh, is that right? Yes, yes, I recognize you. What is it?" he asked, a note of repressed fear in his voice.

"I'm sorry to bother you, Mr. Jackson," Devin began.

"No, no bother. Come in," Josiah gestured and Devin stooped to enter. "Is something wrong? Things are well in South Pass City, I hope?"

Devin realized the man was afraid of bad news regarding his daughter and grandson, so he hurried to reassure him. "Everything is fine. The problem is here in Bryan. In fact, I am the very problem I have come to consult you about."

The man gave Devin a searching glance and then gestured toward a chair. "Sit," he said, perching on the edge of a chair himself in order to pull his boots on over bare feet before standing back up. "I have to go see a man about a dog, and then I'll be back to boil us some coffee."

When he returned, Josiah added more water and grounds to what already sat steaming in a pot on the stove and then bent to stir up the fire in the little stove with its minute cooking surface. He sat across from Devin in a homemade leather and moose horn chair that matched the one where Devin waited.

"Well, then. Has my daughter sent you?"

Devin shook his head, wondering how he might begin. His stomach ached; he felt full of his own misery. He had to confess, and he had to do it soon, before he got himself in any deeper.

"Dulcinetta turned the running of the freighting business over to me. I'm gathering the next load to take to South Pass City. Every day more merchandise comes in on the train. I'm storing it at the warehouse until I have enough for a full load."

"Very wise of you," Josiah said encouragingly, one eye on the coffeepot so it wouldn't boil over.

"I've been keeping all the bills of lading and the invoices in my head," Devin said. "You see, Mr. Jackson . . . the problem . . . that is, I mean—"

Josiah looked at him sharply. "I think you better just spit it out, son, before you choke on it. Whatever it might be."

"Mr. Jackson, when Dulcinetta hired me, uh, promoted me, I didn't tell her . . . she doesn't know. . . . The thing is—I can't read. And so you see, sir, if I should make a mistake, it's not only going to cost me. It's going to cost the company. And her. And anyone else who has an interest in Schering Forwarding. That's you, I guess. And Lou herself, if she's still around. That is, no offense, if Lou is still among the living, I mean."

"I know what you're trying to say." Josiah got up to tend to the coffee. "Have a bit of a problem, don't you?" He poured coffee into two delicate porcelain cups, handing over one on a saucer that felt as thin as paper in Devin's big paw.

Devin nodded glumly. Yes, he definitely had a problem.

Josiah continued: "I have to admire your honesty, however. I had wondered, when Dulcie was considering elevating such a young man to the superintendency of the forwarding company, if she weren't making a mistake. It sets my mind at ease, your coming to me with a problem of this magnitude and not trying to conceal it until things got out of hand."

"Would you consider playing the role of superintendent? Just come down to the warehouse as we're loading up, and take over? I don't know all the details, you might already own the place. I could be called manager or whatever you like, so long as no mistakes are made and the right merchandise gets delivered to the right place. I don't need a fancy title, I'm just a working man. I wouldn't ask you, but I don't know who else to consult. I don't want Dulcinetta, that is, your daughter, to be disappointed in me."

Again Josiah studied Devin, this time over the rim of his steaming cup. "That's important, is it, young man? Dulcie's good opinion?"

Devin ran a nervous finger under his collar. "It is, sir. Ducinetta's estimation of me is very important. I hope you don't mind my saying so, but I'll tell you true, I've never met the like of her anywhere before. And I've been quite a few places, Mr. Jackson."

"All right, Devin. May I call you Devin? I'll help you. When is the next trip to South Pass City?"

Devin nodded at the first question. Josiah Jackson could call Devin anything he liked, if only he would help him out of this predicament. "I think we'll be ready the day after tomorrow, if all the freight arrives here by then."

"Not to worry. We will take care of business at this end of the road, Devin." He held up a finger. "But I will have a promise in return."

"Anything." Devin felt lightheaded with relief that Josiah would help him without making a big fuss over his inability to decipher the mounds of paper in the freighting office.

Although the gleam older man's eye should have given him some warning, Devin was wholly unprepared when Josiah continued, "Swear to me that you will make a clean breast of your weakness to Dulcinetta at the very first opportunity upon returning to the Sweetwater Country."

"I . . . Ah," Devin said. He swallowed a hard lump lodged in his throat.

"I will share a truth with you, Devin Cavanaugh. I don't think this is just a business arrangement with Dulcie. I think my daughter has begun to have feelings for you. But as her father I will not stand by and watch her be deceived once again by a man about whom she cares greatly. Bare your soul to her. Give me your solemn oath that you will divulge all."

Devin was flummoxed. Dulcinetta's own father thought she held him in tender regard? He had considered himself beneath the notice of such a mature, alluring creature. It was flattering to even entertain the thought that Josiah might be correct, but Devin suspected the man had probably mistaken his daughter's immediate need for a manager for admiration of the man who had ended up with the position. It would be too much to even dream, Devin suspected, that a woman like Dulcinetta would look on him in a positive light.

But . . . how could he begin to confess his deficiencies to such a paragon? Where would he find the words? Would she turn on him and never invite him back for one of Ju's dinners? Would she throw him out of the Goldust? Might she perhaps fire him from his new job for incompetence, no less than for hiding the truth?

"Well?" Josiah demanded as Devin failed to respond immediately. "Yes or no?"

"Well, Mr. Jackson," Devin hedged for just a moment more. "Yes, of course I will. I should have told her when she offered me the job. I guess I was just so . . . dazzled by her. By her and by the trust she was putting in me to handle her business. I didn't think it would be such a big impediment. I thought I could just remember everything. I haven't been in the freighting business very long. I didn't know how quickly how complicated it could all become."

Josiah waved away Devin's explanations with a secret smile of delight hovering at the corners of his mouth. "It is a good man who can face his own imperfections without flinching. My daughter and I are lucky Lou happened upon you in our hour of need. Now, Devin Cavanaugh, I really must get some rest. I will be at the warehouse the day after tomorrow and we will see you safely on your way back to South Pass City with all the transfer goods in order."

Devin handed the flimsy little cup and saucer back. "Thank you. Thank you very much, Mr. Jackson."

Josiah, stifling a yawn, flapped a hand at Devin to speed him away, turning the lock as soon as the door had closed behind him.

Chapter *8*
New Clothes

*T*HEY WERE LITTLE MORE than one day away from South Pass City, wagons piled high and animals straining. The weather had been hot and cloudless. Barely a breeze stirred the powdery dust of the road. Even from where he sat atop the wheeler, Devin could feel the ground radiating heat. Always sorry to leave the brush-covered lands where it was possible to see for miles and distinguish any distant speck as benignly inanimate, or perhaps menacingly animate, they had been climbing for most of the day toward canyon and juniper country.

To most people, the high desert looked gray of plant, brown of soil, and utterly devoid of water. Most people did not prefer the arid lands, but Devin did. Fortunate to have worked for a time alongside a college man, a botanist, during the building of the railroad, he knew this country had many plants that might resemble each other, but were actually different. He could distinguish some as they passed: bitterbrush, bladderpod, milkvetch, big sage, fringe sage, and spiny hopsage. He knew those starting to bud—larkspur and yarrow, primrose, bee plant, aster—and those already in bloom, including the rose-like flower of the prickly pear cactus. And he knew the grasses, at least two of his favorites, whose common names were their description, needle and thread, and Indian rice grass.

As they continued to climb, the animals could smell water and pulled hard to get to it. The landscape had begun to change. Now here and there Devin could spy mountain mahogany and service berry. The crossing of the Sweetwater was just ahead, and they had entered the evergreens lining the riverbed. The trees beside the rutted road cast long shadows on the heated earth, and suddenly, for no reason he could have explained, an uneasy feeling began to creep over him. He looked around, turning his head from side to side as if he could scent danger if not see it. "Look lively!" he called back to Moroni.

"What's up, boss?" the boy hollered back.

"Can't tell! Maybe something, maybe nothing. Just keep your eyes peeled." Devin followed his own advice, but still didn't see it coming.

Almost on the verge of drawing his rifle, at the same time he chided himself for his fear for spooking at nothing. Then a shot rang out. A splinter of wood chipped off the wagon behind his right ear and lodged in the meat between his thumb and index finger. Suddenly the fingers of the hand he needed for shooting wouldn't flex. Struggling to pull his rifle out of its leather covering with his left hand, it slipped with the sweat of fear. He couldn't work the weapon free. Without warning, some of the shadows that had caused concern moved out of the trees to surround the wagons. The road blocked by a cohort of some fifteen or so whooping Indians brandishing weapons, the confused mules came to a dead halt. Now Devin didn't have time to continue trying to wrest the rifle from the scabbard. He had only a pistol, and sliding from the saddle of the wheeler he tried to take careful aim before pulling the trigger.

"Take cover!" he yelled at Moroni. The boy sat high on the rear wagon, an unmoving target, mouth agape in astonishment. But Devin's warning came too late. There shone a spray of red against the horizon like a single-color burnished rainbow comprised of tissue and blood. Moroni's once-blond head slowly sank below the side boards.

Devin scrambled beneath the front wagon until all he could see besides the wheels and the ruts were the legs and hooves of horses as riders circled. As yet not many shots had been fired, both sides conserving their ammunition, and Devin knew why. If the Indians had any interest in the commodities freighted from place to place in Wyoming Territory, it wouldn't be the beans, flour, or corn Devin hauled. It would be, in descending order of interest: knives and guns, powder and lead or cartridges, horses, whiskey, tobacco, kettles and pots and awls and nails and other metal items, cloth and blankets, and any furs they could trade for any of the preceding items. They might perhaps have a bit of interest left over for coffee and sugar—if they were the half tame sort of Indians who hung around the white man's forts and had developed a taste for such.

In the winter Chief "Washke" and the Shoshones remained near, precisely because the troublesome Sioux and Cheyenne weren't raiding. But it was late spring, almost summer, and there was no Indian ally within hundreds of miles to help the freighters. With young Moroni down and quite probably dead, Devin was entirely on his own.

His heart sank as he saw the receding dinner-plate sized hooves of his tall Shire wheelers as they were led away, cut loose from the team and destined perhaps to haul travois next time a camp belonging to these Indians moved. Devin cursed, pulling the sharp sliver of wood from his gun hand, trying to stanch the blood which flowed freely. He was enraged at his inability to prevent the murder of his young swamper or the theft of his prized horses. A mediocre mount could cost a hundred dollars; massive, trained wheelers like the two draft horses could fetch five hundred the pair. The mules, which at this moment were being cut loose and driven away with the Shires, didn't deserve to end up in a Sioux stew pot. And how in hell would he ever hope to replace any of them, the eager-to-please boy, or even the horses and mules, if he did somehow manage to get away himself?

Time passed. It seemed hours as he lay there in a cold sweat beneath the lead wagon, but in reality it could only have been minutes. Above him, as someone rummaged through the supplies, he heard thumps and bumps and the scrape of wood on wood. A cloud of flour drifted down, and then several sacks of grain smacked to the road bed, followed by a small brown eruption of Arbuckle coffee beans. Explosions of breaking glass like hurled bombs came next, accompanied by exultant yips and yells and the small thunder of discarded tin cans rolling down the road. Horses whinnied amid blood curdling shouts and the vibration of hooves pounding the ground.

The same thing was happening in the rear wagon, all sorts of precious commodities being tossed over the side to the roadbed. Devin could only hope the Indians didn't stumble on the kegs of Lou's fine sipping whiskey that Josiah was shipping to Dulcinetta.

Devin heard ominous crackling and smelled smoke. A pair of bronzed legs ending in two leather moccasins appeared in front of his face. He lifted his pistol, trying to steady it with the painful hand still dripping sticky blood. The long barrel of a musket pointed under the wagon in his direction. He saw a fall of long raven hair appear, followed by a grinning, painted face. The Indian seemed to know Devin had expended all his bullets and that the gun pointed at him was a sham. He gestured with his chin for Devin to come out.

Devin wondered what would happen if he refused. One way or another he was going to die, and he supposed being crushed by the collapse of a burning wagon was preferable to being tortured to death by the Sioux. Making up his mind to try and make a break for it, Devin started to back out, away from the ominous beckoning and the frightfully-daubed features. He had a glimpse over one shoulder of poor young Moroni's body splatting to the ground, and then before he could fully credit it, the Sioux peering at him numbered two instead of one. They watched with eyes devoid of expression, from either side of the burning wagon where he had scuttled toward the rear like a beached crawdad.

He didn't think he had any choice left in the matter. He surrendered and started to crawl out. When he wasn't fast enough to suit, the nearest Indian grabbed him by the collar and finished yanking him out, a task he didn't seem to realize would not have been successful without the big white man's collaboration. The painted Sioux said something which Devin couldn't begin to understand, and shook him like an old dust rag when he failed to answer. Devin's useless pistol clattered to the ground as his bloodied hand lost its grip. The clouds of smoke surrounding them were a thick roil, threatening to choke them all if they didn't soon get away from the burning wagons.

Devin jerked away and started a mad dash for the trees, his hat tumbling to the ground and pitching away behind him. His pursuer easily outran him and soon caught him by grabbing a handful of hair. Then he tried yanking Devin over toward one of their horses. He pulled a stone war club from his belt. Devin hardly had time to raise his hands, when he received a sharp blow on the temple that made his eyes cross. The shock didn't knock Devin out completely, but his legs grew rubbery and his vision blurred at the edges. He wasn't putting up much resistance as his arm was nearly pulled from the socket and his hands tied behind his back. He stumbled to cooperate and climb atop a rock so he could be mounted on the pony, his feet tied together beneath its belly.

Whooping, the Indian's companion soon joined them. This one had obviously discovered the secret of the false floor of the second wagon, as he now had several kegs of St. Louie Lou's pride and joy strapped to the sides of one of the horses. He leaped up behind Devin, wheeling the pony while jerking the lead of the keg-burdened packhorse. Even laden as they were with casks and a captive, the party set a good pace behind the fleeing mules and draft horses, away from the road and through the trees, westward toward Atlantic Peak.

The air was cooler. Devin didn't know how much time had passed but the sun must be going down. Swaying from side to side on the horse, he doubted himself capable of lasting for even another yard without losing consciousness, the party halted. The Indian behind him dismounted. Devin tried to focus his eyes, and raised his bound hands in an attempt to wipe away some of the clotting blood oozing down his face from the split skin of his temple. His head ached fiercely now, he was seeing double, and he only succeeded in smearing more blood into his eyes.

One of Devin's feet was tugged downward, the thong under the horse's belly cut, and he was dumped off to the ground. He knelt there, incapable of raising his head. Incapable of doing more than awaiting his fate, whatever that might be.

The sound of hoofbeats came to his ears. He could feel the reverberations in the ground beneath his palms. He realized, with a sense of incredulity, the attackers were beginning to retreat, accompanied by victorious yells that caused his head to ring. He thought he must have missed something. Maybe he passed out? He had to be dreaming—why would they bother leaving him alive?

He waited, kneeling in the dirt, slumped over his bound hands, wishing his head would stop pounding. Eventually, perhaps a short time or perhaps a long time later, there came a voice. One that he recognized.

"Behold how the once mighty have fallen," Cal Wilson intoned.

Devin felt the tip of Wilson's boot prodding him in the side. One shove too many, a touch too hard, and the big man blinded by his own blood toppled right over on his face, to the accompaniment of Wilson's cackled laughter, which sounded even wilder than that of the Sioux.

"Get up. We got plans to make."

"I'm not making any plans with you," Devin mumbled around a mouth full of dirt.

"Listen, you dough-head natural, I have little patience left. You will do as I say," Wilson said, "or I will kill ya right now. It's your choice."

Devin rolled over on his back, raising bound, shaking hands to the pulse hammering in his head. "Go ahead. Kill me," he muttered. "I don't care."

"Then if you don't care for your own self, I will kill her! The woman! The expensive piece you admire so much down there in S. P.

City. I will get her alone and I will commence to take my time killing her, Cavanaugh. Mark my words."

"Shite!" Forcing himself to sit upright, cradling his sore head and feeling the urge to puke, Devin said, "You've burned the wagons, run off all the stock, ruined the cargo. You've ruined me! What more do you want, Cal?"

"Well, I'll tell ya." Wilson bent to slice through the thong still tied tightly around Devin's wrists, before sitting back on his heels and running the flat of the blade contemplatively over his lips. "Do ya know why we're called muleskinners, Cavanaugh? To skin means to get the best of, and I proved that time and again with savvy old Beery, eh? I had to get the best of that sorry, grizzled mule, one way and another, in order to get the best of the whole team. So, you see, a man can skin an animal, or he can skin another man, or perhaps even . . . skin a woman. To skin means to take all that someone has. So are ya beginning to catch my meaning, now? Are ya beginning to see yet how it's going to be between me and that fancy mulatto trollop sitting down there in her golden bum-mill thinking to herself that she has *skint* old Cal Wilson?"

Devin studied the wavering image of twin Cals. It was mighty worrisome that he wasn't cursing every other word. The fact that he had given away some excellent whiskey to the Indians was most troubling. And Cal appeared completely sober. It appeared Cal had made a plan, and he was determined to carry it out. He wanted to wound Dulcinetta.

~

Ailis measured and cut and measured and cut, and then began sewing, all through the daylight hours and long into the nights. She stopped only when Dulcie insisted she come downstairs and take a meal. Sometimes, in the late afternoons before the girls started work in the saloon and dance hall, Bethenia joined them.

"You're certainly sewing up a storm, Ailis," Dulcie said on this occasion. "Are you in a hurry to finish up and leave our fair city?"

Ailis and Bethie exchanged glances. Bethenia lifted an eyebrow as she tipped a glass of wine toward her lips, allowing Ailis to fill the conversational void if she wished.

Ju leaned in front of Ailis to set a serving platter of rice and fish with vegetables on the table in front of her, momentarily blocking her view of Dulcie. Although Ju still refused to sit with them and continued to wait on them, Ailis noted fewer sullen glances cast in Dulcie's direction. It seemed to Ailis that perhaps Ju pouted a bit less and was becoming more resigned to her position. And then again, knowing Ju, perhaps not. It was hard to tell with someone so aloof.

"Ju," Dulcie said. "Must you, really? You knew I was talking to Ailis, and so you chose that very moment to lean in front of her to block my view? Don't think for a minute I don't know exactly what you're doing. You are trying my patience severely."

Ju turned and made a silent retreat to the kitchen. Dulcie turned away from the sight, exhaled aloud, and rolled her eyes. "You were saying, Ailis?"

"I only meant to say that there is some talk in the town about the miners starting to think they're barking at a knot."

Dulcie stared at her, her face turning a little pale beneath the rouge on her cheeks. "No. You can't mean it's becoming common knowledge already? They're thinking of giving up?"

"You don't get out of this saloon enough, Dulcie. Apparently no one wants to be the bearer of bad news, so nobody talks to you about it. Many have already left and gone home." Bethenia took another healthy gulp of wine. "You haven't noticed your business falling off lately?"

"I have . . . a bit," Dulcie admitted. "But the Goldust has always been so popular, I might be the last saloon keeper here to really realize custom was dipping. After all, the mines are still operating. The Young American, the King Solomon, the Buckeye, they all seem to be going strong."

"Last in, first out," Bethenia observed sagaciously, throwing Ailis a knowing look. "The Carissa still seems to be doing all right. Maybe your gaming tables do a good business amongst the independents who are yet bringing out enough dust to gamble. But at a dime a dance, my girls notice quickly when their partners become stingy about paying for their drinks, or for dances . . . or for other pastimes. When a man can't afford a good tumble in a mining town, it's a sure sign the place is almost done."

Dulcinetta gazed at the two of them a moment before saying anything further. "And so you are in a hurry to leave also, Ailis? Couldn't you bring yourself to stay on with me a while?"

Ailis lowered her gaze from Dulcie's beseeching one. "I travel with Bethenia. You know that. I wouldn't feel safe traipsing around the country all alone if I let her go on ahead."

"No. No, you're right. Women do travel alone, after all, and I mustn't be selfish. As you know, Josiah has relocated to Bryan to oversee Lou's interests there. I just hate the thought of being left here without another soul close to me except one stubborn, almost useless Chinese girl." She paused, then added, "Oh, of course I don't mean that! Of course, Ju is priceless. I don't know what I would do without her." She lifted her glass before asking, "Have you at least finished my clothing order, Ailis?"

"I've completed the others," Ailis said. "Not yours. I need a few more days yet."

"Well." Dulcie was obviously making an effort to sound cheerful. "How long have I got you both for, then? A few more days, surely, Bethenia? Perhaps Devin will be back by then."

"Devin is coming back soon?" Luther asked with an anticipatory grin. It was doubtful the three women had taken notice of him sitting there until he spoke.

"Yes, soon, I think," Dulcinetta answered.

"The two of you certainly seem to set much store by that man." Ailis was curious, hoping to draw Dulcie out about her relationship with Devin. Ailis had been shocked to hear her elegant friend discussing in glowing terms the rather thick-headed young man Ailis once knew in Cheyenne. Dulcie was surely several years older than Devin Cavanaugh, and Ailis found their connection interesting, to say the least.

Dulcie shot her a sharp glance while holding up a hand to stop Luther from interrupting again. "Do you know of any reason I shouldn't admire him, Ailis?"

"That's not what I meant. Not at all," Ailis hurried to say. If Devin had good prospects here with Dulcie and her son, far be it from Ailis to muddy the waters for him. She thought him rather staid and dull, it was true, but he had a good heart. She wished only the best for all of them. But she still had to look out for herself first. "I brought down what I've finished so far," she said, changing the subject back to dressmaking. "Would you like to look?"

"Why don't we do that?" Dulcie continued to look at Ailis speculatively for a moment, but let the subject of Devin drop as she rose from her chair. "Just let me get Ju."

"I'm going to get ready for work," Bethenia said to Ailis as Dulcie left the room. "Tell our hostess thanks for dinner when she gets back."

"I will." Ailis rose also and walked to the sideboard where she had laid her creations in neatly folded piles. She picked up the top garment and shook it out. It was a long sage green silk jacket with billowing sleeves, its neck and cuffs trimmed with dark green ribbon. Below it lay a matching dress of gray-green silk with a high collar and mother-of-pearl buttons. When Dulcinetta led Ju by the hand back into the dining room from the kitchen, Ailis watched Ju's sulky expression transform into something resembling joy as it slowly dawned on her that the new clothes in the Chinese style were hers. She wiped her hands on the much less impressive attire she presently wore before tiptoeing toward Ailis and the green outfit, a worshipful look of awe softening the features of her face.

"For Ju?" she whispered. One hand reached out, but she stopped short of actually touching the long tunic.

"For you, Chrysanthemum," Ailis said. "From Dulcie."

"But why? I don't understand." Ju looked truly puzzled as she turned her face toward Dulcie.

"Because I wanted to. Because you are my friend. Because you have earned much more than a new dress."

Ju nodded at this last, as if it were only permissible to accept the beautiful dress and outer garment if she had purchased them with her labor. She gathered up the jacket and gown and hugged them to her with a look of pure bliss.

Besides the money, these were the moments Ailis lived for, when she knew absolutely and without doubt that her talent was real, and was appreciated. Ju turned and hurried with her precious new clothes toward the room she shared with Luther at the back of the building.

Ailis took up the next item in the piles of clothes, a jacket of navy blue worsted. Dulcinetta gestured for Luther to approach, which he did, head hanging dejectedly and with as slow a step as he could manage without drawing a reprimand from his mother. New clothes were obviously not near the top of what motivated the boy.

"Take off your jacket, Luther," Dulcinetta said.

And so when his friend Devin and the mule man, Wilson, burst in to the family's private dining room with guns drawn, the boy stood helpless with his arms trapped in the sleeves of his coat. Luther heard his mother's sharp intake of breath before she spun him toward the kitchen door. "Go," she said in a harsh whisper. "Go to Ju. *Now!*"

She shoved Luther away, his arms still entangled in the sleeves of his old jacket, which was proving too tight-fitting for a growing boy to quickly wriggle his way to freedom.

Chapter 9
The Deal

"GET THAT BOY BACK in here," Wilson ordered.

"No." Dulcinetta squared her shoulders and faced him.

Wilson sneered. "Well, I guess you'll just have to do, then."

Ailis, standing stunned with her mouth hanging open, suddenly snapped it shut. She said, "Devin? Is that really you with a face full of blood and bruises? What in the name of *Jaysus* do you think you're *doing?*"

"What does it look like we're doing, slut? We're taking us a captive." Wilson's piggy eyes narrowed as his attention swung to Ailis. "I came for that little sissy boy we hauled up here from Bryan City. But the fancy madam here is who I have business with, anyway. Unless you'd like to take her place, that is?" He eyed Ailis appraisingly.

Ailis backed up a step. She raised a hand to her mouth, eyes wide as she stared at the fellow New York City orphan she hadn't seen in almost two years. Ignoring Wilson, she said, "I remember you, Devin Cavanaugh. I remember our talks in Cheyenne. I truly thought you were a decent man. Of all possibilities, I never once guessed you would end up a common *criminal*," she said. Her voice quavered.

"Ailis. This is not what it looks like," Devin said.

Wilson said, "Shut up, the both of ya. Let's go somewhere we can talk in private." He gestured with his gun for Dulcinetta to precede them into her bedroom. Once there, he kicked the door shut in Ailis's face as she tried to enter behind Devin. "Have a seat," Wilson said to Dulcinetta.

She sank onto the mattress, her gaze never leaving Wilson's face as he locked the door.

Devin said, "Dulcinetta—"

Wilson said with a snarl, "I *told* you to shut the hell up, Cavanaugh."

"I just thought if I tried to explain, she would be more cooperative." Devin held a gun as well, but it wasn't aimed in any particular direction and assuredly not at their captive.

"You make a poor bandit," Dulcinetta calmly observed to Devin. After studying him a moment more, she added, "Your forehead is bleeding."

"Believe me, this wasn't my idea. I didn't leave the Five Points, the auld fight for my square patch of ground, to travel all the way out here west to take up a life of hooliganism." Devin dabbed at his forehead with the tail of his neckerchief, glaring at Wilson through the lashes of the eye that wasn't presently swelling shut.

Wilson aimed his gun, a pepperbox pistol useless in a firefight but deadly in such close quarters, at Devin. "Will ya force me to make you shut up, ya miserable cowan?"

Devin aimed his own gun back at Wilson, as well as he could with a hand marred with a still seeping hole in it. "If you think killing me is going to make her any more cooperative, go ahead."

Wilson said with an evil grin, "I ain't told you this part yet, chum, but your gun ain't got any bullets in it."

Relieved, Devin laid the gun down on the bed. "Then I guess this farce is just about half over."

Dulcinetta, her head turning back toward Wilson, asked calmly, "What, exactly, is it that you want, Cal?"

"I want what I always wanted. I did a good job of work for you, it was a soft snap, and I want it back!" Wilson shouted.

Devin crossed his arms and leaned back against the papered wall. "You need to take into consideration the fact that Cal burned up the supply wagons I was driving up here. His Indian friends killed my swamper and ran off all the horses and mules. By my reckoning he's cost you more than five thousand dollars so far today, Miss Jackson."

"Tell me, if all Mr. Cavanaugh says is true, why in the world should I agree to return your employment to you, Mr. Wilson?" Dulcinetta turned her gaze from Devin to Cal, clasping her hands in her lap. Devin noticed there wasn't a sign of them shaking. She was either truthfully not afraid or else hiding her fear very well indeed.

"I told you that you would be sorry. If I don't get back what Miss Lou gave me—which was my *livelihood*, which you proceeded to take away for no just cause and bestow *undeservingly* on this muff *puppy*—I will be forced to take steps. That boy of yours will pay! Are ya following me yet, Miss High-and-Mighty?"

"It seems to me you've already taken some steps here, Mr. Wilson, rather serious steps. Do you expect me to just give you your job back and forget anything that led up to this particular moment ever happened? Give me one good reason I should ignore the facts that you've taken me prisoner at gunpoint, beat up my supervisor, and destroyed my property."

Boy, Dulcinetta is pretty, Devin was thinking. Color heated her cheeks now that she was getting mad, and her eyes glinted with suppressed fire. Her glossy black curls sparkled in the lamplight. The bodice of her russet dress rose and fell as she fought a battle to maintain control of herself and the situation. Devin felt worthless in comparison, lower than a worm. He had lost her wagons, animals, and merchandise. He had allowed the new employee she had never even met, the Mormon boy Moroni, to be murdered. He himself had been overpowered by Indians, knocked in the head, and forced to accompany the madman Wilson on this attempt to extort employment from her. Compared to her, he didn't begin to measure up. She didn't back down. She didn't dissolve into hysterics. She just stiffened her backbone and dealt with the situation. Watching her in action stole his breath away.

Wilson was saying, "Because if you don't give me my job, I will kill young Luther. That mewling little brat of yours is no loss to me."

"Wait a minute, hold up there. Killing the boy wasn't part of the plan," Devin protested, straightening from his slouch against the wall.

"Shut up, Cavanaugh, I told you!" Wilson said. "What makes you think you know anything about what the true plan is?"

At that moment, a knock sounded at the door. All three people inside the room froze into position like a trio of Madame Tussaud's wax figures. Devin taunted in a low voice, "What's the matter? Not part of your plan, Wilson?"

"Get over there next to her," Wilson said, gesturing with the gun toward Dulcinetta.

"Missy?" Ju's voice sounded in the hallway. "Missy, you all right?"

"Good grief, can things possibly get any worse?" Dulcinetta asked under her breath as she gritted her teeth. "Ju! Go away. See to Luther!"

Before Ju could begin to comply, Wilson turned the handle and whipped the door open. Ju stood there with a lever-action Henry repeating rifle pointed at him. Still training the pepperbox with one hand in the direction of Dulcinetta and Devin, Cal grabbed the barrel of Ju's gun with the other and jerked her inside the room.

Slamming the door behind her, he held her small body immobile against his chest, her feet dangling above the floor, the rifle trapped between them pointed at the ceiling. Then he aimed the pepperbox at Ju's jaw and said to Dulcinetta, "You ready to deal yet?"

"There's no need for that, Cal," Devin said, making a move toward Wilson.

"Back off, Cavanaugh!" Wilson pulled the pistol away from Ju's neck to wave it at Devin before jamming it once more against Ju's jaw. "What do you offer me, Miss Jackson, in exchange for your son's life and the life of this here plucky little Chinee gal?"

"Well, I'm afraid I can't give you your freighting position back, not even as second in command. I'm sorry to say that here, today, you've proven yourself completely untrustworthy." Dulcie bit her lip and looked at Wilson and Ju through lowered eyelashes, as if she were trying to hide the fact that she found this whole negotiation somehow humorous.

"Then they're dead!" Wilson screamed. Ju's eyes bugged out a bit as both his grip on her and his finger on the trigger of the pistol tightened.

"Mr. Wilson," Dulcinetta held up a manicured hand and said in a serene voice almost as if Cal bored her, "calm down. You haven't given me a proper chance to even try and tender you a decent offer. But I will tell you this much for certain, if you succeed in shooting Ju, all deals are off." From the pocket she had Ailis sew into every gown she ordered, Dulcinetta calmly drew her tiny derringer and aimed it at Wilson.

His eyes widened. Then he snickered. "I can surely shoot this Chinee gal before you can hit me with that little pea shooter."

"Perhaps." Dulcinetta shrugged her creamy-skinned shoulders as if the threat to Ju made no difference to her. "Put down your gun, Mr. Wilson."

"*Are you crazy?* I have the upper hand here, in case you ain't cottoned to that fact yet, missy!" Spittle flew from the corners of Wilson's mouth.

Ju echoed in a strangled plea, "Missy . . ."

"Listen to me, Mr. Wilson. If you want to talk business, put Ju down. And put away your gun." Dulcinetta gave Wilson a steely-eyed glare. "Otherwise I will shoot you, you will shoot Ju, and then where will we be?"

Ju's toes reached the floor as Wilson appeared to think about what Dulcinetta was saying. He finally said in a sulky voice, "I'll put it down if you will."

Dulcinetta gestured with her gun. "You first."

Devin raised his hand as if to wipe his mouth, when what he was doing was attempting to smother a grin. Wilson was fast losing his grip on his hostage situation. *I do believe Miss Dulcinetta Jackson could have single-handedly taken on that whole band of Sioux out there on the road*, Devin thought to himself.

Wilson let Ju down until she could stand on her feet, slowly tucking his weapon in his belt but keeping his hand on the butt in case Dulcie was playing some kind of trick. Dulcinetta didn't take her eyes off him as she replaced her little gun in her skirt pocket. Ju backed away from Cal, rifle still aimed at the ceiling.

"As you know, Lou is gravely ill," Dulcie began. "She has business interests in places other than this location, but the only one she has that exists here alone, without counterparts elsewhere, is the Goldust. She owns only this single saloon and dance hall. I would like to take Luther somewhere a little more cultured than South Pass City, a place where a proper education for him can be resumed. I have authority to sell this place if I so choose. I propose that you buy the Goldust, Mr. Wilson, payable in monthly installments, so that I may take my family and promptly go elsewhere."

For a moment, Devin thought Wilson was going to choke on surprise. His eyes widened and his mouth opened and closed like a hooked fish, but no sound came out. Devin, too, felt something akin to astonishment. He certainly hadn't foreseen this possibility. Dulcinetta had just succeeded in raking in all Wilson's chips. She wasn't merely unpredictable. In a dangerous standoff she was downright frightening. He had never encountered anyone even remotely like this incredibly beautiful woman. Would she just surrender the Goldust to a sneaking, thieving blackmailer like Wilson? Would she just walk away from everything she had so carefully built up in South Pass City?

"Well? What do you say, Mr. Wilson? There are customers waiting. I'm not making any money sitting here chatting with you. It's really past time for me to get to work. Do we have a deal? Perhaps we should go out to the saloon and have a drink together, to seal our bargain?"

"Why, I . . . why . . . why sure," Wilson managed to say, beginning to recover what scraps of wits he possessed and bestowing a wide, brown toothed-grin on Dulcinetta.

She got to her feet, rose-colored taffeta dress rustling around her legs. As she neared Wilson, she held out her hand. He shook it, and then still holding on to it, placed it in the crook of his elbow. In his best gentlemanly manner, he opened the door and escorted Dulcinetta across the dining room of her private quarters and out into the hall that connected with the saloon.

Devin drew in a huge gulp of air and slowly let it out. He wanted to shake his head, but didn't dare since it still hurt and he didn't want to make his double vision any worse.

Ju, with a curious lack of expression on her face that made Devin think she had many times before this seen Dulcinetta in action, watched as the two former opponents walked away together. When she couldn't see them anymore, she lowered the rifle, turned, and approached Devin. She peered up at him, shaking her head at his injuries. "You hurt. Ju fix. Come." She, too, headed for the door, turning only once to make sure Devin followed.

"Do you really know how to shoot that thing?" he asked, trailing along behind her.

"Sure, I know." Ju shrugged and kept walking.

~

Much later, cleaned up and fed, Devin was beginning to feel better, although the occasional sharp twinges of headache from the blow to his temple lingered and his injured hand was starting to stiffen up. But questions remained, questions that became more urgent as the hours passed and Dulcinetta continued to act as if nothing out of the ordinary had occurred. After a short break where she disappeared into her private rooms without inviting any company, she once again trod across the plank floor of the saloon, her beribboned skirt swishing and her confident smile beaming bright enough to rival a thousand candles. She circled the room toward her faro table, stopping here and there to chat up the customers as if it were any ordinary evening in the Goldust

Saloon in South Pass City. Wilson, who had headed straight for the bar after their confrontation, proceeded to sink steadily into an alcoholic stupor.

Well, and why not? Devin thought as he eyed the crowd upon entering the main room of the saloon after Ju released him from her attentions. Wilson as good as owned the Goldust now. He could swig every bottle dry if he felt like it. Devin smiled. No one would ever suspect that Cal had been threatening Dulcinetta's life, and those of her child, and Ju, and Devin himself, just a short while before. And most certainly no one would never guess from Dulcinetta's behavior that she and Wilson had just recently been in a deadly standoff, aiming pistols at one another.

Ailis cornered Devin as he stood watching the action from the door of the dance hall, waiting for the night to wind down while nursing the single beer he'd been clutching in his still-intact fist all evening. Of the two breweries in town, he preferred the Tyrolean beer over that of the Germans, but he just didn't think his head would tolerate more than one bottle of either brand.

"What has gotten into you?" his former friend hissed in his ear. "You hold people up at the point of a gun now? You should be ashamed of yourself, Devin Cavanaugh, as well as grateful Dulcie didn't call the city marshal on you after the pathetic display you and that drunken lush put on here a while ago."

"Hello, Ailis. It's been a while. How have you been?" He raised his bottle of warm beer in salute. "Buy you a drink?"

"Don't try to distract me. I want to know what you think you're up to."

It was somewhere near two in the morning by then, and Devin was weary to the bone. "If you wouldn't mind waiting an hour or so until Dulcinetta can close up, I'll tell the story just once. Anyone who wants to can listen."

Ailis offered him a gimlet eye, and then nodded agreement, her auburn curls jouncing. "I can hardly wait for the telling of your tall tale," she said, a sneer overtaking her pretty features.

But wait she did, standing impatiently beside Devin until the saloon finally closed up.

~

Some forty-five minutes later all the patrons of the Goldust had been convinced to leave or else were physically escorted out the door. Those reluctant to call it a night were reminded they could take their patronage to one of the twenty-four hour joints. After seeing the last of them out and locking up, Dulcinetta leaned her back against the stout wood with a sigh.

Devin escorted her, and Ailis, back to Dulcinetta's quarters, where Ju had a pot of hot coffee waiting. Devin waited until Ailis and Dulcinetta had both been seated before sinking into a chair himself.

Without preamble, he plunged in. "Here's my report, such as it is: The draft animals are gone, all run off by a band of Sioux. Both wagons are burned to the ground, along with what few supplies are left after the Indians got through dumping the dry goods in the road and taking what portion they wanted of the arms and ammunition and whiskey. I apologize most sincerely for my failure, Miss Jackson. It will take years for me to repay you. You'll have my resignation now if that's what you require."

Dulcinetta rubbed her forehead briefly before answering. "Tell me, what good is your quitting going to do me? As you heard tonight, I have forfeited the Goldust. Shall I surrender the freighting business as well?"

Brought up short, so sure had he been that he would be dismissed for incompetence if not for participating, however unwillingly, in the evening's shameful activities, Devin felt his mouth drop open in shock. He finally said, "Then I will surely do whatever you think is right, Miss Jackson."

"Fine. In that case, please call me Dulcie." She lifted her cup and took a deep swallow. "The freight is always insured, so you may rest your mind on that count. The customers won't be happy to wait, but it can all be replaced."

"I haven't yet got to the boy who was killed in the raid. A Mormon I hired as swamper. I feel responsible. I didn't warn him in near strong enough terms what could happen on the road." Devin met her gaze reluctantly.

"You mentioned a boy earlier. I am sorry for him," she said in a quiet voice. She blinked at this sad news. "But, Devin, are you truly responsible? Could you have somehow prevented his death and failed to do so?"

Devin said without hesitation, "No, ma'am. There was no way I could have protected him, not even if I took a bullet myself. There were just too many of them and it happened too fast."

"We'll send out a party at daylight to retrieve him." Dulcie rubbed her forehead with her fingertips, as if she too now had a headache.

"Questions are bound to be asked." Devin grimaced. "Are you going to notify the marshal?"

"And what good would that do? I assure you our local lawmen aren't heroes. He might go out and look at what's left of the wagons, but he won't be riding out after any band of Indians, and especially not Sioux."

"But Wilson—"

"Caleb Wilson. Yes, indeed, let us speak now of Mr. Wilson. May I ask how it happens that you accompanied Wilson here to threaten me and my boy and to scare the daylights out of Ju? I could tell you weren't a willing actor, Mr. Cavanaugh, but still I find your behavior entirely reprehensible."

"Oh, climb down off your high horse, why don't you, Dulcie?" Ailis said. "Just inform the man outright that he's behaved like an ass. I can assure you he'll understand the smaller words better, and it won't be news to him." She slanted a glance at Devin while one corner of her mouth twitched.

Dulcie looked at the two of them, as if trying to decide if they meant more to each other than either had disclosed.

"I was wounded in my gun hand, knocked in the head, tied up, and delivered half conscious to Wilson by Indians," Devin retorted hotly, glaring at Ailis. "It's plain to me this whole episode was Cal's by design. The Indians were merely tools, paid off in stolen mules and whiskey."

He turned his attention to Dulcie. "Can I ask you one question? Why in the hell did you reward Wilson with the Goldust after what he's cost us today?"

Dulcie hesitated. "I didn't think I had any choice. I couldn't let him threaten Luther," she said at last, adding, "I couldn't let him have the freight company either. What, then, could I offer that he would accept?"

"So you just hand over Lou's saloon and dance hall? It doesn't make sense."

"But, I assure you, it does make sense—that is, if you know what I know. What I say here is confidential, is that understood?" She looked around, getting mute agreement from all present before continuing. "The mines have stopped paying their investors. They will soon start folding, one by one, at first fast and then faster. It's like a contagion, this gold fever. It arrived here in the Sweetwater district swiftly. It will leave us just as quickly, letting businesses die here without a jot of remorse, while it spreads to a new area as rapidly as it infected us here. Soon there won't be enough customers to go around, and South Pass City will begin fading into obscurity. In a few months there may not be enough custom left to support even just the Goldust, assuming all the others fold first. If I get six months of payments out of Mr. Wilson while I establish myself elsewhere, I'll consider it my good luck to have washed my hands of the deal."

"So you did know all along." Ailis studied Dulcie, a look of respect in her eyes.

Dulcie nodded. "Of course I knew. I was hanging on as long as I could, not wishing to be the one to sound the death knell, making money while the making was good. Now it's almost too late, the rumors are flying that the Sweetwater is a humbug."

Devin watched Dulcie carefully for signs of delayed symptoms of her ordeal; perhaps she would weep, or faint, or exhibit some other typically feminine reaction to having her life endangered. But he saw none, and finally decided he wasn't likely to see any sign of weakness in Dulcinetta Jackson. She seemed always to be on top of whatever was going on around her.

Yet he wondered if she had truly considered every detail of her proposed deal. "So what's to keep Wilson from coming back later to kidnap you in an attempt to get more out of you—when the Goldust truly fails?" he asked.

"Nothing. There is nothing to stop him. That much is true. Nothing except the papers of sale I'll have him sign at my lawyer's office in the morning."

"Perhaps he'll die of alcohol poisoning or something," Ailis offered with a hopeful note in her voice.

"He's been much more fortunate than that so far," Devin grumbled. "The man has the luck of the devil."

"Yes, he seems to be a fortunate man. But also an intemperate one. Perhaps, Ailis, he will succeed in drinking himself to an early grave." Dulcie took a sip of hot coffee.

"You don't have to leave," Ailis argued. "Why don't you just send Luther away? Somewhere he would be safer."

"At one time, that would have been the obvious solution. But now with Lou in ill health, someone needs to take over his care. There are only my father and myself. I have nowhere to send him."

"What about his da's people? Could you send Luther to them to keep him safe?"

Dulcinetta gave a low sound in her throat that was meant to pass for laughter but didn't fool anyone into thinking she was actually amused. "You've got to understand a few things, Ailis. Luther's father and I never married. He made promises that I firmly believe now he would not have kept even if he hadn't been a casualty of the war. Luther's father's people owned the plantation where my father was once enslaved. Josiah was a *slave*, do you understand? Luther's father's people will never, never, *never* acknowledge any grandson with even one drop of African blood."

Devin shot Ailis a scathing look for insisting on prying out Dulcinetta's obviously painful secrets. Ailis shrugged. "I'm sorry," she said, looking back at Dulcie. "I was just trying to help."

Dulcie glanced aside for a moment, as if pausing to catch her breath or deciding how much more to say. "There's nothing for you to be sorry about. Facts are facts. I believed Luther Brandingham Junior because I wanted so much to believe him. I was young, and desperate to become someone I wasn't. Or at least to appear to be someone else." She paused, calling in a louder voice, "Ju, were you planning on joining us or do you wish to continue skulking around corners, eavesdropping?"

For a response the kitchen door swung closed. A tiny smile curved Dulcie's lips. She turned her attention once again to Ailis and Devin. She took a deep breath, then let it out. "My mother was Lou's sister," she said. "A white woman. You have no idea what that meant where I come from. A German immigrant didn't have the same prejudices against negro people that white people from the South do. Lou bought my father's freedom after my mother turned up pregnant. Lou paid for Josiah with dirty money, some might say, earned from liquor and gambling and prostitution. But those things are all Lou and her sister knew to do and, although I am educated, those avenues of commerce are almost all I know as well.

"My son does not have the legal right to use Brandingham, but although it will do him no financial or familial good, he will know who his father was. I come by my name, Jackson, honestly. My father and mother did marry before she died in childbirth. So you see, Devin, I know what it is to have lived through a death that I feel I caused, but that I was nevertheless helpless to prevent."

She paused to swallow another drink of cooling coffee. "Now . . . I trust you two might have a happier history than I?"

It was Ailis's turn to snort a laugh. "I grew up in an orphan asylum in New York City."

Devin said, "I was a big city guttersnipe. My parents died within a few years of arriving in this country—at least I know my mam is dead and I think my da is. He just never came home one night, and Mam died a year or so after that." He swallowed hard, clenching his fists before continuing: "I have another confession to make. I promised Mr. Jackson that I would tell you when the opportunity presented itself, and so now here it is. Here I go."

The women looked at him expectantly. He ran a finger around a collar suddenly grown too tight. "I . . ." He looked beseechingly at Dulcinetta.

"Whatever it is, Devin, it can't be any more personal than what we've already shared with each other here tonight. Please, say what you have to say." She smiled encouragement at him.

"All right then, I will. I can't read," he blurted out. "A few words, maybe. My name. That's about it."

Ailis said, "You were told in Cheyenne that you were never going to amount to anything if you didn't learn to read, but would you listen? No, you—"

"Ailis, please," Dulcie interrupted. "Recriminations are not helpful at this juncture."

"But she's right." Devin would almost rather swallow strychnine than admit it to her face, but Ailis was right. She settled back in her chair with an exultant smile on her face at having wrung the admission from him.

"Yes, your illiteracy is a problem." Dulcie shook her head, as if to clear it. "But we will deal with tangential eventualities later. Right now, I really need a few hours' rest if I am to conduct the business of transferring ownership of the Goldust today. Ailis, I still expect my new clothes, no matter what, so you had better get to your sewing. Devin, we will talk later today, after I meet with the lawyer." She rose, covering a yawn with the back of her hand, and retired to the door of her bedroom, saying over her shoulder before she disappeared, "Good night to you both for now. Or perhaps I should say good day?"

Ailis didn't budge as her gaze followed Dulcie's exit. Then she turned her attention back to Devin. "So what's the deal with you and Dulcie?"

"Well, it's like this," he paused, grinning. "I'm going to marry her." Even as he words left his mouth he was hugely enjoying the look of astonishment that stole over Ailis's face.

"H . . . how can you even think it?" she sputtered. "You? Marry Dulcinetta? The very idea is laughable."

"Because Dulcie's got negro blood? That's beneath even you, Ailis." Devin felt angry heat rising as far as his ears.

"No, silly. I can't picture the two of you together because Dulcie is educated, and so refined, and much too good for the likes of you. A freight wagon driver. It's unthinkable. I predicted as much for you, do you remember, Devin?" Ailis smirked.

Once again, Devin admitted Ailis was probably right—but he acknowledged it only to himself this time. Once a day or even once a decade was often enough for him to tell this pretty, insufferable young Irish woman that she was correct in an argument, and not he.

"Believe what you like, Ailis. We'll just have to see what happens, won't we?" he asked as he pushed his chair away from the table to go seek his bed. *At the freight office, where a freighter would logically bed down*, he thought with a grimace.

Ailis's hearty, unrestrained peals of triumphant laughter followed him out the door.

Chapter *10*
A Promise and a Proposal

ARLY THE NEXT MORNING Devin, despite his still aching head and swollen eye, accompanied a mounted party south out of South Pass City. The freight wagons, wisps of smoke still rising from them in the still air, proved a complete loss along with most of their contents. The men took a short while to sift through what remained of the boxes and barrels and crates and bags shattered in the roadbed, before shaking their heads and giving up further attempts at salvaging anything of much value.

Devin gathered up as much of the lines and harness as was still usable, as well as the chain, and what small bits of merchandise he thought might be of use to anyone. He retrieved a few cans that were not too badly dented. The merchants of South Pass City who had been expecting fresh commodities for their businesses instead returned with only the body of a blond Mormon boy laid out in the bed of a wagon. Moroni's remains were given over to the care of the undertaker, with instructions from Devin to send word to the Saints in Salt Lake City to come and claim their own.

Devin was back at the Goldust by late morning. When he sent word with Ju that he was waiting for Dulcinetta to rise and dress because he wanted to see her, Ju returned in a few minutes, delivering an invitation to breakfast. Luther was already seated and waiting in the small dining room, fork and knife clutched in his fists. "My mama says we're moving to Bryan, and that I'm getting a tutor so I don't fall behind on my lessons," he blurted with uncharacteristic enthusiasm. Luther wasn't usually an overeager student.

"That sounds like a grand idea." Devin moved aside his own silverware to shake out his linen napkin and place it in his lap. Ju set a steaming cup of coffee near him and he thanked her.

"My mama says you are in need of lessons, too, and so you and I will share the tutor."

Devin choked on his coffee. He dabbed, with a clean white napkin, at the trickle of brown liquid dribbling from one nostril. This bit of news explained Luther's excitement. "Your mam says that, does she?"

"I do," Dulcinetta confirmed, entering the room in a swirl of layers of ribbon and brown velvet, trailing the scent of attar of roses. "Do you have an objection?"

"I'm supposing that acceptance of tutoring along with Third is a condition of my continued employment with Schering Forwarding Company." Devin rose to his feet to help Dulcie slip her chair in toward the table.

"You know that it is. Will it be an insurmountable problem for you to knuckle under to my demands?" She looked at him over her shoulder. He noticed she had wondrously long and curly black eyelashes.

"I must admit, learning from a private tutor is a better prospect than attending classes in a schoolroom with a bunch of little tykes a quarter of my advanced age." He re-seated himself next to Luther.

"It occurs to me that I never would have guessed that you were an Irish street urchin off the streets of New York City." Dulcie looked at him appraisingly. "You must have taken diction lessons at some point."

"Sure, and are ye meanin' t' say I don't display the gift o' gab loike ye were expectin', lass? I'm that sorry to disappoint ye, but I've tried me best to leave all hint of that guttersnipe past far behind me. 'Tis true that I'm lacking formal education, but I pick up a bit here an' a bit there, tryin' to fit in—as I expect you have had t' do over the years, me bonny colleen." He gave her a meaningful look which he hoped Luther was too young to understand.

"You're funny, Devin," Luther observed as he dug his fork into a stack of griddle cakes Ju had just placed in front of him. "I already know how to read and write, so I guess this new tutor must be mostly for you."

"I'll make you a wager, squirt," Devin said. "I'll bet that I will be able to out-read and out-write you before you're out of short pants."

"I told you my name is Luther!" Bits of buttered griddle cake escaped his lips to bounce across the tablecloth.

"Luther, don't talk with your mouth full," Dulcinetta chided. To Devin she said, "You really must learn to read and write. It's vital to the business. I assume you must be able to cipher, since you can follow the cards and the betting."

"Making money has always been one of my abiding passions," Devin said. "I know numbers well enough, and can add and subtract.

But I will learn to read as well, since the ability is essential to our future."

She shot him a questioning look, but Devin only shrugged and smiled. Ailis was the single person so far who was privy to his plan to marry Dulcie. But he would have to let his intended bride in on the proposal soon, he thought, or Ailis would be sure to open her mouth and ruin the surprise.

"Since we're on the topic of money, I can order more livestock from Chicago if I can't find enough mules nearer to Bryan. The Mormon, Byrne, has some at his Piedmont place, but I'm not sure I can trust a man who abandons his first wife and three children in England to come here, marry two more women, and proceed to have fifteen more offspring—thus far, that is."

Dulcie glanced at him sharply. "But you will do business with the Saint, Byrne, if he has the mules you need?"

Devin sighed, divining from her tone the answer she wanted. "Of course I will."

"Good. Squeamishness has no place in commerce." She folded her hands together and gave a decent appearance of trying not to look haughty.

Devin smiled. She was gorgeous. He was so lucky. "I will look into purchasing mules from Granger and Company at the Black's Fork Ferry as well. But I'll need time to train the draft animals, and Phillip Harsh, the blacksmith, will need time to fabricate and deliver new wagons. I'm sorry it's going to set us back so much in time and expenditure, especially since you're now giving up your business here in order to relocate. I only hope I can lure back in the future the customers who will be forced to look elsewhere in the interim."

Dulcie shrugged her shoulders as if Devin's worries were of no consequence. It was true that she was sacrificing the Goldust but, in truth, without her it was just a building and a collection of spirits bottles. It would go on, but it wouldn't be anywhere near the same enterprise. And she wouldn't be any help repairing the damage to the freighting business. That would be up to him.

"Do what you need to do," she said. "I'll have the money for you this afternoon, after I see the lawyer about transferring title to the saloon and then the Iliff and Company Exchange about closing out my accounts. I will need a little time to inquire whether anyone here would be interested in my stakes in the Mountain Jack, Grand Turk, Golden State and Nellie Morgan lodes, which I initially invested in alongside John Morris. He may actually have the immediate funds to buy out the partnership and I will not have to go looking elsewhere. But if he doesn't have the cash and wants my portion of the ownership of the claims, I will be forced to accept his note."

"You do understand that I don't have much money of my own. I've been trying to save, but so far have not made much progress toward a personal stake." It made Devin feel squirmy to admit his poverty, but as they were clearing the air and making plans for their future together it seemed best to exercise total honesty.

"But I *do* have money." Dulcie seemed completely unflustered by throwing her lot in with a man of Devin's dubious history, financial and otherwise. "And you soon will have money as well, so don't vex yourself about it."

"But won't it concern you to be marrying someone who is as penniless as I am?" Devin grinned at her across the table. He still had a picture in his mind of how she had fearlessly faced down Wilson. Starting over from scratch didn't seem to bother Dulcinetta Jackson one way or the other.

"Why, Mr. Cavanaugh, do I detect a proposal in there somewhere? If you're already talking marriage, you anticipate me." Dulcie fluttered her extraordinary eyelashes. "I will confess I was going to ask you if you didn't ask me soon. Lack of romance aside, I don't think your paucity of funds is a factor, only your illiteracy. Promise to amend that single shortcoming, and we can proceed."

"I've already said I will. Would this be merely a business proposition between us that you are intending, or more like a true marriage?" Devin felt a little hurt that Dulcie continued to act as if they were two commercial firms set to merge rather than a couple in the throes of newfound love.

She rubbed her sensuous lower lip reflectively with a slim fingertip. "In all truthfulness, I suspect it's a bit of both, Mr. Cavanaugh. Lou sent you to me to prop up the business. She didn't indicate she expected me to marry you. That part is all my idea."

"In that case, Miss Jackson, I have a stipulation of my own." He looked at her, so beautiful and so sophisticated. What would happen if they disagreed? Would she be willing to dispense with another of her money-making enterprises just because he didn't like it? Or would she show him the door? "I ask—" he glanced at Luther, wondering how he should put his request so that the boy didn't get an inkling of what the adults spoke about. "Once we are married, I would prefer that we dispense with the, uh, upstairs activities."

"Ah." Dulcinetta pursed her lips. "You do understand that the girls are free to do as they wish on their own time. I have no monetary stake in their activities beyond renting them the rooms."

"Still, I would prefer not to become known as a . . . procurer, or whatever the proper term might be."

Dulcie laughed. "Why, Devin. You have a hidden Puritan streak! And here I was under the impression you rather liked evaluating the assets on display around these premises."

Devin glanced at Luther to make sure the boy continued to attack his breakfast even while wearing a slight frown of bewilderment. Luther's expression assured Devin the child wasn't catching on to what the adults were talking about. Then Devin looked pointedly across the table at Dulcie's prominent, powdered attributes.

"You know very well that I appreciate such a view. But, as you must be aware, all assets are not created equal. My singular interest is in the properties which are owned only by you."

"How sweet," Dulcie murmured, casting him a meaning-filled glance from beneath dark lashes. "You know that my father has taken over one of the businesses in Bryan? In truth I never had much to do with that one, but once we leave here I am done with it forever. I will admit that sometimes I get a hankering—and don't you dare laugh at me—for respectability. One of your more potent attractions is the possibility that you can offer me that commodity. Does that put your mind at ease, or increase your reluctance?"

Once again Dulcie had anticipated him. He wondered just how astute she really was beneath all that Southern belle charm. "I would not call myself reluctant. And I would never laugh at you or your aspirations. I'm honored you have such a high opinion of my prospects that you would agree to my stipulation even if it costs you to do it. So then, what are your plans? What will you do in Bryan once you get there? Open another saloon?"

She patted her lips and then laid the napkin down beside her plate. "I think not," she said. "I'm ready for different kind of livelihood. I will see what is available. But I will discover some way to pass the time in the meanwhile, never fear."

Devin felt embarrassed heat reaching his ears. "Don't misunderstand me. I wasn't looking for a pledge of financial support from you."

"Nevertheless, you have it. You understand, Mr. Cavanaugh, my family has a bit of a legendary golden touch. We must have King Midas in our ancestry somewhere. We can't seem to help making money. Lots of money."

He swallowed a huge grin. The one attribute he had discovered so far that Dulcinetta couldn't claim was modesty. "That's most reassuring."

"Yes, it is. You may put your mind at ease. Now, Mr. Cavanaugh, shall we move along?"

"Very well, Miss Jackson, I will proceed with asking for your hand in the time-honored manner." Devin pushed his chair back and rounded the table, dropping to one knee beside Dulcie.

Luther's fork clanged onto his plate as he dissolved in a sudden fit of giggles, bits of pancake dropping unnoticed by him onto his shirt.

Ignoring the boy's hilarity, Devin said in all seriousness, "Dulcinetta Jackson, will you do me the honor of marrying me, and be my sweetheart forever?"

"Of course I will." She smiled. "You do understand that I have much to do before the nuptials, but perhaps Judge Morris will consent to take a few minutes to marry us this afternoon."

She certainly didn't waste any time once she decided on a course of action, Devin thought. Once again he considered Dulcie's habit of taking charge. She was certainly a strong personality. But he had already decided he admired that trait in a woman, and so he didn't hesitate to smile back. "I like the way you think. I'll pick out a ring at Cornforth's Mercantile, if you'll stop by and fetch it on your way home from the bank." He whispered, "I'll have to ask you to pay for it. I promise to reimburse you for it someday."

"Indeed, you will repay me, sir." Dulcie lowered her voice to a feline growl, licking her lips like a cream-fed cat as she leaned to whisper in his ear. "You will pay . . . in ways you cannot imagine . . . and you will pay many, many times over, Mr. Cavanaugh."

So involved were they in their personal performance, neither of them noticed the kitchen door softly closing. Ju stood with her back pressed hard to the simple wooden panel, her chest heaving as she sought to contain frightened tears. Dulcinetta was going to marry the young muleskinner and leave South Pass City. Not one word had she revealed to Ju about these plans. The only thing Ju had known up until now, even if she couldn't read them, was that Dulcie was receiving letters of application for the position of tutor to young Luther. Maybe Dulcie didn't anticipate needing Ju's services at all once her newly reconstituted family reached Bryan.

What would happen to Ju then? Did Dulcie intend to just sell the Goldust and move away, leaving Xiang Ju behind in South Pass City like a piece of discarded luggage?

Fragrant Chrysanthemum decided she would have something to say about that. Whether she owed Dulcie her life or not, perhaps it was time to decide her own direction and not keep depending on Dulcie to guide her every move.

Ju shook her head and, fighting for resolve, raised trembling hands to dash the tears from her eyes.

~

While Dulcie conducted her business that afternoon, and while Wilson was away from the premises for the appointment with the lawyer, Devin busied himself with some lengths of sawn wood. With hammer and nails and fabric donated by Ailis for a new lining, he fashioned a false bottom in one of Dulcie's trunks.

Upstairs, Ailis was working on an emergency order for a special traveling skirt for Dulcinetta and a custom vest for Devin. Both of these garments had numerous concealed pockets and compartments carefully sewn in. By the time they were stuffed with a portion of Dulcie's money, it would look like the pair might have gained a bit of weight, but they should be able to safely transport more gold than just the trunk would hold.

Neither of them knew exactly how much money Dulcie had stashed in the bank, or how big a pile it might make. She would probably get the bulk of it in a check, Ailis assured Devin, but he thought better safe than sorry, and continued sawing and pounding and gluing until he was satisfied that the trunk itself would have to be dismantled in order for anyone to discover the secret compartment.

At the bank, Dulcie strove to reassure banker W. C. Campbell—
no relation to the governor—that she truly wasn't selling out because
of the South Pass humbug rumor which was already beginning to
spread like a wildfire. "I assure you, I leave at this point only because of
illness in the family." She looked the banker straight in the eye.
"Otherwise, I would not think of abandoning such a first-rate
investment as I have in the Goldust."

"Harrumph. I suppose, knowing you, you wouldn't at that."
Campbell, a rotund man whose belly strained the buttons of his
maroon brocade waistcoat, looked as if he was struggling to believe
her.

*He probably does want to believe me. His livelihood depends as much on the
city's success as mine has.* But with a sinking feeling, Dulcie admitted to
herself that Campbell wouldn't waste a moment spreading the word
about her selling out as soon as the door of the bank closed behind
her. And that eventuality would likely set the worth of her remaining
investments in the Sweetwater Country plummeting.

Hurry! Before it all starts to collapse, she urged herself, almost running
to the Morris place. Not only did she intend to consult the justice of
the peace about a hasty marriage ceremony, but also to have a
discussion with the judge's husband about the possibility of him buying
out her interests in several ledges in the area.

The Honorable Esther Morris, a plain-looking woman who was
the mother of two grown sons, gave Dulcie's waistline a sharp, if
discreetly fleeting, glance when she heard her request. But she agreed
to meet the lovebirds in her office at four o'clock. As to Dulcie's
business with Mr. Morris, she remembered it was rumored that John
Morris was a drunk who beat his wife. Despite being partners with the
man, Dulcie knew little for certain about him. Partnerships in frontier
towns were made as convenience dictated and as swiftly broken, which
was one reason South Pass City boasted so many law offices.

Morris didn't offer her a seat. She judged by looking at the gleam
in his eyes that she wasn't fooling him a bit, he was presently sober
enough, and had either already heard the rumors or could detect the
faint whiff of panic she was starting to exude. She was terrified the
acrid scent of fear would soon permeate the entire town, at which
point she would almost be forced to give away her mining ventures.

Local merchants habitually suppressed an undercurrent of dread at the very real prospect of losing everything, but she definitely felt it beginning to waft toward her, settling like a film of high desert dust from the road leading into the gulch.

Morris listened to her explanation about her impending marriage and her need to relocate for Luther's sake, studying her as she stood before him like the lowest supplicant but offering no encouragement. A man of few words and none when that option would suffice, he rubbed his chin and when she finished, and shrewdly threw out a lowball figure. The sum was for all of her holdings at once. It turned out to be less than half what Dulcie had been hoping for, but reassuring herself that half of something was better than all of nothing, she gritted her teeth and shook hands on the deal.

At least she would be spared having to find any additional last-minute buyers, thereby contributing to the spread of the town's anxiety, she reassured herself as she hurried on her way.

Chapter *11*
Humbug

*H*AMPERED BY THE WEIGHT of a large carpetbag stuffed with money, after her errand at the bank Dulcie made another stop to retrieve the simple gold bands Devin had reserved at the mercantile. She also purchased a rather gaudy concoction of curlicued gold wire and rose-cut diamonds that caught her eye. *After days like today and yesterday,* she thought, *I deserve a reward. This little filigreed fillip will do nicely.*

After all, it wasn't as if a girl got married every day. Or sold all her holdings. Or started all over once more. She told herself she wouldn't cry, that she was happy for the chance to be reinventing herself once again, and dashed a gloved finger beneath her wet lashes, hoping the clerk in Cornforth's wouldn't notice as he wrapped up her purchases.

"I hear you're leaving town, Miss Jackson," the young man said as he handed her the parcel.

Aghast once again at how fast news traveled in the little city, Dulcinetta said, "Yes, family business takes precedence over commerce, I'm afraid."

"And congratulations are in order, I take it? Am I correct that you're set to marry the boy—er, young man—who was in earlier today to choose the rings?" He grinned weakly, heaving a deep sigh. Apparently he was unable to control the pair of wandering eyes which Dulcie noticed giving her a thorough once-over. She wondered if he might be regretting not previously stating feelings of his own toward her.

"Yes, that's correct. Would you like to come by the Goldust and help us celebrate tonight?" Dulcie hid her annoyance behind a practiced smile, reminding herself it was all part of the game. "I would be happy to buy you a drink."

"Very kind of you, indeed." He tugged down the points of his vest before another thought occurred to him. "But tonight? You can't mean to say you're marrying this very day?"

"That's exactly what I am saying." She adjusted her stance a bit so she stood sideways to the clerk, the better for him to see for himself that she was not in such a hurry to wed because hers was a match of the shotgun variety. If he was going to spread gossip about her, he may as well have at least a few of his facts straight. Then, annoyed with herself for caring a whit what anyone in South Pass City thought of her or her activities, she snatched up her package, completed her turn and headed for the door, lugging her carpetbag. She called an abrupt "good day" over her shoulder as she left the store.

When she reached the Goldust, a celebration was already in full swing. Wilson hadn't waited for her to deliver the completed documents transferring title to the property before kicking off the party, and instead had relieved the bartender in order to start pouring everyone generous libations. Apparently he hadn't heard any rumors of the town's imminent demise from his new post behind the bar, or else he was choosing to ignore them in his newfound personal success. Relieved of any explanation, Dulcie handed over the papers.

"Miss Jackson," Wilson shouted as he grabbed the documents which identified him as the new owner of the celebrated South Pass City Goldust Saloon, "have a drink! It's on the house!" And he proceeded to laugh uproariously at his own waggishness.

"No, thank you, Mr. Wilson. I still have a few things to do yet before I can begin celebrating." Dulcinetta turned toward the hall which led to her quarters, and also to her fiancé Devin Cavanaugh and his preparations to conceal her money. She closed the door of her former bedroom behind her, leaned against it, and asked, "Is it ready?"

"Ready as it's going to be." Devin grinned at her. "Are you ready?"

"As ready as I'm going to be. I confess, although all brides are reputed to be nervous on their wedding day, I'm actually shaking. I hope this plan works." She placed the bulging carpetbag on her bed and tried to remove dainty kid gloves from trembling fingers.

"What's making you skittish? The trunk, or the transfer of the Goldust to Wilson? Or maybe—the thought of marriage to me?"

"Oh, all of it!" Dulcie waved a long-fingered hand. "Now that the final curtain is about to fall here in South Pass City, I just want to be done with it and move on."

"You really are worried." Devin rather liked that she wasn't coolly taking all the sudden changes in stride. He had begun once again to be rather in too much awe of her, not a good thing on one's wedding day. To be nervous and frightened made her human, brought her more to his level, and he liked her better for it. He took her hand, drew her close, and kissed her lips soundly. "There," he said. "Better now?"

She raised dark eyes to his. "Much. Thank you, Devin." She drew away to open the money bag. "Can you handle this alone? I'd like to go check that Ju is getting Luther dressed, and then I have to change myself. We're due at the judge's office at four." She looked approvingly at Devin's new clothes. He wore polished black shoes, dove gray trousers, a starched boiled shirt with black velvet vest, and a black suit coat. He looked so handsome. And for store-bought apparel, it all fit his large frame nicely if a bit snug in the shoulders.

His eyes gleamed with laughter as he shoved his hands into the bills packed in the carpetbag. "I've never in me life imagined such an amount of money," he said gleefully. "But as it belongs to you who has earned it with honest labor, I will force myself to pack it with care and not fling it about the room like flower petal confetti!"

Dulcinetta laughed as she exited the room. One of the things she liked best about Devin Cavanaugh was his unsophisticated attitude toward her wealth. He never made a pretense of acting as if it didn't matter to him. She was sure having money mattered very much to a poor boy. And yet she was also absolutely sure her wealth was not the reason he wanted to marry her—or at least not the sole reason.

Once in the room Luther shared with Ju, Dulcie nodded approval at the fit of the new clothes Ailis had made for her son. "Very nice. Sit right down here and don't you dare get dirty. We have to leave for the judge's soon. Ju, get dressed so we can be ready by at least a quarter till four. I'll need you to help me with my hair."

"I not going." Ju crossed her arms over her chest, hands in her sleeves. She had the obstinate tilt to her head that Dulcie had come to dread, especially now when she didn't have time to deal with Ju's tantrums.

"What do you mean, you're not going?" she said as she crossed back to her own room, followed by her stubborn friend. She opened the door to find Devin just shutting the lid on the trunk.

"I'll transport this over to our room at the hotel while you get dressed. Should we meet up at the judge's or do you want me to come back here to escort you?"

Dulcie smiled. "It's bad luck for the groom to see the bride before the wedding. I'll meet you at Judge Morris's office."

He nodded, hoisted the large, locked trunk to his shoulder as if its weight were negligible, and left the room.

"Help me out of this dress, please." Dulcie turned her back to Ju, lifting a bun of heavy hair with one hand so Ju could start undoing the line of tiny buttons down the back of the gown. "And what do you mean, you're not going?" she repeated. "I want you at my wedding, Ju."

"Ju not going wedding. Ju not moving Blyan."

Dulcie whirled, tearing a button out of Ju's grasp. "What are you saying? What do you expect you'll do if you don't move to Bryan with us? Stay here?"

"Yes. Stay here. Ju work for Wilson."

"Doing what? I demand that you look me in the eye, Xiang Ju." Dulcie grasped Ju's chin and tilted her face up. "Have you spoken to Wilson about this? What, exactly, will you be doing for him?"

"Anything I want," Ju said in a sullen tone. "Cook, clean, maybe work in saloon. Maybe some Fan-Tan."

"Gambling. Okay. I can see that. But do you have it in the back of your mind that Wilson might marry you one day, now that he's got the Goldust? Is that what you think, Miss Chrysanthemum? I rather think you might be mistaken. Don't you understand? When he tires of your company, he'll have you working upstairs." Dulcie put a hand to her mouth, her eyes wide with dismay. How could she stop this madness? For someone who supposedly owed her life to her rescuer, Ju was inordinately pigheaded when it came to doing what Dulcie wanted her to do.

"I do what I want," Ju repeated.

"And is that what you want?" Dulcie whispered fiercely, her hands dropping to seize Ju's narrow shoulders. "You had better think this over carefully, Ju. I told you that you would *never* be forced to that life again. I promised when you left San Francisco that you would always be safe with me. But you have to *stay* with me in order for me to begin to keep that promise! If you remain with Wilson, you will have to do as *he* says."

"Anything *I* want," Ju reiterated stubbornly, refusing to meet Dulcie's eyes.

"I can't believe it." Dulcie was trembling for certain now, and not just her hands. "Ju, you're making such a horrible mistake."

Ju sidled along the edge of the bed until she was once more behind Dulcie, and raised cool fingers to finish unbuttoning the dress. The rest of Dulcie's clothes that Devin hadn't taken to the hotel, except the gown she planned to be married in, were already packed and waiting to be moved to the freight office. Ju smoothed this last addition into a waiting trunk and shut the lid. She held out a heavy satin gown for Dulcie to step into, and buttoned it up. Then she waited silently for Dulcie to sit so she could style her hair.

I'm feeling her hands in my hair for what might be the final time, Dulcie thought with a kind of despair as she let Ju help her get ready to be married. Fragrant Chrysanthemum, without any detectable emotion, undid the pins holding the heavy fall of hair in a plain bun at the nape of Dulcie's neck. She began to brush out the shiny black curls.

~

Devin held his breath as the vision that would in only a moment's time become his bride entered the courthouse. *Courthouse, such a grand name for another batten board building set flush against the main thoroughfare, itself a dusty track*, Devin thought. But if courthouse was too ostentatious a name for the building holding her, he couldn't come up with a word impressive enough to describe his Dulcie. Dressed in a creamy yellow satin gown bedecked with numberless yards of delicate white lace, her hair fastened in an elaborate coiffure with dozens of pearl-headed pins, she held in her hand a carved bone fan, and the toes of dainty white slippers peeked from beneath the hem of the sumptuous gown. She wore a large filigreed gold and diamond ring on her right hand, but her left was bare, awaiting his wedding band.

Following close behind her and crowding each other in the small space were Ailis and Bethenia and few of the girls who had roused early for the occasion, all dressed in their finest, most colorful apparel, resembling a flock of exotic birds.

"Although you do make a handsome pair, I still can't believe this is happening," Ailis whispered to Devin. "That she would choose *you* from among all available men—it's simply beyond understanding or belief."

"I know. I agree. I am a wondrously lucky man," Devin said as he held out his folded arm for his bride to grasp. He refused to take offense at Ailis's friendly insult.

The ceremony was short, just a reading of the vows, an exchange of rings and "I do's," and soon Ailis Tierney and Mr. Morris were signing the marriage certificate as witnesses.

Then outside and just a few steps down the street, and they were back at the Goldust, where the revelry had continued without them. They had no sooner entered than Wilson was clambering drunkenly atop the bar. Swaying, he yelled, "Listen up! A toast. A toast to the happy couple! Mr. and Mrs. Devin Cavanaugh, may you live long and have many children—and enjoy every moment in the making of them!"

The patrons of the saloon hurrahed deafeningly and stamped their feet in rough rhythm. Dulcinetta looked at Devin. She rolled her eyes toward the ceiling, mouthing "buffoon" so only he could see.

"He is an idiot," Devin said, trying for a low tone next to her ear, meant for her only to hear over the din, "but aren't you kind of sorry you're fooling him into buying the short end of the stick? It isn't a mistake, is it, Dulcie, to sell him the Goldust? You're certain the mining around here is set to collapse?"

She glanced quickly around them to ensure no one paid their conversation the least bit of attention, holding a finger to her lips. "Shh—not so loud." She moved closer so she could speak into his ear. "Hell, no, I'm not sorry! Why should I be sorry? He tried to kill you, he threatened to kill Ju, and he would have killed me and Luther if he didn't collect something he considered at least as valuable as his lost wages from the freight company."

As if to reinforce her declaration, she lifted a hand to smooth back the hair from Devin's forehead so she could examine the painful knot where he had been struck.

Even though the happy newlyweds had yet to drink to his toast, Wilson wasn't quite finished. Waiting for the noise to die down, he added, "And a toast to the new owner of the Goldust Saloon! The next one's on me, fellas!"

More huzzahs erupted as Wilson attempted to climb down from the bar without falling on his face. The task was made more difficult because he refused to relinquish his glass, and what whiskey remained in it, held in the tight clutch of one fist.

Dulcie watched the spectacle with hooded, expressionless eyes as Devin approached the bar to get them each a drink.

As the evening wore on and any guests who had come only to wish the newlyweds well had long departed, the party got more raucous. Devin began to wonder why he and Dulcie stayed. What was her purpose in hanging about? Longing to wring a last bit of excitement from the place she had given up? He didn't think so. Dulcie didn't seem the broody type. From what he'd gathered, she felt what was done was done and it was time to move on. She wasn't attempting to work the faro table tonight, she didn't even glance in that direction. She sat quietly, watching the activity in the saloon and sipping now and again from a glass of sherry. Some men just getting off work in the Carissa approached to offer congratulations, and she stood to accept chaste busses on her cheek with good humor, even as some of the more intoxicated of her former customers who had already kissed her once stumbled over to line up and follow suit.

Before everyone got too inebriated, Devin rounded up help to move the rest of Dulcie's bags and trunks. At last, when he went to gather up the sleeping Luther to take him to the hotel, it began to come clear what Dulcie was waiting for. Free now of child care duties, Ju entered the main room of the saloon. As Devin stood with the child in his arms, Dulcie watched with a strange glittering fever reflected in her eyes as Ju began to work the room. When Ju quickly made her choice and started for the stairs, Dulcinetta abruptly stood. "All right, time for us to go," she said, beginning to walk toward the exit.

Following, Devin said asked, "What about Ju?"

"Not coming," Dulcie said.

"Not coming to the hotel tonight, you mean?"

"Not coming to the hotel tonight. Not coming to Bryan tomorrow. Not coming with us at all. Ever."

Devin could see her gritting her teeth. "She's staying on here . . . with Wilson?"

Dulcinetta nodded, a single jerk of her ringletted head. "I will admit that our Fragrant Chrysanthemum makes me crazy. After all I've done for her, the first fork in the road of freedom and she chooses that . . . that worthless *drunkard* over what I could provide."

"But it is truly her choice to stay? I mean, Cal doesn't have anything to hold over her, does he? She would be staying of her own free will?"

"It's what she says she wants. A horrible, horrible mistake—but, yes, it is what she chooses."

As they entered the hotel and began climbing the stairs, Devin said quietly, "Dulcie. I can see how hurt you are. I'm sorry for it. Perhaps your friend will change her mind later."

Dulcie snorted an unladylike laugh. "Perhaps."

But some time later, after he'd settled the boy in a cot and turned down the covers of the big bed, he would have had to say, if anyone asked him about it, that he didn't mind the absence of a lady's maid that night. He didn't mind at all undoing the tiny buttons resting along Dulcie's spine. He didn't mind helping her remove all the pins from her long hair, and he especially didn't mind letting the long, crimped tresses sift through his fingers to drape over her bare shoulders like a sumptuous black waterfall.

Chapter *12*
An Eye for an Eye

EVIN PUT DULCIE AND Luther on the stage to Bryan the next day. He would follow later when he had finished his business in South Pass City. Ailis, unsure of her welcome on the second floor of the Goldust now that Dulcie no longer owned the saloon and unwilling to pay the fee she suspected Wilson might want to charge, was going with them. After seeing Dulcie's trunk—it wouldn't have drawn a second glance from anyone who didn't know its secret—and Ailis's precious machine stowed in the boot, Devin handed Ailis up alongside his new wife and stepson. Bethenia and the dancers were planning to follow in a few days.

"Why aren't you coming with us?" Luther demanded, tears trembling on his lashes and his lower lip protruding in a pout.

"I will be there in a couple of days, boyo. Don't be so impatient. Watch out for your mama, and say hello to your grandpa for me." Devin knew Dulcie was dreading this journey in the company of her child, this child she had never been very motherly toward and consequently hardly knew. Luther was a good boy. Devin hoped that the time spent together would strengthen the bond between mother and son, but knowing Dulcie's feelings about the onus of maternal duties he wasn't holding out much hope, especially if Luther continued to mope and pine for his new stepfather's company. He stood on the rung to lean in and kiss Dulcie, then backed down to street level and shut the door. With a salute from Devin to the driver, the coach took off trailing a cloud of fine grit and was soon lost to sight.

He entered the Goldust in the late morning, when sunlight lay hot and yellow as melted butter on the sawdust of the floorboards. He figured Wilson might have had time enough to sober up a bit by now, and was gratified to see that although the former muleskinner was sitting with his head propped on his hands, nursing a cup of coffee, at least he was upright. Devin assumed this accomplishment was probably thanks in large part to Ju, who hovered nearby, hands clutching the cotton cloths she used to shield her hands when transporting the big coffee pot from the kitchen. A wary look stole over her face as she caught sight of Devin, as if she thought he had come to remonstrate with her about her decision to throw in her lot with Cal Wilson instead of following Dulcie to Bryan. But Devin had no intention of second guessing Ju. By his lights, a person had a right to his or her own errors, and Ju was welcome to the chances she made for herself.

After Devin had his pound of flesh, that is. With heavy deliberation he seated himself across from Wilson. When there was no reaction, he gave the table leg next to Wilson a good, hard kick. Cal moaned as he leaned back in the chair, eyelids scrunched shut. "Knock it off, why don't you. My head hurts." He pressed a wet cloth cautiously to his eyes.

"Drink up," Devin said. "You're coming with me down to the livery."

Wilson opened bloodshot eyes and stared for a moment before draping the damp cloth once more across his hands and raising it to his face. "Like hell I will. What in tarnation would I want to do something like that for?"

"Because you owe me some stock, that's why. You're going to come pick out the likeliest mules available in this town." Grateful that he at least still had Tiberius at the livery recuperating, beyond that one animal Devin was uncertain about his ability to judge what constituted a shrewd mule purchase.

"No. I won't go. You can't make me." Wilson refused to open his eyes again.

Devin reached over and yanked the cloth away from Wilson's face. "You owe me, Cal," he insisted. "You know a lot more about horses and mules than I do. I could use your advice."

"Oh. So now you decide you need me to help ya, huh?" Wilson's lips twisted in a sneer as he tried to snatch his wet rag back.

"Only because you let those Indians take off with almost the last animal I had," Devin said with heat. Then he tempered his voice, sure that if he tried to make Wilson feel guilty he would succeed only in driving the man further away from any sentiment toward cooperation. "But yeah, since you insist on making me say it, I need you to back up my choices."

"I'll have you know, I had *nothin'* to do with any Indians." Cal's eyes slitted against the yellow glare of the sun glinting off patches of bare floor where the sawdust had been scuffed aside.

No matter what, this absolute lie Devin couldn't bring himself to let pass unchallenged. "Yeah, that's why they delivered me right to *your* campsite, because they didn't know what to do with me after they almost killed me."

"Coulda been like that." Cal shut his eyes again, adding, "So what? I didn't burn any wagons and I didn't kill nobody. Go away and leave me alone, why don't ya. I ain't feeling up to snuff."

"Too bad. Drink up and let's go pick out some stock."

After another two cups of strong black coffee, at last Wilson admitted, "Yeah, okay, Cavanaugh. If you ain't going to give me any peace about it, I guess I got time to help you out." He tossed back the dregs from his cup and stumbled to his feet. Addressing Ju, he said, "I'll probably feel good enough to eat something when I get back." She nodded, watching them with narrowed eyes as they left the Goldust.

At the livery, Tiberius seemed pleased enough to see Devin again. But at the sight of Wilson his ears flattened and his eyes took on a dangerous glimmer.

"Aw, old Beery turned up lame, huh?" Cal sneered at the mule. "What a shame."

Devin doubted very much if Tiberius's disability was truly news to Cal. The mule's dislike for Wilson seemed to have increased to hatred, probably as a result of the laming. Wilson returned Tiberius's evil-eyed glare in full measure. To distract Tiberius from thinking about biting, no matter how much Wilson might deserve a strong nip, Devin fed the mule an expensive carrot from his pocket and then lifted Tiberius's foot to check how his wound was healing.

Cal watched from a distance, a faint grin on his face. When Devin let the hoof down, Cal said, "First of all, a good-looking mule ain't always the best choice. If they ain't trained right, they're worthless. A mule that don't know you yet, you pick up a hind foot just like ya did there, see how it takes to being handled."

"A few bad habits from the animals I can deal with, and I can ask about any previous training," Devin said. "But what if the answers I get from the owners are lies?"

"Watch a man hitch a mule and then see for yourself how it handles. I gotta tell ya, from what I see here this morning the pickings are gonna be mighty slim. But at least they all seem to be getting along. Ya don't want no animal that can't tolerate others."

Fine advice, considering its source, Devin thought. But he let Wilson put a few of the mules through their paces, and drove the wagon himself once a prospective purchase was hitched up to it, just to get the feel of how the animal reacted. By midmorning he had acquired five new animals, and word was beginning to get around that he was interested in buying harness-broke mules and a couple of big draft horse wheelers, which ultimately would probably prove the more difficult to locate.

By the time they were about ready to call it a day, Wilson was showing signs of needing a drink. His greasy hair hung down into his inflamed eyes and his hands shook with the tremor of the confirmed drunkard whose last bout with the bottle was wearing off. In addition, he seemed to be failing to recall his ongoing feud with Tiberius and stood with his unguarded back to the large gray mule.

Tiberius, not one to ever forget a wrong, suddenly lowered his head and gave Wilson a hard shove. The surprised man landed face first in the muck. Raising up on his elbows, he was already screeching as he swiped a hand across his lips. "Gawdamn! Gawdamn you, ya flannelmouth, chiseling, no-'count mizzle! I'll kill you this time, Beery, I will. You—"

Cal was just getting started on his rant and had made it to his knees when Devin lunged forward, stooped quickly, and planted one knee in the middle of his back. He shoved Cal's face back down into the vile corral mud. Cal thrashed and blubbered, trying to turn his face aside and draw a breath that wasn't comprised mostly of manure and horse piss, but Devin held him down by the shoulders. Outside the corral, an attentive pack of skinny, half-wild hogs that had the run of the town set up a high-pitched, squealing racket.

"What the hell, you moron chucklehead?" Wilson shrieked when he could draw breath. "I just helped you out! Cavanaugh, what the cozening Christ are you doing—"

No match for the former iron man, Wilson was helpless to stop Devin from once more cramming his face into the sludge. "Now listen up, Cal," Devin said in a menacingly soft voice as he bent to speak next to his former boss's ear. "I know you're behind Tiberius's lameness. So this is going to hurt you some, but as the good book says, eye for eye, tooth for tooth, hand for hand . . . and foot for foot." He swung a heavy leg over the struggling man beneath him, then, spinning around, he tried to catch one of the thrashing, booted feet presently churning up mud.

Success came with a cost. As soon as Devin grabbed one of Cal's feet and gave it a mighty twist, the man's other leather heel caught him a grazing blow to the side of the head. Devin rolled off and safely away while Cal fought to sit up, panting and pulling his injured foot up close to his body. He scooted away on his ass in the mud, face and hair dripping clots of fragrant wet soil. Tiberius stood by, watching the action with avid interest gleaming in his eyes as he leaned against the pole corral. "What the burnt-assed hell is wrong with you, Cavanaugh?" Cal yelled. "Ya broke my firkin' foot!"

"That was payback for injuring my mule, don't bother trying to deny it," Devin said. "Your foot's not broken, by the way. I didn't hear any bones crack. 'Tis only a sprain. But I will leave you with this warning—if you hurt anything, or anyone else, I care about, including Dulcie's friend Ju, I will hear about it. And I will come after you."

"It's the little China gash's choice to stay. I don't make her do anything she doesn't want to do." Wilson scrambled to his feet, wincing when he tried to put his weight on his injured foot.

Devin stood up too, near Tiberius and out of the vicinity of Cal's balled fists. "Just so you remember, you were warned. There's worse in store for you than a bruised foot if you ever have a mind to raise a hand to Ju."

Wilson opened the corral gate and began to limp away, muttering imprecations and shooting looks of pain and impotent, burning hatred over his shoulder. Before he disappeared from sight, he shouted, "You better watch yer back from now on, Cavanaugh!"

"You watch your own, Wilson. And stay away from my stock!" Devin roared after the retreating figure, adding for good measure, "Or else!"

Just to make Caleb Wilson's humiliation at the hands of the younger man all the more memorable, Tiberius chose that moment to voice his opinion. He bellowed *haaawww! haawwww!* loud enough for the whole town to hear. The pigs in the audience outside the corral, even though it could not possibly have been the first South Pass City battle they had ever witnessed, grunted and squealed in excited approbation.

~

A few months later the dance troupe rotated back into South Pass, Ailis along with them. She'd lasted but a few days with the newlywed Cavanaughs, feeling like a weed in the flower bed of their matrimonial bliss. Dulcie said Ailis was being silly and that she was welcome to stay as long as she liked. But as soon as Bethie and the girls headed to Fort Bridger for a week or so, Ailis grabbed the next stage and began following the troupe. She didn't like being back in Cal Wilson's sphere, and she especially didn't like the fulminating stare he bestowed on her whenever he was sober, or even the fact that he seemed to be keeping track of her movements in the first place. But there was a lot she didn't particularly like about how she had to go about her chosen occupation, and she did what she must in order to make as much money as she could while such free-flowing funds were available.

She was glad to see Ju again, and to note with her own eyes that she seemed to have come to no harm while here in Wilson's employ. Ju seemed to be carrying on much as she always had, cooking and cleaning for Wilson and offering her services to a few others as she had time to accommodate them in between games of fan-tan, the ancient Chinese game played with buttons, a metal bowl and a simple square.

Ju told Ailis one of the merits of the game over others she could have chosen was its addictive quality, and it truly seemed that once the miners learned how to play they were virtual slaves to Ju, the *tan kun*, and her croupier stick. With few exceptions the same group was at it every night until Ju decided she had enough. All her activities seemed lucrative. She had ordered in bolts of silk in several colors and wanted Ailis to make her as many new Chinese-style outfits as possible during her stay. In some ways Ju seemed happier than Ailis had ever seen her before.

It was Cal Wilson Ailis didn't like and didn't trust. She hated looking at him, at his squinty eyes and the strings of saliva swaying from brown stumps of his teeth when he talked. He gave her the jimmies. She tried to avoid him. Even now, bent over the bar with his greasy head close to another man's, a man she didn't know, the two of them were no doubt engaged in some kind of vile collusion. She tried to slip out the door to get something to eat before Cal could notice her. But, unfortunately, too late.

"Ailis . . ." came the call, Cal's smoke-and-whiskey voice a gravelly growl. "C'mere a minute, would you?" As if he'd been watching for her to come downstairs, which she had little doubt he had. The more she tried to escape his notice, the more he seemed to mark her schedule.

She stopped, turned, glanced at Ju who shrugged the information that she didn't know what Cal was about.

"Come on, don't be shy," Cal wheedled in a tone that caused the hair on Ailis's neck to prickle in alarm. "We have a bit of a proposal for ya." He chuckled evilly as she felt her spine stiffen and her mouth turn down at the corners. "Not that kind of proposition, don't you fret! It's an entirely harmless way for you to make some axle grease, I promise. Maybe . . ." his oily glance slid sideways toward the accomplice who had yet to show anything of his identity other than the tiniest glimpse of profile, "maybe even a lot of money."

His grin caused chill bumps to break out on Ailis's arms. If Cal liked her, she decided with sudden vehemence, it was definitely worse than if he didn't.

But a chance to make money—maybe lots of money? She and Dulcie had talked a bit about setting up in business together in Bryan City in the brief time she had spent there with her friend. There had been some talk of them perhaps sharing a building. They had even toyed with names for her little shop while they got tipsy on wine one evening, French no less: *Couturière et Modiste*. But it was all idle talk, dreaming, on Ailis's part anyway. It would be years yet before she had the kind of funds it would take to open her own business. Dulcie, Ailis suspected, could well afford to back her in order to start such an enterprise. But Dulcie hadn't outright offered, only talked around the idea, and Ailis wouldn't ask. Instead she had hared off again with Bethie and the girls, chasing after her dream. And here she was, back at the Goldust still dressing the dancers, with that creepy Cal Wilson always eyeing her with a pinch-eyed look of speculation. And now he had hatched a *proposition* for her.

It couldn't be anything good. Ailis was pretty sure of that. Whatever the offer was, considering Cal was involved, it probably wouldn't even be legal. Sometimes she despaired of herself. There was little she wouldn't do in the chase after money, stopping short only of bargaining her body for gold or bills. Half ashamed of her consuming hunger for capital, the other half proved unable to resist the lure of riches. Despite Ailis's better judgment, her feet began to slide across the sawdust-covered floor toward the bar and whatever part Cal Wilson might be prepared to offer her in his latest sneaky scheme.

"First of all," Cal said in a voice barely above a whisper as soon as she had approached near enough to hear, leaning toward Ailis as she in turn tried to stifle a grimace of distaste at his proximity, "I want you to make a wedding dress for my Chrysanthemum."

"What?" Ailis shook her head as if trying to clear water from her ears. "What did you say? You're marrying Ju?"

"Shh! She don't know about it yet." Wilson looked toward Ju, where she presided over the fan-tan table. "I haven't said anything to her. It's meant to be a surprise."

"Well, how do you know she'll agree? What if she doesn't want to marry you? That would be a surprise, all right. Then what would you do with the dress?" *Will you still pay me if this pipe dream of a wedding doesn't go through?*

"I'll give her the dress anyways, missy, no matter what. I'll give that little Chinee gal lots of dresses, as many as she wants. And don't you worry none about us not getting hitched; she'll do it."

Apparently she had to come right out and ask. "And you'll pay me either way?"

Cal waved a dirty hand. "I said don't worry about it."

Ailis found it curious and more than a little disconcerting that the stranger who had been so intent in whispered conversation with Wilson just a few moments ago now kept his head turned aside from the present negotiations. She couldn't see his face. A quiver of unease swept over her, but she still hadn't heard the second of Wilson's offers. So instead of turning away as she wanted to, she held her ground.

"As for the other . . ." Cal motioned her closer. Reluctantly Ailis closed the distance between them by about an inch. "We want to hire you to run a little errand for us."

"By 'we' you mean . . ." She motioned toward the silent man still sitting with his back to them.

"Yeah. Me and my partner here." Still the man didn't show his face.

"Shy, is he?" Alice asked with a trace of a sneer.

"More like cautious. A word to the wise: it's a thing you might consider practicing, missy, the weather eye."

"So it's like that, is it? I thought so. Why don't you come right out and say what you have to say, Cal? Why all the pussyfooting around? Is your proposal a tad unlawful, perhaps?"

"Forget it." At last the mysterious man turned to look at her. He had the face of a weasel, or perhaps a rat, with two black, gleaming eyes set close together over a pointed nose. He peered at Ailis with obvious malice. "You've got a big mouth. Ask too many questions. You are a stupid woman. No woman can ever truly be trusted."

Ailis sucked in a breath. Instinctively she knew she shouldn't show fear of this man, even as she felt terror under his icy, penetrating gaze. So instead of keeping quiet as she knew she should, she challenged him. "Stupid? Stupid because I'm a woman, or stupid just because?" she asked.

The small mouth with wet, red lips puckered, hiding a set of sharp yellow teeth as he studied her. His cheeks worked as he sucked on his molars. "Maybe . . . not so stupid after all," he finally conceded. "But untrustworthy. Definitely untrustworthy."

Ailis glanced at Cal. "Is that what you're thinking as well?"

Cal shrugged.

"Then why did you call me over? You're wasting my time, if not your own." She started to turn away.

"Wait." The rat-faced man didn't try to seize her arm to stop her, but his voice held a tone that demanded obedience. "Tell me, Miss Tierney, would it be necessary to threaten your life to gain your silence concerning our plans? Or are you smart enough to know what would happen to you if you ever thought to divulge anything we revealed to you?"

She had allowed her pride let this to go too far. She had to stop it now. Ailis forced herself to turn back to look at the little man who frightened her so. "I have but one question. Is it too late to pretend this conversation never happened?"

The man laughed. At least Ailis thought it might be laughter. His lips stretched over his pointed little teeth and he emitted a strange series of small puffs of breath that sounded similar to a snake's hiss. "Oh, *brava*, miss! Not stupid at all, I see. But, my dear, I regret to inform you that things between us have progressed a considerable distance beyond mere pretense."

Chapter *13*
New Ventures

*T*HE GROWING SETTLEMENT OF Bryan City had a look of smug permanence about it in the years following the railroad's refusal to negotiate with S. I. Field for land in Green River City. Strung out along Evans to the cross streets of the downtown district of Tenth and Eleventh, the little town looked like it might be a survivor, one of the fortunate few destined to prosper after the completion of the great iron road that now spanned the continent.

Devin drove his new team into town, amazed at the ongoing transformation of the settlement, and amused at the change in his own attitude toward Bryan City and the entire Wyoming Territory just since the past spring. Marriage to Dulcinetta had certainly sweetened his outlook on life, and not merely because she suited him so perfectly, nor simply because she was so undeniably pleasing to look upon. The brawny Irishman's constant cheerfulness couldn't even be wholly the result of a complete cessation of any money worries on his part, thanks to Dulcie's personal fortune and her continuing careful management of their business interests.

No, his life had been transformed by becoming a husband and father—statuses he had never thought to seek for himself. Whenever he thought about it, he was amazed all over again at what good fortune had come to pass for such an unlikely candidate.

The tug of home growing ever stronger, he halted the team in the road outside the freight office corral, and jumped down to hurry inside. "Set the brake. Start the unharnessing, get the team rubbed down and fed," he called to his new swamper, another of the flood of refugees earning his way home, hungry and penniless, from the gold camps of South Pass and Atlantic City and probably available only until he earned enough to buy a third-class railway ticket. Devin no sooner got a man trained than he quit and it was time to start over with another one. They were mostly faceless and interchangeable. Devin had no real connection to any of them. After his sad experience with Moroni, in truth he wanted none.

As he entered the office, his clerk, a skinny man named Willoughby in a starched white shirt and sleeve protectors, rose to greet the boss.

"How are things?" Devin asked.

"Fine, just fine," Willoughby replied, passing over a pile of invoices and bills of lading for the freight stacked against the walls of the warehouse, of which the office occupied just one small corner.

Devin thumbed through the papers, astonished as always that he could actually decipher most of the words printed on the sheets. He'd progressed quickly once past the initial stumbling blocks of the alphabet in print as well as cursive, and some phonics which allowed him to begin to sound out words. He wasn't the fastest reader by any means, but he was coming along to the point where Dulcie could once again focus completely on her own interests while he took over sole management of the freighting company. More routes, more wagons, more responsibility. He couldn't do it all; he had had to learn to delegate. As it was, he now went out with the wagons only about once a month, just to keep an eye on things on his routes, which were ever expanding as the surrounding area began to be developed. The territory was still rather sparsely settled, it was true, but even the most far-flung ranch ordered supplies for delivery once in a while and, in addition, he had won the coveted civilian contract for delivery of goods from Bryan City to Camp Stambaugh up north.

And these days anything that anyone desired could be brought in on the rails. Gazing over the stacks on his desk, he spotted the copy of *Woodward's National Architect* he had been awaiting. He scooped it up while simultaneously depositing the hastily-approved documents for Willoughby to attend to, and headed out the door toward home.

What he and Dulcie and Luther presently called home was Lou's small house in Bryan, which they shared with Josiah. He knew he had only to open the door and call out "I'm home" when he would be pounced upon by a small boy bearing books. Today, it was immediately obvious Luther had been expecting him.

"Devin!" Luther cried. "Let's do homework!"

"Aw, Third. I've only just got in the house. Can't it wait?"

"No! I need help reading, you know that."

Devin knew what the boy actually meant was that they could both do with some extra reading practice. Luther spent his weekdays at the little clapboard-sided school that had been hastily erected by the town mothers with the secret financial backing of Josiah Jackson. Then, with after-hours schooling from a private tutor, he was rapidly threatening to outstrip his stepfather in both reading and writing.

"All right, all right. Where's your mother? I wanted to talk to her."

As yet no one had summoned the heart to inform the boy that the adults in the family sometimes preferred each other's company to his. And also as yet, Luther was of the age that he still thought the whole world revolved around him. Neither of the doting adults, meaning Devin and Josiah, dared disabuse him of the notion, and Dulcie happily left the matter of Luther's supervision to them. Lately Devin had developed the distinct feeling that the child was, perhaps, becoming spoiled completely rotten.

"She's not here. She went shopping." Luther tugged at the cloth of Devin's trousers, trying to urge him farther into the house.

Josiah entered the small front hallway. One eyebrow arched at the sight of his grandson clinging to the oversized Irishman. "Glad you've arrived home once again, Devin. How was your trip?" Josiah smiled, adding, "Maybe it's not my place to tell you this, but Dulcie is planning a surprise for you."

"Granddad, you weren't supposed to tell!"

"*You* weren't supposed to tell. But I knew you would, so I just saved you the trouble." Josiah grinned fondly at Luther.

Devin smiled at Josiah while detaching Luther's sticky hand from the cloth of his trousers. "I'm thankful to report that once again the trip was entirely uneventful. And, where Dulcie is concerned, I've begun to suspect that your daughter is a never-ending source of surprises." His mind made quick inventory of the shopping available in Bryan City, trying to guess what his wife might have bought to surprise him. The perusal didn't take him long. The business district was fairly small as yet: a watchmaker, a druggist, a tobacconist and news shop, a hardware store, and a general merchandise store. Most of Bryan's commerce consisted of wholesale grocers who shipped to the Sweetwater district, a couple of restaurants, a hotel that sheltered some of the local population and those alighting from the stage or the passenger train cars, a lunchroom, and of course, several saloons. Most of the liquid refreshment businesses advertised the availability of Kentucky bourbon and rye whiskeys from makers ranging from Willow

Run to El Dorado and Chicken Cock, although they also included a purveyor of brandy, at least one of wine, and one of gin.

"How's business?" Devin asked, knowing Josiah wouldn't go into any detail in front of the boy.

"Getting along," the older man replied. Always stiffly dignified, Josiah never gave a hint of the nature of his enterprise, not by even so much as a twinkle in his eye. And in truth he was usually a rather solemn man who took the responsibility of seeing to the steady and safe transaction of the favors of Lou's girls quite seriously, as seriously as he had taken his barkeep duties in South Pass while he kept a watchful eye on his daughter. He had largely ceded that latter duty, it seemed with some relief, to his son-in-law. "Well, now that you're home, I think I will just go attend to some things that I've been putting off," Josiah said, reaching for his top hat and placing it on his head.

Left alone with just the boy, Devin gave up on any idea of adult conversation. Looking down into Luther's expectant little face, he said, "I guess you win, Third. Let's go read."

~

Dulcie held out the signed contract accompanied by a bank draft for a quite hefty sum. Once the document transfer was complete, she shook the grinning man's hand across the gleaming surface of a glass and oak display case.

It should have been a happy time. She should have felt exultant. But she didn't. It wasn't often that she questioned her own motives or actions, so the distinct lack of enthusiasm that crept over her as she closed on this much-anticipated deal surprised her.

What's wrong?

She kept asking herself the question, but thus far had come up with no definitive answer. Buying the business itself couldn't be what bothered her, it was a solid concern and a definite step up in societal terms from the South Pass saloon and her previous career dealing cards. Josiah had been all for the deal when she discussed it with him. Her father still served as her sounding board when Devin was absent from home, and she felt no guilt about having made the final decision without consulting her husband. Devin trusted her judgment in all things commerce, as she, in turn, unreservedly trusted Josiah's counsel.

So what could be wrong? She felt exactly as she had when the inexplicable notion settled on her that South Pass City was headed for a bust and that she had better get out while the getting was good. Although the South Pass *News,* as reliable as ever, still published every Wednesday, she knew in her bones that this summer would be the last good season for the Sweetwater district. She had done the right thing to get out. But had she done the right thing by buying in here today?

She looked around at Bryan City as she began a slow walk home. Most of the canvas and half-board dwellings were being replaced by more permanent homes and false front commercial buildings. The railroad's machine shops and roundhouse had a substantial air of redbrick permanence, and the community had even rallied to build a schoolhouse, for heaven's sake. Surely, if the Union Pacific Railroad brass made the decision to anoint Bryan the division point, there was no earthly reason for Dulcinetta Jackson to be skittishly detecting ominous rumblings of disaster. She should just focus on the kind of temblors that could be attributed to the regular arrivals and departures of the huge iron steam engines, those noisy, sooty symbols of the single giant business that was the basis for the existence of all the rest. The businesses of Bryan rather reminded her of a bunch of small barnacles clinging to life on the sides of a large chugging tugboat—the railroad—in the middle of a fast-flowing river of sagebrush.

She just hoped she and her new little business wouldn't be scraped off if the railroad tug somehow crashed on hidden rocks. She lightly ran gloved fingers over the pages folded inside her cloth handbag. She told herself the new contract was safe as safe could be. The seller's history was solid. The research she had done on him had shown no irregularities, everything was on the up and up. All merchandise had been appraised and guaranteed, the business itself was indisputably a going concern, its books tiptop and without blemish. Not the least question of any sort about the seller or the business had arisen during the audit or at any other point in the proceedings. Everything pointed to a successful new venture for her.

And it was a thing she'd always yearned for, to own such a reputable and proper business. She was buying something more than a profession. From here on, stretching out as far as she could see the future, there would be no more sly glances cast her way, no appraising looks down people's noses as they weighed her decency and the depth of her conformation to the strictures of proper society. Just so long as she was standing behind that hefty edifice of beveled glass and wood with its gleaming and glittering display of merchandise of undeniable quality and value, she would be a fine, upstanding member of the growing community of Bryan.

She wanted this. She had no doubt of that. Josiah supported her, and she was confident Devin would applaud her decision. She would spend the rest of her days hobnobbing with a better class of people than miners, dance hall girls, and gamblers. And while that particular segment of the population had been totally acceptable to her up to this point, those sorts of people were so . . . transitory. There was no true building of relationships with them. They came and they went like puffs of smoke the moment any impulse stimulated them to arrive or to go, and especially as their personal fortunes waxed or waned. Just look at Ailis and Ju, who had both chosen to let Dulcie go her own way without them.

Dulcie wanted permanence. It was one of the reasons she had tumbled into such a precipitous marriage to a man she scarcely knew. But there again she had trusted her instincts and Devin had so far proved her right, in more ways than she could have imagined. He trusted her with his secrets. He took a lot of responsibility for Luther off her hands. He treated Josiah with respect, a quality essential to any bond she built with a man. He was younger than she by a few years and still had some growing up to do, but she'd never met anyone who looked at her with such frank admiration, merely for who she was. Devin openly adored her. In his eyes, she knew, she could do no wrong.

And it was that very aspect of their association that was enough to make her pause and question whether she was truly making the right move now. If it turned out she was wrong about this, she dreaded seeing huge disappointment in her written on her young husband's expressive face.

But, oh, how she craved respectability, to be able to claim a place in society. She was willing to gamble to get it. As Devin's freighting business grew, as they started to fit in with the town's growing communal structure, as Luther made friends and yet more connections were established through school and perhaps one day even church activities, the Cavanaughs would inevitably rise in people's estimation. She would leave far behind her the woman who had sat dealing cards all night in a miasma of cigar smoke and whiskey fumes with strange men across the table salivating at the sight of her bosom. She would be somebody, somebody in her own right and somebody as Mrs. Devin Cavanaugh as well, and not just the woman who controlled her aunt's rather questionable businesses.

Although she would continue as long as necessary keeping an eye on Lou's concerns, while focusing on her own ever-increasing fortunes. She had taken the first step. It was all within her reach now. She had the future she'd always dreamed of nestled right here in her handbag. She could feel the heat of it, of her triumph, so tantalizingly close. It was all falling into place. It was so right—she *knew* it was right, as if she had planned it all down to the last detail and the opportunity hadn't just tumbled into her lap.

And yet . . . something about it didn't *feel* right. She still felt that niggle of doubt, that worm of fear so far still contained in its chrysalis but coming ever nearer to bursting out of its wrappings.

What could *possibly* be wrong?

~

Devin listened to Luther read with half his usual attention, ears attuned instead to the anticipated sound of the front door opening.

At last his impatience was satisfied as Dulcie swept in, removing her hat and gloves and walking toward them with a smile. "Two of my favorite men!" She bent to kiss the top of Luther's head, and then bestowed a chaste peck on Devin's lips as the boy looked on, frowning. Luther's disapproval had nothing to do with propriety and everything to do with the fact that he considered Devin his discovery. It was only right that he was therefore the proper recipient of the bulk of Devin's attention, and he jealously guarded against encroachment.

"How was your trip?" Dulcie swept aside her skirts to join them at the table.

Devin shrugged. "Mostly unexciting, although I did discover Ailis back in residence at the Goldust when I stopped by to check on Ju."

"What! That . . . that disgusting reprobate has them both in his clutches now?" Dulcie picked up Luther's copy book and began to fan herself in her agitation.

Luther observed with interest. "Who are you talking about? And what's a reperbate, Mama?"

Dulcie drew herself up. "Never you mind, Luther. The subject is not fit for a child's ears. Go on to your room now. You can read to yourself for a while. And close the door behind you."

The boy shot a look of rebellion toward Devin, clearly willing to stand up and disobey his mother if his stepfather gave the slightest sign of support.

"Do as your mother says. Go." Devin pointed toward the boy's small bedroom. Luther slid off his chair and departed in a droop-shouldered sulk, casting looks of injured offense over his shoulder at the adults.

Devin ignored the boy after seeing that he obeyed, then covered Dulcie's small hand with one of his own big paws. "Ailis seemed fine. Don't worry, they both seemed fine. In fact I think Ju almost runs the place now, the gambling and the food and the upstairs rooms, with Cal just minding the bar."

"And Ailis? She turned aside my every effort to tender an offer of going into business together, simply to return to that kind of life? I don't understand."

"Ailis is proud, very proud. She comes from humble beginnings. Perhaps she didn't understand that your idea wasn't a gift. She would want to carry her own weight in any undertaking."

Dulcie sniffed. "Which is pretty silly, if you ask me. *You* didn't have any trouble letting me set you up with the freighting, and Ju is still insisting on paying me back from her earnings. I would have gladly lent Ailis the money if she wouldn't accept an outright gift, but she resisted even speaking of anything approaching a partnership."

"Speaking of Ju, that reminds me, I've got another installment for you from her. I'm sorry things didn't work out for you and Ailis. But you are right about one thing, I would be happy to inform the entire world of everything you've done for me."

"You are too sweet, darling. And I don't mean to keep throwing money in your face. As you well know, I didn't earn the greater part of it on my own either. I'm just taking advantage of the golden opportunities my aunt's connections have presented to me. I'm more than happy to share my good fortune. Which reminds *me* . . ." She retrieved her bag from her lap and placed it on the table, drawing out a sheaf of papers. "We bought another business today. A jewelry store. If you have no objection, I already have a name. I would like to call it *Nonpareil*."

Despite Josiah's warning that Dulcie had a surprise for him, Devin was indeed astonished. He whistled as he reached for the documents. "Jewelry?"

"Well, at present a watchmaker's, if you want to be precise. But I plan to expand. We will still carry and repair watches, but I've always liked the look of gold and silver and precious stones."

"Of course you have. I know how you love your shiny baubles. I don't know why this comes as such a wonder to me. But, uh, what exactly does nonpareil mean?"

Dulcie put her nose in the air, affecting an upper class snobbery. "It's French, of course. Nonpareil means matchless, without equal, the *crème de la crème*."

"Oh, well, I should have been able to guess that." Devin laughed, at himself and his stunned reaction to the unexpected situation. A surprise, indeed. "You are nonpareil, that's for sure."

Dulcie blushed prettily. "You flatter me, husband."

He looked around to make sure that Luther wasn't eavesdropping and then waggled his eyebrows at his wife, whispering, "I will be pleased to indulge in a lot more flattery . . . later."

Dulcie giggled behind her hand, batting her lashes suggestively at him.

"But right now, I want you to look at something." Devin reached to slide the copy of *Woodward's National Architect* closer. "It's time for you to pick out the plans for our house, Dulcie. Any house you like, you select it and I will get it built."

When she hesitated, he added, "It's not that I've got anything against us continuing here with your father. It's just that I always wanted my own home, and now I want to make our first home a brand new house, one that we built together."

"Well, it's not so much that I don't want to leave Josiah. It's . . ." She hesitated as the creeping uncertainty overtook her again. So long as Devin was supporting *her*, she felt safe and confident in the decision to invest in their new life. But as soon as he asked her to support his putting down roots here, she wanted to shake her head, push the building publication away, say, *No, no, it's a mistake.*

She couldn't begin to put her feelings into words. Not so long as Devin had such clear hope shining in his eyes. She could plainly read expectation on his face, the anticipation that she would encourage him as he bolstered her, the anticipation that she would be a good wife and not a naysayer, that she would help him realize his dreams.

Until she could find some answer to her foreboding, a solution to the puzzle of what could possibly be wrong when everything seemed on the surface to be so right, she told herself she would just have to pretend. She pasted a smile on her lips and slowly slid the periodical of house plans nearer.

It wasn't the first time she had thumbed through one of these publications. Her husband had accumulated stacks of books, brochures, catalogs, and booklets: *The Manufacturer and Builder;* an architectural journal called *Building;* and many others. He had studied all kinds of books containing all kinds of instructions for everything from how to transplant trees—useful information if one were interested in importing shade to this almost treeless high desert environment—to "full and complete sets of specifications and an estimate of the cost of each design" for entire houses. Despite her unease over she-knew-not-what, she felt quiet pride in how far Devin had come in his quest for self-education. She remembered when the first of his building instruction manuals had arrived, how he stayed up late studying it, head bent in the lamplight, trying to puzzle out the words, which were clear enough if a bit tentative in their spelling:

> *Furnish all the Timber used in the construction, of good sound square edged quality, free from any and every imperfection tending to impair its durability or strength, and as well seasoned as any convenient market will afford. The Sills, Posts, Floor Joist and Rafters, to be of Chesnut, Pine or Spruce, and the remaining framing timber of Hemlock, Pine or Spruce, at the option of the Contractor. Dimensions of the timber, as follows . . .*

Devin had always had a knack for numbers, and now his reading and comprehension had improved immeasurably. It was obvious he would wait no longer. He wanted her to pick out her house, and she had no doubt at all that he would move heaven and earth to get whatever house she chose built as quickly as possible. So she started flipping through the designs, each with instructions for everything from cellar walls, to plumbing specifications, to window casings, to plastering and fireplace mantels. The booklet contained nineteen different projects, each drawn to working scale. These particular plans were meant to be placed in a builder's hands. Others of Devin's collection featured scale drawings of entire houses that could be mail-ordered and delivered by freight train from Chicago to the selected building site in far off Bryan City, Wyoming Territory. With the great road connecting east to west, anything could now be had by anyone with the means. Any housing dream she fancied could be fulfilled, from a simple cottage estimated to cost a couple of thousand dollars to an Ornamental Brick Villa with French Roof and Tower projected to cost a mind-boggling thirty thousand.

"Hmm," she said, trying her best to sound excited and eager, "how about something like this cottage?"

Devin frowned. "That's awfully small, Dulce, and such a simple design. Wouldn't you like something bigger, fancier? We can surely afford it."

"Why, think of all we have to learn about building, darling. We have lots of time, an entire future, to think big . . . later. This first little house of ours could be just the inaugural home of the many houses we'll build. Wait! Tell me you can see it: Cavanaugh Constructors!"

His lips stretched in a broad smile. "You never stop, do you? There are always those little gears turning in your head. I can almost see the teeth meshing."

"Should I stop, darling? Do you really want me to?" She nudged the booklet aside to grasp his hands. "Would you like me to become just an ordinary housewife, all my concerns centered on cooking and cleaning and child care—but perhaps in the process becoming just a *little* boring?"

He had to laugh. "Not you. Never, my lady!" He leaned in to kiss her thoroughly, now that they had a bit of privacy. No mere little peck would do, not for his incomparable and outstanding Dulcie.

She leaned away after the completion of his complete bussing, her eyes gleaming with laughter. "Lady? Have you been reading fairy tales? Do you fancy yourself the prince awakening Snow White? Or perhaps one of the knights of Arthur's Round Table—Lancelot, I presume?"

"Oh, aye, I would like to have ye see me as yer Lancelot, my lady. As I said . . . later."

They shared a laugh of an intimate couples' nature before turning back to the serious business of their new house, and contemplation of perhaps one more new avenue of commerce.

Chapter 14
A Secret Mission

*A*ILIS BENT HER HEAD, lifting her skirt and extending a dainty booted foot to step down from the doorway of the stagecoach. A couple of cowpokes lounging against the wall of the train station eyed the sight of the trim calf emerging from beneath the ruffle of a white petticoat, nudging each other while one gave a low whistle of appreciation. Ailis smiled as she stepped to the dusty street, the tilt of her head and the glance from beneath long lashes in the young men's direction an acknowledgment of the compliment they sent her way.

The stage driver rounded the coach to the back to begin unloading the passengers' luggage. Ailis didn't have much. She didn't plan on a long visit to Bryan City this time. She meant to conduct her business and catch the next stage north, and so she had left most of her things behind in South Pass.

Hefting her carpetbag, she headed toward the hotel. She was anxious to complete her mission so she could return to the Goldust, finish Ju's dress, collect her precious one-of-a-kind machine, and be on her way. She would be glad enough if she never saw Caleb Wilson or his rat-faced friend ever again. She would miss Ju, but sometimes the price for remaining alive was a steep one.

Luggage deposited and room key in hand, she emerged once again onto the street. Heading for the small business district of Bryan City, she walked at a determined pace until she reached what should have been her destination. She raised a hand to shade her eyes, looking up and down the street at the false fronts and windows painted with store names and advertisements. She was in the right place, everything looked familiar—except for the one merchant she sought.

She felt like stamping her foot. It would be just her luck for the man to have gone out of business in the short time she'd been gone. It happened all the time out here: deliveries went awry, incomes didn't meet expectations, families far away ran into difficulties and needed help at home. Shops closed up and shopkeepers disappeared without a backwards glance.

She looked around again. Where she remembered a watchmaker, timepiece repair shop, and jeweler, the sign now read *Nonpareil*. And she realized at once what she'd missed the first time: Dulcie. The plan, which they had hatched while overindulging in some good wine one night, was a dressmaker and hat shop for Ailis, and a fancy jewelry store for Dulcie. They even dreamed up French names: *Couturière et Modiste* for Ailis, and next door, the *Nonpareil* for Dulcie.

The stunning reality stole her breath, the realization of how quickly Dulcie had proceeded alone, going on to fulfill her part of their plan. If Ailis had only let Dulcie stake her, bent a little instead of being so stiff-necked and stubborn, she could have had the still-elusive dream shop by now. Instead . . . instead she was on some mission to further the as-yet veiled plans of devious Cal Wilson and his shifty, evil-eyed friend.

Ailis imagined entering the jewelry shop and trying to explain to Dulcie her requirements without raising her friend's suspicions. It was hopeless. Dulcie was probably the least easily fooled person Ailis had ever met. What possible explanation could Ailis manufacture for having to buy a few bagsful of expensive stones from Dulcie that would begin to seem plausible?

She thought of all the money residing in her pocketbook, Cal and Weasel Face's money. She could follow through on their plan, buy as many loose gems as she could get her hands on, and return to South Pass City safe and sound. From there she could run as far and as fast as she could in order to get away from the two men. Or she could take the money, and run now . . . and look over her shoulder, living in fear for her life for the rest of her days.

She raised a gloved hand, bit back a sudden sob. How had she ended up in such a fine mess? In her own estimation, she was a good enough woman. Not perfect, but she had never deliberately harmed any creature, man nor beast; always dealt honestly with her customers; and sometimes even offered up a prayer if she happened to recall the day of the week was Sunday. Although more often than not lately, Sunday usually found her sleeping until afternoon along with the rest of the traveling troupe.

From the corner of her eye Ailis caught movement behind the plate glass fronting the shop. Turning her back, she hurried off before Dulcie spied her lurking in the street outside Nonpareil. She didn't have much time, a few days at most, until Cal and his associate would come looking for her. She would tuck herself away for a while, she decided, and hide until she could make up her mind what she should do now.

~

Josiah sat in his office behind the purple door at the so-called White House, going over some accounts. He straightened in his chair as the office door opened and a well-dressed woman with a rich cascade of auburn curls was ushered inside. He pushed his chair back and stood, while she set down the carpetbag she carried, and began removing her gloves.

"Miss Tierney, isn't it?" Josiah asked. He hesitated—surely this friend of his daughter couldn't be seeking the kind of work he offered here—then added, "Please, take a seat. Tell me, how may I be of service to you?"

She sat, still clutching and twisting her gloves in her hands. "Mr. Jackson," she began, and then halted as if she couldn't discover the words.

"Josiah," he said. "Call me Josiah."

"Josiah, then," she agreed. "I need a place to hide out for a few days, and I was hoping you could help me."

"Miss Tierney . . ." He cleared his throat. "I hope I don't have to explain to you what kind of house this is. You shouldn't be here. You need to go to the hotel, or better yet, I'm sure my daughter and her husband would be glad to offer you accommodation."

"Call me Ailis. I insist." A ghost of an impish smile tugged at the corners of her mouth as she duplicated his informality. "See, that's the problem. I had a room at the hotel, but I can't stay there. It's too public. I can't be seen right now. And I can't stay with Dulcie and Devin because I have a problem that I need help solving, but I can't involve them. Either of them. It's too dangerous. They would go running to try to rescue me, and then they too would be in over their heads. They have each other to answer to now, and they have a son. I can't ask them to endanger their family. I won't."

"Am I right in assuming you think, then, that *I* can help you solve your problem?"

"I think you can help me puzzle out a solution, yes. I'm not asking you to do anything beyond listening to me, and perhaps helping me to discern a way out of my dilemma. I would never ask you or anyone else to put life at risk just because of my own carelessness." She raised a hand to rub at the worried creases of her forehead. Almost in a whisper, she added to herself, "Fool! Why didn't you just walk away?"

Josiah steepled his fingers, resting his chin on them as he studied the distraught young woman seated before him. "Perhaps you should start at the beginning, my dear. Would you like a cup of tea?"

"Would you think ill of me if I asked for something stronger?" Tension showed in the set of Ailis's shoulders and the clench of her teeth.

"Not at all. What will you have? Some wine?" When she just shook her head, he said, "Gin? Or whiskey?"

"Whiskey. In a cup of hot tea. A bit of false courage would be most welcome right now."

"Think of it as fortification." Josiah picked up a little wooden-handled bell to summon the serving girl. At this point he was afraid he was as much in need of some bucking up as his anxious guest.

When they were both holding a fine Queensware cup of steaming tea strengthened with a splash of whiskey, Josiah said, "All right. Let's hear what it is you think you've done that could imperil so many lives."

Ailis took a deep breath before plunging into her story. "You know Cal Wilson, of course." At Josiah's nod, she continued, "Well, he's got company. I don't know the man's name, but he's as shifty a character as I've ever had the misfortune to meet."

"Go on," Josiah said.

"I. . . I challenged them. Instead of turning my back when they conspired to convince me to cooperate, I opened my mouth and got impertinent. I was used to it being just Cal, you see. I felt safe in dismissing Cal because his usual mode of operation is to drink himself into insensibility each night, forgetting the day's unpleasantness and his intimidation of others. He seems harmless. Pathetic, really. Ju appears completely unafraid of Cal, and so the rest of us have begun to take his persistent, if largely ineffectual, sour nature for granted."

"You don't think Ju is in any danger."

"No. Not at the present time, at any rate. Oddly enough, I think Cal really cares for Ju, and in return she seems to hold his number. Ju does almost exactly as she wishes, and Cal seldom says a word to deflect her from whatever course she chooses. Now he even tells me he plans to marry her."

Josiah raised one eyebrow at this news. "Interesting. But now you feel unsafe?"

"That little . . . *weasel* friend of Cal's makes my skin crawl. And he as much as said they would kill me if I didn't do as they say."

"And what is it they want you to do?"

"I was to purchase as many loose gemstones as I could, or gems in as cheap a setting as I could find, and return with them to South Pass City. If I could not obtain a good quantity of stones, I was to order them and return here to pick them up when they arrived. It was all to be done as quickly as possible."

"And have you done so?"

"I didn't even step inside the door of the jeweler's! Once I saw the name of the place had been changed, and that what used to be mostly a watch dealer and repair has become a fancy jewelry store with a French name, I knew what happened. I knew Dulcie had worked her financial magic once again, and opened the kind of place she had long envisioned owning. Don't get me wrong. I am glad for her—overjoyed, truly, that she seems to have such a charmed life. A handsome young husband who is also becoming a successful businessman, a clever young son, the ability to enter and exit various business ventures and always on the side that will make money. I know it sounds like I envy her, and in a way I confess that's true, I do. But I also love her, Mr. Jackson. I would never bring any harm to her."

"Josiah," he reminded her.

"Josiah, yes. I would never do anything to hurt Dulcie, Josiah. And so I cannot go through with this plan because she will immediately see that my actions make no sense. She would soon worm the entire story out of me, and then she and Devin would want to immediately come to my defense and gallop off to South Pass City to confront Cal Wilson. I can't allow that. I can't do anything that would do the slightest damage to their perfect, storybook life."

"Well, first of all, my daughter's life hardly fits the definition of perfection. She spends a lot of time planning her moves, and works endlessly hard to see her ideas come to pass."

"Oh, I know that! I do. You know what I mean, though. You can't deny that Dulcie has a golden touch. Where others in the exact same situation would flounder or fail, your daughter always finds a way to come out on top. And if I am jealous, or not, of her good fortune, the fact remains that she *is* blessed with uncommonly good luck."

"Perhaps." Josiah rested clasped fingers against his lips. "And you don't know what the ultimate need is for the stones?"

Ailis shook her head. "I don't. But it's nothing good, I can assure you of that much."

"Why don't you just take the train east, go somewhere else to make your purchases? There's Cheyenne, or you could go all the way to Chicago, buying a few gems here, a few there. Such a course would arouse less suspicion, and you wouldn't have to involve Dulcie at all."

"There isn't time. I'm supposed to take the next stage north."

"Hmm. And you don't know what Wilson and his friend are up to?"

"No."

"Well, you cannot stay here at the White House—or the blue house with the purple door if you prefer." He smiled at her. "If your reputation is not your own first priority, it does matter to me what people would say if you remain here in this place of notoriety. And if, in the future, you were ever to revisit your position on partnering with Dulcie in business, it might harm her prospects if anyone took notice that you had any business dealings with us here."

"And what about her, if I may ask? You're Dulcie's father. You live in the same house."

He tipped his head toward her in acknowledgment of the seeming contradiction. "My daughter and son-in-law do live in my house. I suspect it will not be long before that situation is remedied. And, as you must admit, things are different for a man than they are for a woman, no matter how enlightened the population of this territory appears in granting women the right to vote. Dulcie living in my house with a husband carries a completely different connotation than Dulcie, alone, living here in the White House."

"Please reconsider. I am a seamstress. I've worked in a lot of morally-questionable locales, but my virtue remains intact. I design clothing and sew for the ladies. I don't join them in their subsidiary activities."

"Be that as it may. I can't think why you would be willing to take such an unnecessary risk with your good name. Here's what I think you should do instead. . . ."

~

Thumbtacked to the door with a string, the little bell jingled. Dulcie looked up from where she sat at her desk going over the books, a smile breaking over her features when she saw who came through the doorway of Nonpareil.

"Ailis! How good to see you."

"And you, Dulcie." Ailis turned in a circle, her skirt belling out as she took it all in. "You did it! Nonpareil, just as you said. And you did it all so quickly, too. I am impressed."

The urge to once again try to convince her friend to come in with her as a partner stole over Dulcie. She stifled the impulse with some difficulty. Ailis was the best at her craft, and it was Dulcie's nature to push people to perform to the utmost limits of their ability. But with this woman, she knew, that course of action would probably be a bad idea. Trying to drive Ailis hadn't shown any sign of working up to this point. There was no reason to believe such a tactic would work now.

"Come in. Are you here to visit? Say you will stay with us while you're here."

"I have a room at the hotel. I'll only be here until the next stage north arrives."

Dulcie reached for her friend's hand, giving it an affectionate squeeze. "Well, what are you doing here on such a short trip?"

Ailis smiled. "I'm on the hunt for gemstones. I've bought out the entire stock available in South Pass City, even resorting to some personal transactions. I need as many precious stones as I can find. Loose gems preferred, but I will take them in the less expensive kinds of settings if I must."

Dulcie spent a moment reflecting, testing what she thought might be going on here. The rapid explanation rang false somehow, as if Ailis had practiced it before coming in, and the smile on her face seemed strained. "Any particular type of stone, or cut, or color?" Dulcie asked.

"It doesn't matter. Any precious stone will do. They just have to be real jewels, not paste."

"I don't have much in stock," Dulcie said. "I have only recently taken over the shop from a man who specialized in men's watches. I could order loose stones from Chicago, and have them here within two weeks or so. May I ask what is the need behind your request?"

"I . . . I have a customer. You know, there are lots of rich Englishmen wandering around the West looking to establish large spreads of free grazing land. A . . . a woman, a titled heiress, has ordered a custom, bejeweled wedding gown made. I need to obtain as many gems as possible, as soon as possible, to fill the order for her."

"I wasn't aware many European women were in the habit of wandering the frontier, only men." Dulcie said slowly. "And I would suppose such an event, the appearance of a titled heiress, would be the talk of the territory. You know how the newspapers love tittle-tattle."

"This woman . . . she could make my reputation, Dulcie! Think of the business that might come my way as a result of just this one order."

Ailis was lying to her. Dulcie became more and more certain of that fact as her friend's voice rose and her fantastic story grew. But why? What could possibly be the purpose of spinning such a tale? She could barely keep the suspicion from her own voice: "Tell me, how much do you have to spend?"

Ailis placed her bag on the counter and began to loosen its strings. "I . . . I've hardly counted it, but here, here it is. We will see how much I can afford. And, and, oh! Look, I almost forgot. Speaking of weddings, Ju is marrying Cal! Here is your invitation I promised to deliver."

Probably nothing could have worked better to distract Dulcie from teasing the truth from Ailis's web of falsehoods than the news that Fragrant Chrysanthemum was set to marry that worthless scoundrel Caleb Wilson. Ju, another of her friends of long acquaintance who refused her outstretched hand of friendship. Dulcie couldn't begin to understand it. She didn't think she lorded it over anyone. She didn't consciously try to rub their faces in her prosperity. Why couldn't they just seize the help she offered? She could have made their lives so much easier. Why would they rather deal with such a poor excuse for humanity as the drunkard who now owned the Goldust? It was inexplicable. Counting herself extremely fortunate to have escaped South Pass City on the winning side, Dulcie would have thought her friends would be happy to join her in turning their backs on the place. Instead, one chose to remain there and make her living on her back, and the other seemed only too eager to get *back* to the situation from which she had offered them both the means of liberation. Why could the women she knew accept not the least little bit of help from her?

Why did they prefer to remain enslaved, in a manner of speaking—defined by her as their stiff-necked refusal to accept help and continuing inclination to remain in situations injurious to their health and possibly their future financial well-being?

Hands shaking, Dulcie reached for the envelope. The attendance of Dulcinetta Cavanaugh and any guests she cared to invite was requested on Saturday, September 10, at 2:00 p.m. to celebrate the union in matrimony of Miss Xiang Ju and Mr. Caleb Wilson, in the office of the Honorable Esther Hobart Morris, South Pass City. She felt faint, as if her undergarments were too tight and choking the breath from her. "I don't understand. How could she?"

"It's her choice. Ju more or less runs things at the saloon. Cal mostly just tends the liquor dispensing."

"Of course. He couldn't bring himself to leave overseeing that part of the business to anyone else." Dulcie tasted bile, afraid she was going to be sick. She held spread fingers over her mouth. "I can't believe this."

Ailis shrugged. "Face it. Anti-Chinese sentiment is growing. With legal marriage to an American, Ju will probably be safe from future deportation. Returning to China would mean slow starvation for her. She seems happy enough on her own account. I think she would want you to be happy for her as well."

Dulcie grimaced. "Don't show up for the ceremony with a long face of doom, is that what you're telling me?"

"We all make our choices, and then we live with the results. Your disapproval may be neither here nor there in the long run, but believe me, your opinion has the power to wound."

Bought up short at the tone of Ailis's statement, Dulcie stared at her friend. "Have I done something to offend you, Ailis?"

There was the merest hesitation before the answer arrived. "No, of course not. I'm a little pressed for time, that's all. Could we get back to the real purpose of my visit to the bustling metropolis of Bryan City?"

A neat turn of topic with a bit of lighthearted facetiousness, Dulcinetta thought. "Excuse me just a minute. I may have some of what you need." She turned toward the small back room and the safe which contained a couple of velvet-lined trays of loose stones. She snatched the more valuable gems from the top tray and added them to the lower tray. Closing the safe door and locking it, she returned to the front of the store with only the top tray and the cheaper selections.

She laid the display in front of Ailis.

"That's it?"

"I'm operating on the basis of your story, darling. Real but cheap, that's what you said, isn't it?" Ailis raised a face stamped with misery. Dulcie felt sorry for her, but not enough to abet her obvious deceit. "Still care to stick to your story, or would you like to enlighten me as to what's really going on with you, Ailis?"

A small moan escaped Ailis's lips. "Dulcie, please don't start questioning me. If you want to help me, just let it rest. Do I have enough money to purchase these stones?"

"Just enough, I think." Dulcie studied Ailis for a moment longer, but when it became clear that no clarification of the situation would be forthcoming, she stooped to retrieve a small velvet drawstring bag from a shelf beneath the display case. After straightening back up, she scooped the gemstones into the bag, tightened the strings, and handed it over to Ailis. Then she watched as her friend, unshed tears trembling on her lashes, turned and almost ran from the shop.

Chapter *15*
Some Shooting and a Wedding

EVIN GRINNED AS HE surveyed the stacks of lumber being unloaded from the flatcar on the siding behind the depot onto one of his freight wagons. He had ordered the entire kit for his and Dulcie's new house from a lumber mill in Chicago, only having had to oversee the cutting and laying of the stone for the foundation in Bryan ready for the arrival of the house materials.

He was excited to begin construction, and still in awe at how quickly his new contracting company had come together. The speed at which deals could be accomplished out here in the West continued to amaze him. The rapidity of agreements reached, arrangements made, and a construction foreman and laborers hired were all accomplished seemingly at the speed of a transmitted telegraph message. With Dulcie's money paving the way and greasing the wheels, there didn't seem to be a limit to what an ambitious man could accomplish, and he was itching to get started learning all he could about building houses.

Unfortunately, he had a wedding to attend in South Pass City, so he would miss seeing his new abode begin to rise from its little patch of cleared ground. He would be sorry indeed to miss the initial steps of construction, especially because the reason was just to make the trip to watch Dulcie's friend Ju tie the knot with that hopeless ne'er-do-well Cal Wilson. The leaves of the cottonwoods along the river had already turned, and winter would soon arrive. Devin would much prefer to stay behind and let Dulcie go on to the ceremony, but Ailis had delivered the invitation in person several weeks ago and Dulcie was set on them both attending. So, to please his wife, he would make the trip, even if the whole thing seemed a great waste of time.

He could understand Dulcie's worry. She wanted to check up on Ju, and he respected that. She had always worried about Ju, but this latest decision of her Chinese friend to tie her fate to Cal Wilson seemed to work Dulcie into a suppressed froth of frustrated apprehension.

"Ju is of an age to be making up her own mind," he had insisted the night before as they readied for bed. "I wouldn't advise interference in her plans, especially at this late date. She will only resent you for it."

Dulcie, having removed the tortoise-shell pins holding up the mass of her curly hair, had tossed her head, causing the gleaming spirals to bounce, and flicked a dismissive hand toward him. "Pfft. Ju has resented me before. She would get over it."

"So she might. Eventually. And I'm not any happier than you about her choice for a husband. But right or wrong, would you deliberately set out to spoil her wedding day?"

She narrowed her eyes at him, knuckles prominent as she gripped her hairbrush. "I'm not without self-restraint. I've kept quiet so far, haven't I? I've stayed right here in Bryan and haven't gone rushing up there to interfere. I've selected a lovely silver service for a wedding gift. I wouldn't make a fool of myself on the very day of the nuptials."

"Sorry. Of course I know you wouldn't cause a scene at the wedding." He raised his arms, inviting her to join him in the bed.

She sat on the edge of the mattress, but didn't lie down beside him. "And I'm worried about Ailis. That cock-and-bull story about the rich English woman and her bejeweled wedding dress belongs in a book of fairy tales. There's something going on there in South Pass City, and I don't like being kept in the dark."

"Can you think of any reason Ailis wouldn't trust you?"

He reached for her but she snatched her arm away. "No, damn it! They've shut me out, both Ailis and Ju, since we moved away. We three were the best of friends at one time, and now I have no friends, neither here nor there."

"You will make new friends." He kept his voice as low-pitched and reassuring as he could. But Dulcie was having one of her infrequent storms of self-pity and wouldn't listen.

"But that's it, isn't it? The real heart of the matter. I've left behind, or been left by, my old friends. And no one here in Bryan City has made the slightest move toward accepting my overtures."

"Did you place your advertisement for the inauguration of the ladies' literary club? Surely, with the lack of refined activities in this town, you should get a good response."

She dabbed at her eyes. "One. Just one acceptance, Devin! A reply of acceptance from Mr. Abernathy's old spinster sister. Abigail Abernathy hardly presents the entrée into society I was anticipating."

He scooted over to wrap his arms around her waist. He had to be careful not to sound the least bit disparaging of Dulcie's ambitions. Her standing in the community had reached overarching proportions. Somehow she had convinced herself that buying a decent business would endow her with a corresponding measure of approval from the local ladies. She wanted respectability, and she wanted it immediately. Devin had never seen this starry-eyed side of her before they moved to Bryan. At South Pass City she'd been such a hard-headed businesswoman. It had come as quite a shock to him to discover that Dulcie had a hidden vulnerable—did he dare think *immature*—side to her nature.

"This is hardly New York or New Orleans." He felt her spine stiffen as if she inferred he thought she was such a ninny she didn't know where they were or what difference it made, and hurried to add, "They're just not ready for someone like you around here, Dulce. Give them time. They'll eventually discover, as I did, your true worth."

She had turned, eyes glistening with unshed tears, and lifted a hand to stroke his face. "Oh, Devin. I'm sorry for breaking down like this again. Thank you for building my confidence, sweetheart," she said. "You are so good to me."

And that's how the silken lasso of wedded fidelity dropped once more over Devin Cavanaugh. He was so quickly ensnared, his plans for the immediate future now pivoted, merely to please his wife, toward a wedding he didn't want to attend. He would so much rather be helping to raise the walls of their new home in Bryan City.

~

Ailis had handed over the gems as soon as she returned to South Pass City. Without even removing her wrap, she approached Cal and they retreated to the hall behind the bar.

"Is this all ya got?" Cal exclaimed as he eyed the small pile of stones in his palm. He looked up as she nodded. His face began turning an alarming shade of puce. "Well, I'll be a cunny-thumbed swad. You thieving little Ourang-Outang. I should'a knowed better than to trust you to do any honest commercing for me. You thought to jockey me, didn't you, ya infernal cotton-mouthed miss!"

Ailis began to tremble. She knew once Cal started with his purple-faced swearing, the episodes often ended in a high dudgeon of alcoholic violence, recrimination, and self-pity that could last for days. "That's all that was to be had. I swear it, Cal. I gave Dulcie every penny you provided, and this is what I got in return. I would have gone on—

to Cheyenne, or even Chicago, but I wanted to return expeditiously to show your faith in me wasn't misplaced."

"And polished baubles you bring me! *Polished*, by damn. You think I'm a goney, to be taken in by the likes of you? I told you *raw*. I told you *uncut*." Spittle flew from between his rotten teeth as he raged. "How might we think to conduct the grand suck-in with *these*—these pretty, shiny little rocks? I ask you—"

"That's enough, Cal." The sharp-faced little man, unnoticed by either of them, appeared beside Ailis's elbow. Speaking so soft-voiced, he was all the more terrifying to her. "She did exactly as I told her, didn't you, madam?"

"I . . . I did. I did just what you said. I was trying to explain. I'll be glad to go out again. Soon. Whenever you say. But I wanted to come back to finish Ju's wedding dress, you see. It's important. Important to her, and . . . and to you, of course, Cal." She turned beseechingly to Wilson, who was still scowling down at the little collection of jewels in his hand. But now she knew for sure, oh, yes, she did, that Cal and Weasel Face were planning a great shave. Cal had just confirmed it. They were going to stick it to someone. And she didn't want any part of it.

But she must see reality. She had to admit to herself she was already part of it. She knew that was the only way she could begin to discover how to extricate herself from this mess. Cal was just outright hotly lunatic, as Weasel Face was an unfeeling, emotionless reptile. She had to get out, to find a way to escape, or she might soon find herself dead.

"You would be willing to try again, miss?" Weasel Face asked. "If we entrusted a little bit more currency with you, and showed you a likely sample or two of exactly what it is we require?"

Oh, no! Ailis cringed. Weasel Face trying to be friendly was much more frightening than Cal's absolute fury. She didn't want to get any deeper into the schemes of these two. She wanted only to run. But how? How could she possibly get safely away from them?

"I think we should negative that idea," Cal said, his voice grating and whiny. "The wench is noticeably deficient; she don't know a shitepoke from a shinplaster."

Weasel Face paused to indulge in his sinister, breathless imitation of a laugh, the sound that always sent shivers up Ailis's spine. "Caleb, I must say I find your colorful and inventive use of language most diverting. However, when it comes to creating anything other than tortuous sentences, I think you need to leave all the planning to me."

"I'd like to repay some of the torment I've suffered all my life, I tell you that. 'Tortuous?' I've been straight on with you. It's her that's messed things up, not old Cal. Can't you see it? You're letting her pretty little face addle you. But . . . sure, I'll step aside. You go your own way, and you'll know soon enough which of us makes costly misdecisions."

Cal extended a closed fist, poking Weasel Face in the chest. The little man held out his hand and Cal passed over the small pile of stones. Cal glared at Ailis, and then once more returned a baleful look to Weasel Face, as if he couldn't decide which of them angered him more at the moment. "You obviously don't need me no more. I guarantee you my assistance in this matter ain't to be sneezed at. I'm sure you know how to proceed, only feel free to refer with me in the future in the certain case that you can't get the whole scheme well verbalized between the two of you, eh?"

Cal turned away from them, headed back toward the bar and the bottles on shelves behind it, their contents his solace and his compulsion. Ailis found herself hoping Ju would be lucky, that the bottle would take care of Caleb Wilson soon and she wouldn't have to suffer a marriage of long duration to the man.

"The look in his eyes. He would kill me if he could." Ailis inhaled as Cal turned his back on them, and shut her eyes tight while continuing to hold the breath.

"Never fear, madam. Cal just has no subtlety. Sending you out was merely my little test, to see if you would do exactly as you were told— and also to see if you would come back." He reached for her arm. Opening her eyes and catching the movement, Ailis tried to fight instinct and not flinch away. "Come, let us go somewhere we won't be disturbed, shall we, and discuss our next move. Cal will recover from his bout of high dander. He always does."

He began leading her toward the stairs. Ailis desperately wanted to pull her arm away. The only things upstairs were her bedroom and the rooms of the dance hall girls. But as soon as she tensed to resist Weasel

Face, his grip tightened. Glancing at him from the corner of her eye, she could see his sharp little teeth revealed. She realized then that he enjoyed causing her discomfort, and the more she wanted to fight him the more he enjoyed it.

"I don't take men to my room," Ailis grated in a low voice. "I'm not that kind of girl."

"Please. Don't get yourself in a pucker, as Cal would say. I want only privacy. I don't intend to partake of your particular . . . charms."

If that statement was meant to provide reassurance, it missed the mark. She could see he really was amused by it all: her naiveté, Cal's anger, her fear. Being alone with Weasel Face for any reason got her in a pucker, all right. She felt like one big pucker, all the muscles from her abdomen up to the top of her head tightened in dread. But what could she do except go along?

It didn't help matters that as the two of them climbed the stairs, she caught Ju giving her a thorough inspection full of speculation. When they reached the top and her room, Ailis closed the door on a look of resigned recognition from her friend, as if one more heretofore spotless woman had fallen from the pinnacle of propriety to the dung heap of soiled sisters at the foot.

Once inside her room with the door closed behind them, the man finally let go of her. His gaze took in their surroundings, as if he could evaluate it all in a glance. In front of one wall stood the desk with her open machine case atop it, Ju's partially finished silk dress draped over it. Two wooden chairs to either side of the desk held more clothing in various stages of completion, their colors piled one atop another like the riotous petals of giant flowers. Her bed was neatly made, covers drawn tight as she had been taught in the orphanage so long ago. Her own few items of clothing hung from hooks attached to the wall, two dresses and a coat. The rest, her stockings, chemises, and petticoats, remained modestly hidden in her traveling trunk.

"Not at all what I expected," Weasel Face commented. "No extravagance. You live like a nun."

"I save my money, yes. Do you know a lot about nuns, Mr. Whatever-Your-Name-Is?" Ailis rubbed her reddened wrist. He might not be big, but those small fingers were plenty strong.

"We will leave my identity a mystery, if you don't mind. You'll find you will be much safer that way." This declaration was accompanied by a few puffs of laughter, as if the thought of her in peril pleased him. She supposed it must. He gestured toward the bed. "Sit."

Instead Ailis gathered up her sewing from one chair, placed the dresses on the bed, and lowered herself to the seat of the straight-backed chair.

Seemingly unconcerned with propriety, Weasel Face sat on the bed across from her before removing a jeweler's loupe and a few gemstones from his pocket. "Now, for our first lesson," he began. . . .

Ailis allowed her taut muscles to loosen a bit. It seemed all he really meant to do while the two of them remained locked in her bedroom was instruct her in the art of evaluating and acquiring raw gemstones.

His voice droned on, and on the one hand Ailis found the oration about hardness, luster, refractive specific gravity, fracture, and other new and unfamiliar terms fascinating. On the other, Weasel Face's murmuring voice threatened to put her to sleep. She reminded herself that it was probably a grievous mistake to relax in front of this man. She straightened her spine and shook her head in an attempt to remain vigilant.

"I trust I'm not boring you, madam?" he asked, noticing her efforts to regain a state of watchful alertness. "Ah, well, I suppose not everyone shares my personal absorption with the world of precious stones. It's probably a good thing I never aspired to be a school teacher since I seem to be lulling you into a doze. And you only really need to know enough to complete your assignment. I will let you get back to your own preoccupation now, so you can finish Miss Chrysanthemum's wedding dress. We will have further lessons in the next few days, until I think you know enough to proceed, and then Cal and I will fund your next expedition . . . which, no doubt, will turn out to be a bit more rewarding than the first."

He pocketed his supplies, rose to his feet, showed her a glimpse of his sharp little teeth as he passed, and went out the door. It latched gently behind him.

~

All eyes in the small crowd were raised to watch the bride descend the stairs at the Goldust. Resplendent in a magnificent crimson silk gown and matching brocade jacket, Ju took each step slowly, her eyes lowered—but not to make sure of her footing. Instead a small smile curved her painted lips; she seemed to be enjoying the open admiration.

At the bottom of the staircase, Dulcie waited to hand Ju a nosegay of bright paper flowers. Luther had possession of the bride's ring until the ceremony, a duty he seemed to be performing with the utmost seriousness.

Ailis watched from her position at the top of the stairs, assessing the effect her latest creation had on the wedding guests. Satisfied that she had once again delivered an utter sensation, she waited until the bride reached the bottom and then moved to start down the stairs herself, followed by the dancers still in residence, all of them attired in Chinese-inspired gowns of shimmering silk in various jewel-toned colors.

Cal took Ju's arm, her wide sleeve with its gold accent trim belling out as she raised her hand to clasp his. They left the saloon and led the procession up the street to Mrs. Morris's abode and office.

Following behind, it looked to Ailis as if Cal had a head start on the celebrations, as he stumbled once or twice and seemed to be using Ju's hand for support. *An omen of Ju's future, surely*, Ailis thought with sour conviction.

Dulcie left her husband's side to come up alongside Ailis and nudge her in the ribs. "Happy, happy, remember?"

"Hush up, Dulcie," Ailis hissed, trying to will her features into some semblance of joy for their friend Ju on this supposedly auspicious occasion.

As many people as possible crowded into Esther Morris's small parlor, which also served as her office. She waited while the onlookers finished coughing and clearing throats and settled themselves, and then began the short ceremony, finishing with "Xiang Ju, Fragrant Chrysanthemum, do you take this man, Caleb Wilson, as your lawfully wedded husband—"

She didn't get to proceed to the "love, honor, cherish, and obey" part of the vow, before Ju broke in, saying, "Sure, I take. He take me too."

"Well, good," Mrs. Morris said, amid hearty laughter abandoning any effort at trying to get Ju to repeat traditional pledges. "Who's got the ring?"

"I do," Luther said proudly, elbowing his way up to the judge, who motioned that the ring belonged with the groom. Cal took it from the boy, slipped it on Ju's finger, and then bent his bride backward in a sloppy, possessive kiss.

Ailis shuddered at the thought of the state of the man's dental hygiene, but what did it matter to her? She wasn't marrying him. The party waited outside for the bride and groom, where some in the audience tossed flakes and tiny bits of gold to wish them prosperity in their new life. Watching the oblivious wedding guests as they trooped off behind Ju and Cal, eager to start the post-ceremony revelry, Ailis remained behind. As the others entered the Goldust, she knelt and scooped as much as she could of the discarded bounty into her pockets before trailing the merrymakers back to the saloon.

Once inside the door, she saw Dulcie trying to catch her eye, gesturing for her to join them. She raised a hand for her friend to wait, and hurried up the stairs instead. She finished her packing, closed the lid on her trunk and locked it, then laid her traveling costume beside her carpetbag on the bed. Giving everything a last once-over to make sure she hadn't forgotten anything, she placed her sewing machine, already closed up in its wooden case, nearest the door. She dumped the wedding loot from her pockets into her handbag, on top of the money Weasel Face had provided for her trip to Chicago. Deciding she was in too big a hurry to worry about the dirt mixed in with the gold right now, she tied the bag shut and draped the cords around her waist, hiding the bag itself under her clothing.

Once more she descended the stairs, a false smile of reassurance pasted on her face as she took a seat at the table where the Cavanaughs sat.

"Everything all right?" Dulcie asked. Devin, having known Ailis the longest, gave her a penetrating stare.

"Fine. Just seeing to some last minute details," she said with a tinkling little laugh, glancing sideways at Devin to see if it looked as if she might be fooling him. "I'll be catching the stage to Point of Rocks later on, so I won't be able to stay for the whole reception. I'm sure I won't be missed."

"I'm sure you will," Dulcie insisted. "Why don't you stay over another day and return with us to Bryan tomorrow? You can take a few days, surely, to visit with us there and see the progress of our new home?"

"Oh, Point of Rocks is closer. A shorter journey and I can catch the train there and save fifty more miles." Ailis caught herself fidgeting nervously. Catching Devin openly weighing her uneasiness, she halted the telltale motions of her fingers rubbing together and her knee bouncing under the table.

"Are you in a hurry, then?" Dulcie prodded. "Where are you headed, anyway?"

"Nowhere in particular. Just for a holiday. I don't think I'll be touring with the girls for much longer, so I thought I'd take a look around the country and see what comes up."

Dulcie leaned forward and placed a hand on Ailis's arm. "Ailis, are you not telling us something? Is there, perhaps, a man in this secretive scenario?"

Ailis turned her head aside, not meeting Dulcie's smile. "Dulce, please do stop prying! I promise you, there's no man."

"The offer to go into business together is still open. Anytime, Ailis."

Devin placed a warning hand atop his wife's to try to stop her nosiness, but Dulcie just sighed and rolled her eyes at him.

"All right. I'll think it over. Thank you again, Dulcie." Ailis pulled her hand from beneath Dulcie's. Her knee was jumping spastically once more and she gritted her teeth, compelling it to stop. A couple of musicians were tuning up in the corner, and conversation swirled around the trio seated at the table, making it almost impossible to hear. In a very short time, the party was in full swing, dancing and drinking at a fever pitch. Part of the reason for the general urgency to have such a good time was attributable to the lateness of the season. Most of those still left in South Pass City intended to remain dug in for the snow months. Those who preferred to go elsewhere to escape the usual harsh high country winter weather had already departed, except for the few stragglers who had stayed for the wedding.

Ailis was to journey to Chicago and return as quickly as possible. She had tarried as long as she dared, wanting to make everything as perfect as she could for Ju's wedding. She did not want to risk becoming trapped in a blizzard on a closed road, and she feared the longer she delayed the more likely her mission would end with a bad result.She glanced at her bracelet watch and rose to her feet. "The stage is due any minute now. I really must change. It's been wonderful to see you."

Dulcie had also risen and leaned to bestow a parting kiss on Ailis's cheek. Ailis had started to walk away when the front door banged open and a wild-eyed man barged in. He was well-dressed, if a little dusty. Ailis realized the stage must have arrived and she hadn't heard it in the general din inside the Goldust. She'd have to hurry. But she watched in paralyzed horror as a pistol materialized in the stranger's raised fist and he headed straight for the bar. Terrified people quickly opened a path for him. The musicians caught on that something unusual was afoot and they set aside their instruments. Silence descended on the Goldust.

"You! You goddamned cheat!" The man advanced unmolested toward the bar. Cal had his back turned, but as he glanced in the mirror a look of utter shock froze his features. Calm, standing next to her new husband, Ju slowly reached toward the shelf below the bar. All the man's attention centered on Cal, and Ju was so short he didn't seem to see her stealthy movement . . . or didn't consider her a threat if he did see.

Cal, hands raised, started to turn toward the man. Before he could pivot even halfway the gun went off. A bottle on the back bar shattered, and Cal dropped to the floor. Bright red blood, almost the color of Ju's dress, and white bits of bone splattered the mirror and the bottles on the shelves.

Without the slightest change of expression, Ju raised a shotgun to her shoulder and pulled the trigger. The stranger, an expression of complete surprise on his face, looked from the little Chinese woman to the front of his shirt and vest where gouts of blood suddenly bloomed. Then he crumpled to the sawdust.

Immediate confusion reigned inside the Goldust. Weasel Face appeared out of the melee and grabbed Ailis's arm. "You've got the money on you?" he demanded.

She nodded, the only sort of answer she could give. Her throat had closed up and she could barely draw breath, let alone speak.

"Let's go," he said, turning her toward the door.

"W . . . wait. Where are we—"

"The stage. We've got to catch it. Now move."

"But my clothes. My machine!" She glanced down at the fancy silk dress she still wore, entirely unsuitable for traveling on a Concord stagecoach through the choking alkali dust of the Wyoming desert.

"You can replace everything later. Go, go, go!" Weasel Face said, his grip on her wrist becoming tighter and more painful.

If Ailis had ever wondered if the man was capable of emotion, she now had her answer. Weasel Face was scared. The fact that he was frightened translated into utter panic inside her chest.

She caught a single glance of Dulcie's blurred features as her friend climbed on a chair to try and see better what was happening. Devin was starting to push his way toward Ailis, blocked by the shocked, milling spectators.

As the town marshal entered the saloon to see for himself what all the commotion was about, Ailis and Weasel Face slipped past him and out the door. Down the street, the last of the stage's replacement horses was being backed into harness. Weasel Face towed Ailis toward the dusty conveyance, waving a piece of paper that might have been a ticket and shoving her up the step and into the coach. "There's been a shooting. Nobody else is riding out today, so let's go," he yelled at the driver.

"Don't you have any luggage?" the man asked.

"No! Let's go, I said!"

The driver shrugged. It was true there had only been one ticket sold for today's stage to Point of Rocks. There were usually more, sometimes even a gaggle of hangers-on atop the coach in addition to the passengers sheltered inside. But there were some kind of big doings going on in South Pass City today, and a corresponding dearth of tickets sold. Traffic had been slowing anyway as summer faded to fall. He knew to expect the lady, curiously dressed though she might be in a fancy gown for the ride to Point of Rocks and lacking any gear, but the unexpected man apparently had paid a fare as well—if the paper he waved was indeed a ticket. The whip shrugged, climbed to his high seat where the conductor waited after having loaded the mail, raised his lash, and cracked it expertly near the rumps of the waiting horses. The coach took off with a jerk and, swaying up the road out of town, quickly disappeared. Soon only a faint dust cloud remained to mark the mysterious, sudden departure of a young dressmaker named Ailis Tierney from South Pass City, Wyoming Territory.

Chapter *16*
An End and a Beginning

EVIN WAS HAPPY TO get back to Bryan City and to the construction site of the new house. The well had long since been dug, and by the time he returned from the disastrous wedding at South Pass City, the exterior walls were already raised, an experience he sincerely regretted having missed. One crew worked on installing the windows and doors while a differently skilled bricklayer and hod carrier built up the house's two chimneys brick-by-brick. As soon as the chimneys were completed the roof could go on, and at that point Devin could finally stop worrying. So long as the structure was weather proof, he and his men could finish the interior over the winter.

But Dulcie had trouble finding any peace of mind. Ailis had disappeared. Wires of inquiry sent in anticipation of the stagecoach's arrival at Point of Rocks had produced only a dead end. The return wire said that the stage had overturned on its journey. The driver had been killed. The conductor had been shot and left for dead although it was anticipated that he would eventually recover, and the two known passengers had vanished without a trace. The marshal in South Pass City sent back word that he would like to talk to Ailis and also to the enigmatic male friend of Cal Wilson's to see what light they might be able to shed on the wedding day shootings, but to date there had been no sign of either of them.

The widow, Ju, could contribute almost nothing to the enquiry. She said the man who caught the stagecoach at the same time as Ailis had been hanging around the Goldust for a couple of weeks, and that he and Cal had often been huddled together at the bar, as if over some clandestine arrangement. But Fragrant Chrysanthemum hadn't been privy to the nature of their whispered conversations. She claimed she had no explanation for why the enraged Easterner had burst in on her wedding and murdered Cal, nor the slightest hint of what had become of Ailis or the little man whose name Ju had never learned during his tenure in South Pass City.

As time went on, informational flyers the marshal sent out continued to turn up no clue as to the mysterious conspirator's identity.

The marshal admitted he was stumped about how, or even whether, to pursue that line of investigation. In the meantime, Ju was free to continue as mistress of the Goldust, her shotgun killing of the shootist—who turned out to be a mildly successful stockbroker from Chicago with no previous history of violence—deemed an act of self defense.

Dulcie chewed over the available facts incessantly at first, quite sure that Ailis's tall tale of a rich bride's order of a jeweled dress fitted into the mystery somehow. But as the weeks passed with no word, the weather grew increasingly frigid, and her life resumed its normal framework, if her business was somewhat hampered by cold and wind. Slowly, her focus on Ailis's disappearance began receding from the agitated center of her thoughts to take up a quieter residence at the outer edges, even though she knew consideration of the fate of her missing friend would never entirely fade away.

Much of Devin's freighting business shifted toward Brown's Park, where ranches existed that required supplies and prospectors continued to search for gold in the vicinity, as well as other metals after copper was found in Jesse Ewing Canyon and on Douglas Mountain. From Brown's Park, connections could be made to Colorado and Utah, but the nearest railroad connecting point was Bryan so most provisions went out from there.

It was a busy winter, although a run of horrific blizzards made regular commerce difficult. The first shocking storm roared into the territory on October 12, blockading the Union Pacific line at Rawlins, 140 miles east of Bryan City on the opposite side of the Continental Divide. Three more storms slammed the rail line in quick succession. A further series of storms beginning in December delayed trains for two months and stopped the line dead for nearly a solid month of frigid weather. At one point eight hundred passengers were stranded— including among them Susan B. Anthony and a Japanese delegation bound for the nation's capital—and a thousand cars full of freight sat in a tangled snarl on the tracks, waiting for delivery.

"Shall we starve, do you think?" Dulcie asked Devin at one point when stores in Bryan were at an exceptionally low point. He reassured her they were lucky in comparison to some locations, places such as Laramie. Bryan, a distribution point, had warehouses including his own, and grocery wholesalers, that had begun the winter well stocked.

If the selection of available comestibles in the little town became rather limited, still it sufficed. At one evening meal they dined on salmon caught and canned in Alaska and shipped from California on the railroad, dried and stewed prunes shipped from China to California and then to Bryan by rail, crackers so stale they might have been stored in an army repository from the time of the War Between the States before they somehow ended up in Devin's warehouse stock, and a bottle of Champagne shipped by boat and rail from France.

"Well then, shall the people stranded all along the line eventually starve? I wish there were something we could do for them." She twisted her napkin between her fingers, a nervous habit she had recently developed. "And I worry especially for Ju, and the others who overwintered in South Pass City. I wonder how they're faring, snowed in for months up there in the high country?"

Devin patted her arm. "Those who live in the Sweetwater district, at least, know from experience what to expect. I'm sure the people of South Pass City stocked up on food and fuel for the winter, and are faring well. I'm equally sure the railroad has the snowplows out every available minute and the stranded passengers will soon be on their way. At any rate, the chatter on the telegraph says although they're trapped they have been amusing themselves well enough with games and sing-alongs, even a ball or two."

"Think of that—a ball! Perhaps dancing has a practical purpose, helping to keep them warm. But it does sound as if they're continuing to keep their spirits up, even though provisions are scarce." A tentative smile appeared on her face.

At least he'd got a fleeting smile out of her. He had been worried lately about Dulcie's state of mind. Although she mostly put on a good front, many times she seemed depressed, especially when she confessed she had been thinking once more about Ailis's disappearance.

Hoping to keep her thoughts focused anywhere but on the recent string of troubles, Devin didn't mention the livestock freezing to death in the halted cattle cars along the line. He didn't want Dulcie in mourning over helpless animals. Instead he cleared away the supper dishes and then brought out some sample books. "Would you like to look at wallpaper swatches? The interior of our house is coming along nicely, and we will soon be able to move in."

"In the middle of winter? Darling, I don't think I could entertain the thought. Let's just stay here with Papa, where we're safe and warm." Dulcie sighed, but he appreciated that she restrained herself from rolling her eyes at his suggestion.

"We don't have to move right away, certainly, if you don't want to. But I do have to keep the men busy and paid or as soon as the track opens up they will desert me for more regular work. So it would be good for my business, d'ye see, if you could just bring yourself to pick out the patterns you want on your walls."

She cocked an eye at him. "You do know how to get around me, don't you, you sly devil? All you have to do is hint that I might somehow be hurting your business, and I'm all cooperative putty in your hands."

Devin glanced around to make sure Luther was out of earshot before leaning over to whisper low in his wife's ear. "Shall I be molding you, like putty in my warm hands, a bit later when we are alone?" he suggested. "Or . . . perhaps you would like to try your hand at the molding of m—"

She interrupted, slapping his arm with her linen napkin, although a genuine smile appeared on her face. He knew as he looked at her that she was secretly pleased with his mischievous flirting. "Naughty man! Hand over those sample books."

"Aye, madam. I and your son will be in the kitchen while you make your choices." He raised his voice: "Luther, dishes!"

The boy peeked around the corner. "Aw, Mr. Devin, do we have to?"

"Work doesn't accomplish itself, me boyo! Someone has to do it. In the present case, that's us. Come on, Third." He draped an arm around the boy as he nudged him toward the back of the house.

~

"I've been thinking," Dulcie said as they breakfasted on another thrown-together meal of whatever happened to be left in the cupboards.

"Should I be concerned? Sometimes following the trajectory of your thoughts is terrifying." Devin was in a good mood, willing to tease and play a bit in the early morning after a most pleasant dalliance the previous night, a nice interlude before he had to face another struggle in the snow to the freight office. The sun shone brightly on the banked snow outside the windows, and the room was warm from the fire Josiah, whose normal work day was the Cavanaughs' night, had built up in the little cast iron stove before retiring to his bed. Devin was glad they had received less snow on this side of the Divide than what had pummeled the eastern side, but the rail line was still halted. Each day they awaited word about the estimated arrival date of their shipped goods. But even in the absence of any freight, there were still wages to be paid, monthly accounts to review, and the most important duty for the morning, seeing that his animals being fed and their stalls cleaned. On a normal day, these chores would be seen to by others, but Devin had told most of his freight employees to enjoy a holiday from work until the trains were running. After he finished at the office and the livery barn, he planned to hustle over to the new house, where there was always something novel for him to learn from the construction foreman and building crew.

"Very amusing you are this morning. But when the house is ready for visitors, I would like to begin holding a series of teas for the local ladies." Dulcie fiddled with her place setting, turning her cup around and around on its saucer.

"Oh, yes? Of course you should do that if you like, dear. Your social life is your own affair, although I'll do anything I can to assist you." Devin shrugged a shoulder dismissively, and raising his own coffee cup to his lips, blew across the steaming brew before taking a cautious sip. At least they still had coffee, he thought gratefully. Now if he only had a newspaper less than a month old. In a very short time he'd grown habituated to actually reading a newspaper while eating his breakfast, rather than just looking at the illustrations. *And, while I'm wishing for things unattainable, I believe I'll put in an order for a couple of fried eggs and some bacon.* He smiled at his own whimsy.

Dulcie smiled back. "Really? I'm glad to hear it. But beyond the social aspect—persuading ladies to come to our new house for tea, since my literature society idea seems a bit slow to take root—"

"Temporarily. Only temporarily, I'm sure," Devin interrupted. "You'll have a better turnout when the weather improves. Third, eat your breakfast."

"I hate grits," Luther muttered. "Especially without any cream or butter. Gran'ma always served me grits with cream or butter."

"Your grandma isn't here. However, I am here, and I say eat up," Devin said.

"Thank you for your continuing faith in me, Devin. You are a treasure." But Dulcie's brow furrowed in an expression of doubt about any improvement in the state of her social affairs. She, too, stirred her mush with a spoon, showing little interest in actually eating it and thereby setting a bad example for her son. "The truth is, I doubt if the ladies would consent visit me without some enticement."

"What's enticement, Mama?" Luther asked.

Disconcerted, Dulcie shot Luther a look that plainly revealed she'd completely forgotten her son's presence.

"Something nice to get them out of the house when the weather's bad." Devin hurried to interject and rescue the situation; it was hard telling what Luther might innocently repeat outside the family circle, and the news that the Cavanaughs planned to entice the ladies of Bryan City might not be taken as Dulcie had meant it. But he understood her unspoken thought: *Nobody would ever visit me here, at Josiah's.* If her father's color wasn't enough to turn "respectable" ladies away, his profession would surely do it. It was beyond Devin's understanding why his wife thought the opinion of the local snobs was so important. It could probably be traced back to the fancy schools she'd attended as a girl. But it was important to her, and so it must also be important to him.

"How come you know so many big words if you can't read?" In front of Luther, the handle of his spoon stood upright in his bowl of mush. Obviously, the boy would try any tactic to get out of eating his breakfast.

"I just do, that's all. I'm learning to read as fast as you, and I seem to remember I told you to eat up, so stop talking." Turning his attention to Dulcie, Devin said, "I think it's a grand idea."

"Just listen. You haven't heard the rest of my inspiration. You would have to attend some of the teas as well."

Devin spluttered as he took another sip of coffee. He wiped his lips and checked his shirt front for dribbles. "Aw, you don't want me to do that, Dulce. What help would I be? You know I have the manners of a mule driver, or a New York street rogue. Which, in truth, is what I am."

Luther looked up with interest, perhaps anticipating a tale he hadn't heard before.

Dulcie shot Devin a meaningful look, her eyes cutting toward the boy as if to convey *Please don't give him any ideas.* "Your manners are perfectly acceptable. The aim of your presence would be to answerquestions about the building of the house, of what might be available as far as design, and the quality of construction."

"I'm afraid my foreman would be better qualified to answer those questions."

"You said you would help me. You're the owner of Cavanaugh Constructors. I doubt if many ladies would know enough about building to contradict you. And even incomplete answers would have more heft coming from you than from your foreman."

Leaning his elbow on the table, Devin rested his chin in his hand as he regarded his wife. "Luther, you're excused if you're just going to sit there playing with your breakfast."

He waited while the boy left the room. Now he was beginning to understand what Dulcie was saying. "Two birds with one stone," he said musingly, looking with admiration at his inventive wife. "Community standing for you, and advertisement for the construction business for me. You will attend the teas all smartened up and sparkling, and I will expound a bit on the design and building of Cavanaugh houses before leaving you ladies to your tea and cakes. A quite brilliant way to sell jewelry, and also a way for me to start selling houses."

"You make me sound so calculating, darling. I would attempt to improve our community standing for both of us, surely, not just for myself. And there's nothing wrong with smartly endorsing one's business. If we promote ourselves a bit as well, if people come to see us as trustworthy and admirable, that's all to the good, isn't it?"

"To my way of thinking, if they won't accept you on your own merits, it's no more than they deserve to be invited to our home merely for a sales pitch," Devin said. "But all this is new to me. Until I met you, I was only concerned with having a steady job. Although I sometimes thought about knocking Cal from the driver's seat of the freight wagon, it never occurred to me to imagine much of a future for myself. But I've learned one sure thing since then: wherever you lead I will be more than happy to follow."

"What a good man you are, Devin Cavanaugh." Dulcie patted one of his broad forearms. "I do so appreciate you, darling."

"And I do appreciate how you go about demonstrating your appreciation." Devin tossed a devilish smile her way before rising to don his cold-weather clothing and begin another day as a successful business owner.

~

The house was finally finished. The carpets and a few items of furniture Dulcie had ordered had yet to arrive from Chicago, but for the most part the structure was complete and the Cavanaughs had settled in. Although spring had made its appearance and everyone was overjoyed to see the greening of the cottonwoods and the appearance of wildflowers, they were all still having to make their way through a sea of mud that seemed endless, in order to get around Bryan City.

Devin's freighting crew had resumed deliveries whenever the roads were passable, but he worried about the rapidly-warming weather, which probably meant the Black's Fork would overflow its banks, creating yet more mud in the little town. In the meantime, business of all kinds was booming. The finishing touches had been put on the hotel, and that's where Ju insisted on staying for the duration of her visit.

"I don't understand why you think you have to stay somewhere else." Dulcie was put out with her friend, who, despite everything that had happened to her, was obviously still as headstrong as ever.

"I have money." Ju opened her handbag, displaying the contents to Dulcie. "I pay my bill."

"I won't take your money." Dulcie crossed her arms over her chest.

Ju thrust the bag toward Dulcie. "You take. You buy my debt, I owe to you. I pay, buy back my family honor. You take. Now finished. I free."

"You've been free since San Francisco. But fine, if it makes you feel better, your debt is paid. Would you like a receipt?" Dulcie took the bag. Ju didn't rise to the bait of Dulcie's derision. Dulcie did retrain herself from pointing out that none of Ju's family in China would ever even suspect what Ju had been through to pay back her father's original debt. "What will you do now? Would you consider leaving South Pass City?"

"Where I go? China? San Francisco? No." A lesser woman than Ju wouldn't have been blamed for giving up and leaving the place where so many bad things had happened, by her choice and otherwise, but the thought had apparently never occurred to Fragrant Chrysanthemum. "My home South Pass City. My business now, too. I go home on next stage. Be back with money for you for saloon in summer."

Dulcie shook her head, suspecting if she suggested Ju move to Bryan City she would think Dulcie was simply in the market for a servant. Ju hardly seemed broken up about Cal, but did seem to take pride in being the owner of the Goldust. The best thing at this point would probably be for Dulcie to just let it go and take the payment with good grace. She should know by now that Ju would do what Ju wanted to do. Dulcie could only sit by and wish her all the best fortune. "Will you at least consent to stay and have a cup of tea or coffee with me, Ju? Two business women together. You will be my first guest in my new house, and you will bring me luck."

Ju considered, then, removing her wrap, agreed. It would be the first time in memory that Dulcie had served Ju instead of the other way around. One of the very few times that Ju had ever consented to sit in Dulcie's presence.

Dulcie gathered cups, and sugar and cream, on a tray and brought them to where Ju sat looking around appraisingly.

"Do you like my new house, Ju?"

Ju nodded. "Nice."

"I'm glad you approve. Tell me, have you heard anything at all about Ailis? Did the marshal ever get any word of her whereabouts, or any clue to what became of her?"

"No Ailis. She never come back. She never send letter."

"It's just so strange, her disappearing like that. Without her luggage. And especially without her dressmaking machine. She set such store by that machine, it was almost like a part of her. It's unthinkable that she would leave behind her only means of supporting herself."

Ju shrugged, unable to explain Ailis's disappearance and apparently unwilling to even speculate about what happened. "Maybe she come back."

"Maybe so." But Dulcie had begun to suspect that, sadly, they had all seen the last of Ailis Tierney.

~

There were times Devin wondered why he continued to live here. Bryan City, Wyoming Territory. Why stay? After the winter of snow upon snow, and the spring of flood and mud, now in summer there came drought. Day after day, with no rain. The land grew parched, deep cracks appearing as the arid soil dried and split. Vegetation that had grown tall with the spring moisture now grew dry and brittle, the slightest breeze causing an irritating susurration of sound as if the thirsty land constantly begged in a hoarse whisper: *water, water.*

The Black's Fork was now a mockery of the raging torrent it had been just a few months earlier. A muddy, slow-moving trickle, it dared locals to accurately try recalling the high-piled snow of winter and the flood waters of recent spring. Mother Nature of the West proved herself a fickle goddess, enticing, wet, and seductive at one season, and then suddenly and without warning withdrawing her favor, turning inexplicably spiteful, arid, and harsh. Especially here in the high desert of Wyoming Territory it was easy to see why the native people believed each aspect of nature was a separate spirit, in need of constant recognition and prayer and appeasement. Perhaps it was true that the Indians' Great Spirit was displeased by the iron rails bisecting the continent, isolating the buffalo and also the tribes who depended on the animals for sustenance. Because now the young railroad which had replaced the horse as the fastest means of transportation in the West was left gasping. The great iron engines depended upon a reliable water source to function, and the very existence of the Great Road was now threatened.

And the Cavanaughs, the recently-formed family who had come together to do so well in this raw land, why did they stay? Surely it wasn't continued belief that the U. P. would remain in Bryan. That illusion grew more tattered by the day. The Cavanaughs had money, they could start over, be anything they wanted, anywhere. So why on earth did they stay?

Devin looked out over the miserable little settlement of Green River City, where it was expected the U. P. would relocate after some intense negotiation. Mr. S. I. Field and associates, who, courtesy of having got there first with an Overland Mail land grant from Congress five years prior to the Union Pacific Railroad Act of 1867, owned the entire narrow river valley that the railroad now acknowledged it needed.

Perched in the buggy alongside him, Dulcie sighed. The town of Green River was a mess of roofless shells of crumbling adobe. About the only life discernable recently had been some paleontologists seeking dinosaur bones, and a river expedition led by a one-armed veteran of the Civil War. Green River City was home to a railroad section man's house, S. I. Field's disreputable-looking log store, and a few board and canvas hovels.

The couple had discussed over and over the possibilities open to them. They could follow Josiah, who had decided he was too old to keep starting over. They could go with him to St. Louis and live like civilized people with him or at Lou's grand house, where she still clung to life. St. Louis, where they could be assured Luther would have a decent education. St. Louis, where the Cavanaughs could find another option for making a living. They had money, and Devin had no doubt Dulcie could come up with some way to invest it so they could make even more money.

Or they could remain here, issue another challenge to the harsh high desert of the Wyoming Territory. They could start over. Again. Besides the need for housing, the predictions of the end of freighting with the arrival of the railroad had so far proved unfounded. People who lived away from the rails still needed things delivered from the rail terminals to their settlements, and Devin continued to be ever more successful in the transfer business.

A small forehead thunked into Devin's upper arm. Luther moaned into the sleeve of his stepfather's coat. "Green River is ugly. I don't want to live here."

"Nothing's settled yet. Look at the pretty rocks. They look like castles." Devin attempted to comfort the boy while keeping his eyes focused straight ahead. He didn't want to look at Dulcie. They had already almost agreed to stay, even if he could not bring himself to admit it yet.

"Reassure me again that the house can be moved?" she asked him.

Devin wasn't entirely sure he was ready to ponder buying an overpriced lot in Green River and then to proceed with hoisting up and moving their brand-new house fifteen miles east. His personal triumph concerning the construction of their home was still too recent. The picture of it, rising as it had from the land of sand and sagebrush, like magic, like the illustration of Venus on a clam shell in one of Dulcie's expensive art books, was almost burned on his retinas. He'd just been so pleased with it—and with himself. But he'd hardly had time to savor the thrill of his achievement before all the good feeling associated with his success was snatched away from him. He wondered if it would always be like this out here in the West, a series of brief periods of contentment followed by another time of struggle, the fight for survival followed by momentary satisfaction.

It was starkly beautiful here sometimes, he had to admit. Maybe that was just the way life was supposed to be.

And to look on the bright side, better his own fate than Cal's. Having begun this expedition together little more than a year ago, the two men had been presented with so very many chances to make a wrong choice. The West offered both peril and opportunity, and one's fate sometimes hung on a very thin thread dangling between the two. Cal had grasped that strand of spider silk, swung out over the abyss, and watched it come apart in his hands as he dropped into the void.

Still reluctant, Devin said, "Yes, it's possible to move the house."

Without pause Dulcinetta pounced, moving to the second concern nearest her heart. "And the school? You can move it as well?"

He sighed. "Yes . . . we can move the school, Dulcie."

"Good," she said. "Let's get on with it."

"I guess that settles it," Luther said in a sulky voice. "We're moving here."

"I guess." Devin knew, no matter how he felt now, in time he would be pleased. There was so much opportunity ahead of them. Once again, all they had to do was take hold of it. He'd been worried about Dulcie. She had more or less been putting on a brave front for his benefit since Ailis had disappeared. Now she appeared ready to take the next step and move on. He had a wonderful wife who was once more beginning to look forward, a bright young son who would also undoubtedly enjoy a new location and new friends after the family settled in. They had everything anyone could ask: youth, money, ambition, and family. Dulcie was all he could ever have dared hope for himself, and if she was ready to go forward he wanted to be the one walking by her side. Once more, together, they would claim victory.

He started to turn the buggy around, slapping the mule's haunch with the reins. But the stubborn animal didn't immediately respond, continuing to face the tiny little town for a moment as if to ponder the loss of the old and precious and familiar, contrasted with the shock and stench and promise of the new.

Tiberius suddenly bellowed, as if exceedingly amused by the twists and turns of their intertwined fates, and happy to be included in another new adventure.

Haawwww. HAAAWWW!